# ALL HER CHILDREN

Alyson Radcliffe Ross

*A Summer Hill Irregulars Mystery, Book Two*

*Dedication*


As always, for Jim

# Chapter One

The man wouldn't stay dead.

No matter what I did, he kept popping up, sort of like Rasputin in Russia. I tried bludgeoning, poisoning, stabbing, and shooting the poor guy. He kept coming back. I rolled my head to get the crick out of my neck. I spun around in my chair for no good reason. I tapped my toes. I tapped my pen on the legal pad in front of me. Ink spattered everywhere. Tapping is not a good idea when one writes with a fountain pen.

I leaned back and thought. Maybe I shouldn't kill him. After all, he was flawed in many ways but overall, a likeable person. Maybe he was redeemable. A light bulb went off in my head (figuratively speaking). What if I redeemed him instead of killing him? He could become a sidekick to my heroine. In fact, if I did it right, he could be a recurring character in later books. Oh, I liked that idea. It wreaked havoc with my outline, but I could already see how this book could be much better than I had imagined when I started writing it.

The biggest obstacle to the change was the fact that I was writing my latest mystery novel with a deadline in mind. Making a big change midstream could derail the whole process. My editor was wonderful, but she wouldn't cut me any slack when it came to deadlines. I can do it, I decided. This character could turn out to be a lot of fun. Ideas began to tumble from my brain. My pen flew across paper as though of its own volition. Finally, I ran out of ideas. I read the list of plot twists carefully. 'Well, that's just stupid,' I muttered, striking out one outlandish idea. I kept reading, placing asterisks by things that might enhance my story and making notes about things that I should keep for future plots. I stood at my desk and stretched. My hand was sore. My back was sore. My throat was dry. I had been working for hours and I needed a break. And after this breakthrough I deserved it.

I had read of one famous mystery writer who kept a treadmill next to her desk. When she needed to clear her mind, she jumped on her handy machine and ran. That wasn't for me. First, I couldn't fit a treadmill into my home office. Second, and more importantly, I didn't want to. I was definitely anti-running. It was too tough on the joints and after about one block I got a stitch in my side. It was sheer misery. I had hated it when I took physical education in middle school and high school and I hated it still. My son, Nick, who ran long distance on his high school track team, simply couldn't understand why I didn't run with him. Of course, he was sixteen going on seventeen and didn't understand a lot of things about me. And vice versa. Living with a teenager was a major learning experience. I wondered how he really felt about living with a single mother, and one with an unusual profession to boot. After all, I killed people for a living (metaphorically speaking).

Unlike running, I did understand walking, however. And I much preferred walking in the great outdoors to working out on some mechanical object wedged against my desk. I picked up the leash hanging on a doorknob and called for our boxer puppy, Maggie. She came running, tail wagging, her mouth forming an excited grin. I struggled to attach the leash to the little whirling dervish, my commands for her to sit having either been misunderstood, not understood, or, in all likelihood, ignored. After a short dance around each other we were joined together by a tenuous piece of spun fiber and we headed out to enjoy a beautiful autumn day.

4

Early autumn in southeast Virginia is a wonderful time of the year. The air has a crispness that holds a promise of colder weather and the delight of sitting by the fireplace or, even better, huddling around a fire pit in a friend's back yard, drinking hot beverages and planning holiday parties. Today the leaves were beginning to show off their fall colors. Spectacular orange and yellow leaves were interspersed with the green ones of summer. Fallen leaves crackled underfoot as we set off on our walk. The crackling made me remember my resolution to buy a leaf blower. Pretty is as pretty does, but sweeping the driveway and sidewalks clear of leaves was a lot of work. Normally I turned this task over to Nick, who accomplished it with a lot of complaining. A lot of very loud complaining, along with a fair amount of sighing. A year with a little less teenaged grousing would be a good thing. The blower would also help with snow removal if I bought one with enough power. And yes, before anyone asks, we do get snow in southeast Virginia. Sometimes we get a lot of it.

For at least today the thought of snow had escaped my mind. I decided to enjoy the perfect autumn temperatures. The weather hovered in the high sixties, more like Indian summer than true autumn. This weekend my friends on the street and I were going on our annual apple picking trip to an orchard outside Charlottesville. There would be hayrides, bluegrass music, hot apple donuts and sweet apple cider. I could hardly wait. Even if I didn't look forward to the cold temperatures and cloudy days of winter, never mind the snow, fall was my favorite season.

On the other hand, there was spring, with its enticing promise of things to come. And I couldn't forget summer, with bright sunshine and my vegetable garden bursting with harvest.

Let's face it, any season other than winter could be my favorite. I didn't ski and I didn't skate and I didn't like cold weather one little bit, so poor winter would have to remain at the bottom of my list.

A gust of wind tossed a bevy of leaves into the air. Maggie jumped around, snapping madly, doing her best to catch at least one of these unexpected treats. I laughed and threw a leafy handful toward her. She lunged and whirled, frantically biting the air. Then she suddenly threw herself onto the ground, rubbing her back energetically into a multihued pile. I laughed again and bent to tickle her tummy as she lay on her back, four legs waving in the air. Maggie accepted my ministrations for a few seconds before she brought herself to a standing position, shaking grass and leaves off her coat and grinning maniacally. I made a mental note to give her a bath before the day was done. Goodness knew what was lurking beneath those lovely leaves.

I took a deep, invigorating breath and looked around as Maggie and I headed toward our local park. Autumn in the college town of Summer Hill, Virginia, was a glorious time of year, as I may have already mentioned. Summer Hill University was back in full session, and along with that came an influx of students that seemed to give the town an energy it was missing in the summer. Our town is a popular tourist destination so it's not exactly quiet during the summer months, but seeing students walking, biking or skateboarding along the streets was energizing. No matter what one thinks of college students these days, they can be fun to watch. They crowded the outdoor cafes, drinking fancy coffee drinks or beer, arguing loudly about politics, philosophy, upcoming sporting events, or whatever caught their attention at the moment.

Groups of giggling young women poked around the inside of the boutiques and young men invaded other stores looking for the latest in sporting equipment, hopefully on sale. The theater group announced the year's first production, and in the afternoons, you could hear the university band practicing on the football field.

Tailgating is a popular occupation on game days. Summer Hill isn't a super power but it can hold its own against its competitors and most of us who live in Summer Hill enthusiastically root for our team. Tailgating gets competitive as the season progresses, with groups vying for the best decorated venue, the best team spirit, the best barbecue (my personal favorite because you get to taste all the entries) and other honors. Over the course of years, I had amassed quite a collection of recipes of what purported to be tailgate food, some of it amazingly fancy or intricate. My mind drifted momentarily to the long anticipated first tailgate party of the year. I knew I needed to find the perfect new tidbit to try out on my family and friends. My dear friend across the street, Ray, was a barbecue king, but I was our group's queen of appetizers and I loved surprising them with something different.

In addition to there being a plethora of school activities, the local farmer's market morphs into a fall foodie wonderland as autumn arrives. Ripe apples and succulent pears replace strawberries and blueberries. Corn and tomatoes disappear and hard squash, pumpkins and vegetables like cabbage take their places. And the baked goods! There are apple and pear pies, squash and pumpkin pies, apple bread, and apple cake, together with apple butter and apple sauce and candy apples. (Do you sense a theme here?) I smiled and increased my pace. With the thought of all that mouth watering food entrenched in my brain, I knew I needed to prepare by shedding a few pounds.

Maggie seemed to pick up on my mood. She trotted along beside me, head held high, happily exploring the fall scents in the air. We walked to the end of our street, turned right and entered the trail that led to a nearby lake. I was mentally rewriting parts of my book when I heard puffing behind us. I pulled Maggie to one side of the trail, preparing to allow a jogger to pass, but the person's steps slowed and then stopped.

"Jackie!" a voice called out.

I turned to see Marcia, my neighbor across the street, close friend and apple picking buddy leaning forward with her hands on her knees, breathing heavily.

"Since when did you take up jogging?" I asked.

"Since I was trying to catch up with you," she replied. "You must have been on another planet. You didn't hear me calling." She reached down and scratched Maggie's ears. "Even this pup didn't hear me." Maggie gave Marcia's hand an enthusiastic hand swipe. A swift tug on the leash and brisk command kept her from jumping up. If I were being completely honest, however, I might think that she was distracted by another leaf blowing across the path rather than following direction. With a puppy it can be so hard to tell. Whatever the reason, Maggie kept all paws on the ground and smiled up at us goofily.

As we talked, I surveyed Marcia skeptically. It was difficult for me to believe that a short run would cause her to lose her breath. Marcia was as tiny as a ballerina, fit from regular exercise at the gym and from her gymnastic coaching. Today she sported yellow and blue hair styled into a spikey hairdo. What in the world? Oh yeah, tonight was Summer Hill High School's annual football game against the high school from the next town. It was a fierce rivalry. Marcia's oldest son, Bob, was a tight end. I've always wondered what that means.

Certainly, you could look at the back of a football player and admire certain parts of his anatomy, but I was sure that had nothing to do with the position Bill played. Maybe I'd ask Nick. I could already see him rolling his eyes and wondering how his mother could be so dumb. Maybe I'd just ask Google.

Marcia and her husband, Bob, were fervent supporters of the team and Marcia was showing her enthusiasm by coloring her hair in the team colors. Marcia's hair color changed so often that we never knew if she was trying to signal her mood, support a cause (it was pink in support of breast cancer awareness during the annual fund drive) or if she was just having fun.

"Are you going to the game tonight?" she asked.

"Of course. I wouldn't miss it."

"I assume Nick's going."

"Sure is. He's going with some of the other kids in the neighborhood. I know the coach is disappointed Nick decided not to try out for the team this year, but track and swim team take enough of his time. He's satisfied with just being a spectator and rooting for the team this year."

"We'll miss his kicking," Marcia sighed. "Those field goals really help. The new guy's just not as good as Nick is. His scoring hasn't been that great. But I sure understand you not wan ting him to get over committed. Some of these kids are stretched so thin. And they're just doing things for their resumes." I agreed. Marcia continued. "We limited the twins this year. Bob told them to pick two things they want to do and to do them well." Marcia gave Maggie's ears another scratch. "Hey, do you want to walk around the lake? It's such a beautiful day."

I smiled as I listened to my friend. Sometimes it was hard to know what to

9

think of Marcia, given her hair and distinctive sartorial choices. I'll describe her as I would a piece of candy; fluffy center with a surprising hint of common sense surrounded by a quirky shell. Hard to describe but truly delicious.

We started at a reasonable pace. No running, thank you.

"The retirement home is sending a busload of residents to the game tonight," Marcia said, referring to the continuing care facility where she volunteered.

"That should be a lot of fun for them," I responded, wondering where this conversation was going.

"I think it's great," she replied. "Woodford Hall has so many activities for the people who can participate. They have loads of field trips, all sorts of arts and crafts, a great lecture series, and terrific food. I guess Bob and I will end up in a place like that some day. If we can afford it…"

"It's a little early to be thinking of that now," I said, squinting at Marcia. She and I, as well as our other friends on the street, were in our early forties. That seemed young to be thinking about senior living.

"You never know what will happen." Marcia pursed her lips and slid her eyes in my direction.

I knew that only too well. My husband, age forty, had been felled suddenly by a brain aneurism. Talk about a shock! Two years later I was feeling that I was more or less on solid ground once again, but the thought of my wonderful Lars still caused a twinge in my heart and sourness in my stomach. And sometimes, after a particularly trying day, I still hold a one-person pity party, crying in my bedroom and asking God why he took Lars. So far, He hasn't answered. I doubt he ever will.

"But a nursing home?" I asked.

"Continuing care facility," Marcia corrected me. "Many of the people who live there still drive and have very active lives. I guess it gives them comfort to know that if they get sick their care is already arranged." She paused to pick up some fallen oak leaves. "These will be pretty in a centerpiece." Marcia fancied herself an artist and was constantly creating decorations for her home. Sometimes they worked. Other times they didn't. On more than one occasion a weird yard display had vanished in the middle of the night. Each time that happened Marcia was absolutely flabbergasted. Sometimes she convinced herself that the display in question had been so special that a trespasser decided he or she just had to have it. It never seemed to occur to her that no part of her handiwork ever reappeared elsewhere in the neighborhood. I had my suspicions as to the identity of the culprit who made Marcia's decorations disappear but, at least to date, I was keeping mum.

"One of the ladies I visit at Woodford Hall invited me to tea tomorrow," Marcia said. "Would you like to go?"

I thought a moment. "I don't think so. I'm making major revisions in my book and the deadline is closing in. It's sort of like preparing for a hurricane, which my editor will create if I'm late with the book."

"Tea at Woodford Hall is supposed to be very special," Marcia coaxed.

"I know, but no can do," I said adamantly. Sometimes you just had to stand firm, particularly against a friend with Marcia's persistence.

Marcia stopped. She stared at the lake a moment and then turned to me. "Here's the thing," she finally said. "This lady said she wants to talk to me about something important. She said there's something going on at Woodford Hall that she's worried about."

"What could that be?" I wondered.

Marcia shrugged. "It could be someone stealing. You hear all the time about that going on in places like Woodford. Or it could be a new chef." She spread her arms out. "It could be anything." She took a deep breath. "Here's the weird part. She wants me to bring you. And Bernice. And Linda," referring to our other friends on our cul-de-sac.

My eyebrows shot up into my bangs. "What in the world for?"

"If I knew, I'd tell you, wouldn't I?" Marcia asked in annoyance.

"Of course, you would. That was just a stupid rhetorical question." I replied.

"Oh, one of those," Marcia said. "I should have known." She put her hands on her hips. "So, are you coming or not?"

I continued to resist. "Why don't you just let me know what she wants when you get back from tea? I really need to work." I was feeling truly perplexed about the invitation. "How does she even know who we are?" I asked.

"Well," Marcia said, turning the word into one of multi-syllables, "She did mention how we helped solve that murder in the neighborhood. Maybe she wants a detective to look into the new chef or whatever is going on."

"Then she should hire one," I said stubbornly. "Or start a committee. Don't they love committees at places like Woodford Hall?"

"I'd agree with you," Marcia said, "but she sounded really worried." She hesitated. "Actually, she sounded frightened. That really bothers me. I don't think she's the kind of woman who would blow things out of proportion. I've always found her to be very level headed." She spread her hands out in supplication. "Jackie, I'm concerned."

I thought for a moment. This did sound kind of interesting. And Marcia was

12

one of my closest friends. If she was truly worried about whatever this lady might share, it was important that her friends be supportive. Maybe I could work a little longer than I had planned this afternoon. Maybe I could get up early in the morning. Or maybe... "This is too intriguing," I replied. "I'll be there."

Maggie tugged on her leash and the three of us headed for home.

# Chapter Two

Sunday brunch at Woodford Hall is considered quite an event and "scoring" an invitation from a resident at the compound is a coup. With that in mind, I stood in my bedroom closet feeling desperation pour over me as I tried to decide what to wear.

A casual sweater and tailored slacks wouldn't do. I needed to come up with something more elegant than that. Unfortunately, very little, if anything, in my closet ran to sophisticated, fashionable or elegant. I worked from home. Now that I was a widow, I didn't need the pretty dresses and slacks outfits I wore for evenings out with Lars or for law firm parties. Blue jeans and tee shirts were more my current style.

Nothing I pulled off the rack seemed right. I sighed and dialed the number of my fashion consultant, my neighbor Bernice. A former model, Bernice has impeccable taste and is happy to share clothing suggestions. Unfortunately, she's a 5 foot ten-inch-tall African American prone to wearing greens, yellow and oranges, while I'm a 5 foot five-inch-tall blonde who looks like she's been stricken with the plague if she wears those shades. So obviously there is no wardrobe sharing between us. However, desperate times call for desperate measures. Surely Bernice would offer some sage advice. And she better offer it quickly; it was almost time to leave. "Help," I said when Bernice answered her phone.

Bernice's throaty chuckle responded. "Wardrobe problems?" she said knowingly.

"Yes," I replied, "and I really shouldn't be going anyway. I'm going to get behind on my writing and…"

"You're on deadline," Bernice said. "I know."

We'd been this situation before. "You need to go," she urged me. "I can feel this is going to lead to something exciting, and Lord knows I could use some excitement."

Uh oh.

"What's up?" I asked.

"That's the problem," Bernice sighed. "Nothing's up. No crisis at my husband's job. Classes at the college are going smoothly." Bernice, a tenured professor at Summer Hill University, had returned to school after retiring from modeling and earned her PhD in mathematics. Her husband, a former professional football player, was principal of our local high school. "The kids are healthy. Their grades are good. I need something to happen."

Uh oh again. When Bernice was in this kind of mood, she could come up with almost anything to relieve her boredom. The last time she felt this way I had ended up tethered to a bungee cord.

"I don't know what to wear!" I wailed.

"Wear that calf length suede skirt with the burgundy sweater and a scarf." How could she remember so clearly what was in my closet? Maybe the fact that, as I indicated earlier, it was largely filled with jeans, shorts and tee shirts helped. I took the mentioned items off their hangers. "And a hat?"

"And a hat," Bernice confirmed. "Don't forget makeup. Mascara and lipstick are not going to cut it. And get a move on. We're leaving in ten minutes."

I glanced at my watch and stepped into the skirt. "Crap!"

"Indeed," Bernice said cheerfully, ending the call.

I peered at my face in the bathroom mirror. I pulled my make up mirror out

15

from under the counter and looked more carefully. I was blessed with good skin, probably a legacy from my British grandmother. She always credited her peaches and cream complexion, which she had long into her 80's, to the moisture of her native land. I suspected, on the other hand, that it was the result of good genes which I appear to have inherited. That made more sense, since grandma hadn't returned to England after she left, at which time she was a young bride. After Lars died, I had maintained my skin routine, but had stopped wearing makeup for the most part. As Bernice implied, the most I had done was to swipe some mascara onto my lashes and color my lips. If truth were to be known, after I was widowed, I simply stopped caring. That probably accounted for my drab, uninspired wardrobe also. Now, my feminist friends would insist that none of this matters, that our beauty springs from our personality and what lies inside us. To a great extent they are right. On the other hand, there is something to be said for making the most of your assets and, sometimes, for simply feeling pretty. Somehow, I had forgotten this.

I sat in the chair at my bathroom counter and carefully applied foundation, blush, eye shadow and lipstick. I always thought that my green eyes were my best asset and, as I surveyed myself in the mirror, I noticed that they seemed to sparkle with the application of a bit of cosmetics. What an improvement!

I plaited my hair into a French braid, carefully pleated my scarf and placed a tan fedora jauntily on my head to complete my outfit. As I turned to leave Nick walked past my room. He put on the brakes, looked me up and down and gave a low whistle. "Mom, you look fabulous."

Fabulous? Really? How long had it been since someone said I looked fabulous? Sure, the compliment came from my teenaged son, but on some level that made it more special because he rarely noticed anything about my looks. I took a final glance in the mirror.

Maybe it was time to take a little care with my appearance. The made up me felt a little lighter, a little happier, somehow. I decided to put aside questions about what this feeling implied about my psyche for another time and just go with the flow.

As to my wardrobe, I had a little extra money in my bank account. Perhaps I would go shopping and buy a new outfit or two. Bernice would certainly help me with that. And Marcia and Linda would happily join in. I hesitated about asking them. I had the bad feeling that they'd have a great time dressing me and that I'd end up feeling like a walking, talking Barbie doll. Another idea went into the 'think about it later' pile. That pile was getting awfully tall.

I smiled at my reflection, hugged Nick, gave Maggie a farewell pat and stepped outside just as my friends approached my driveway.

As expected, Bernice was perfectly groomed, clad in a dress that flattered her slender figure. She had added a turban that accentuated her high cheekbones, aquiline nose and slightly slanted eyes. Marcia looked prim and proper in a black and white dress with a tight bodice and flared skirt. On her head was perched a tiny fascinator, the type of hats made so popular by the British royal family. And miracle of miracle, her hair was its natural color. Linda, who lived at the end of our cul-de-sac, wore a formfitting grey suit with a large brimmed hat topping her silver locks. Her sleek runner's legs looked even longer than ever, since she was wearing high heels that were about 6 inches tall. I would have taken one step and broken my ankle had I tried wearing shoes like that.

"Another adventure!" Linda said, sliding into the passenger seat of my car.

"I guess," I muttered, turning the key in the ignition.

Bernice tapped me on the shoulder. "You look beautiful," she said. I couldn't help but smile.

As we drove toward Woodford Hall, we speculated on why Marcia's friend wanted to meet us all. Recently we had been instrumental in solving the murder of my next-door neighbor, something we had found ourselves investigating because of our fondness for her high school-aged daughter, whose father had been the prime suspect. We had attracted a fair bit of attention when the case was solved and our involvement exposed, but that attention seemed to fade relatively quickly. At least we thought it had.

"I can't imagine why else Evelyn wants to meet you," Marcia said, echoing our conversation, as I turned the car off the main road and drove down a narrow drive with white fencing on either side. Along both sides of the road horses raised their heads as we passed, one young stallion racing alongside our car.

"Aren't they beautiful?" Bernice asked.

"I wouldn't mind riding again," Linda commented, watching the graceful animals.

"I didn't realize you did," I said, carefully taking a tight turn onto the road that would lead us to the main building.

"Oh yes, my sister and I had horses when we were growing up," Linda said. "I really miss them."

There are a lot of horse farms in our part of Virginia. Secretariat, the Triple Crown winner, was bred on a farm just outside Richmond and as you drive west toward Charlottesville equestrian communities and farms become prevalent, along with wineries.

"Maybe we should all take up riding," Bernice said. "I wonder if the kids would like it."

"As if your kids don't have enough to do," Marcia snorted. "And no, you can't keep a horse in your back yard."

Bernice appeared lost in thought. Oh dear. She really must be bored.

A sprawling white building appeared in front of us as I made another turn. Large pillars supported a dark green roof, and a wide porch filled with autumn flowers and casual seating arrangements spread its entire length. Two wings stood at a 45-degree angle to the main building. On either side we caught glimpses of individual homes, or cottages as they were called, and two roads wrapped behind the structure and wound their way through large fields dotted with occasional groupings of trees.

"This place is beautiful," Linda whispered. "It must cost a fortune to live here."

"It's not cheap," Marcia agreed, "but Bob says that with careful planning we could probably do it." Marcia's accountant husband was happiest when counting the cost of things His grocery shopping spread sheets drove Marcia crazy.

"I'm not sure I'd want to," Bernice said, stepping out of the car. "It's awfully quiet." Indeed, we hadn't seen a single person since we entered the grounds.

"Well, it *is* tea time," Marcia pointed out. "When I'm here during the week there's a lot going on. And as I told Jackie, a lot of the people are still fairly young and fit. Some of them board their horses here and there's an active riding program and a school where some of the residents teach children how to ride. They even have a program that works with handicapped children."

"I hope I'm able to do that when I retire," Linda commented. "Right now, it

19

sometimes feels like getting out of bed is a chore. I don't think I'd have the energy to volunteer with a program like that, although I'd love to."

"That's because you're still working," Marcia replied. Linda was an executive with our local hospital. "I bet it's different when your time is really your own."

"On the other hand, it might give you more energy to involve yourself in something you love," Bernice said, always the one to encourage us to follow our dreams.

"Humm," Linda replied noncommittally. "I'll think about it."

"You go, girl," Marcia said, punching her gently in the arm.

Linda smiled and took a final glance at the horse pasture. The stallion that had raced us was hanging his head over the fence. He whinnied softly at her.

"Humm," Linda said again.

We stepped into the main foyer. Oak floors gleamed under patterned rugs. In front of us rose a cantilevered staircase, spiraling gracefully to the second floor. To the right a stone fireplace graced the far wall, with several groups of flowered chairs set near it. A low fire glowed in the fireplace. As we entered, a tiny woman rose from a wingback chair and approached us with a smile.

"Marcia!" she said.

"Evelyn!" Marcia met the woman halfway and they hugged.

"I'm so glad you came," Evelyn said. She beamed at us. "And these must be the friends of yours I've heard so much about." Marcia introduced us. "Well, you look so lovely and festive," Evelyn said. She patted her coiffured head. "I've given up wearing hats for the most part, but maybe I should rethink that decision."

Linda blew a feather away from her eyes. "I can't see a darned thing with this hat," she said softly. She grinned. "But I look terrific."

Evelyn smiled. "I should warn you that I have very good hearing." Linda blushed. Evelyn's smile widened. "You truly do look terrific," she told Linda. "I'll rethink my ban on wearing hats, but the real reason I don't wear hats any more is that the doggoned things make my head itch."

We all laughed.

Bernice looked appreciatively around the lobby. "This is a beautiful space," she said. "And the fire makes it feel so warm and inviting, even if it is so huge."

Evelyn agreed. "The management does their best to make it feel that way. You must come back at Christmas. The entire place is festooned with greenery and ornaments, there is an enormous tree tucked under the staircase and at least once per week we have live music performances along with wine and appetizers. I'll have to send you a list of concerts, so you'll know when you'd like to come."

We all indicated our appreciation for the invitation.

"Let's go in to brunch." Evelyn led the way down a deeply carpeted corridor and into a large room with French doors opening onto a garden centered on a fish pond. "I don't know why they carpeted this hallway," she complained. "People with wheelchairs have the devil of a time. And a lot of us with apartments do need help walking." She sniffed. "Sometimes decorators don't seem to have much common sense. Occasionally the poor waiters have to lift a wheel chair and its passenger into the dining room. It's a wonder they don't hurt themselves."

The room we entered held an assortment of tables, all covered in white linens and set with sparkling china and cut glass. A waitress clad in a tuxedo led us

21

to a table next to the French doors. "I wanted you to enjoy the view of the garden," Evelyn said. She gestured to the woman who had seated us. "Let's have some wine," she said. She winked. "I'm so glad I didn't end up in a dry county. I do enjoy wine with my meal." Our attendant left to fetch the beverage and another immediately took her place. He set a multi-layered plate covered with pastries in the center of our table. "Help yourselves," Evelyn said as the waiter handed each of us a menu. "I can particularly recommend the crab eggs benedict or the stuffed French toast although everything's good."

We chatted amicably during the meal, enjoying our new acquaintance. When we couldn't eat another bite, Evelyn pushed her chair back. "Let's go enjoy the garden. It's such a lovely day."

We stepped through the French doors and meandered along a trail that ended with benches next to the koi pond. Evelyn gestured to us to sit.

She tilted her head. "I bet you're wondering why I asked you here," she said. She laughed. "My, that was a cliché, wasn't it?" We all nodded and laughed with her.

Evelyn sighed. "I have a friend who has a bit of a problem." She looked at us intently, her gaze finally resting on me. "You're the one whose next-door neighbor was murdered, aren't you?"

"Yes" I admitted.

"I read in the papers how you . . . how all of you helped the police figure out who the killer was."

"Not really," I demurred. Indeed, I had almost become a victim myself, but I didn't want to lay claim to actually solving the case.

"We DID help," Marcia said, kicking my shin. "I don't know if the police would have ever figured it out."

"I'm sure they would have," I disagreed.

Bernice and Linda were scowling at me. "We helped," Bernice said, "not that the police appreciated it."

'I think they would have solved it," I insisted.

"I'm not so sure," Linda said.

"And if you weren't dating a certain person connected with the case, you might not think the way you do either," Bernice said.

I clenched my jaw stubbornly. "Yes, they would have," I said under my breath.

Evelyn's lips twitched. "This must be a story for another time."

I glared at my friends, who rapidly agreed that now was not the time to dissect my love life, such as it was.

"Well," Evelyn said, "modesty is fine in most circumstances, but I know what I've read and what I've heard."

Here I glanced at Marcia suspiciously. She seemed to be avoiding my gaze.

"My friend needs help, and I think you're the people to help her."

"What does she need help with?" I asked.

Evelyn frowned and lowered her voice. "She thinks someone is trying to kill her."

# Chapter Three

Gob smacked. Isn't that what the British say when they're completely taken by surprise? It's such a lovely word, carrying so much meaning in just two syllables. Yep, that's what I was. Gob smacked. I'm sure my jaw had dropped at Evelyn's words and that my eyes were bulging out like those of the koi in the pond. In fact, if the fish were listening, I'd be willing to bet they were gob smacked too. I cast a glance over my friends. Everyone looked equally stunned. They sat staring silently at Evelyn. She had accomplished something never before done in history. None of us was talking.

Suddenly, pandemonium broke out and we were all talking at once. Babbling was more like it. "What? When? How?" Etc., etc., etc.

Marcia turned and pointed a finger at me. "You talk." Bernice and Linda nodded their heads vigorously. I took a moment to collect my thoughts.

"What makes your friend think someone's trying to kill her?" I finally managed. Evelyn shrugged. "There have been several incidents. At first, she could explain them away, but gradually they became more blatant. The last one was very obvious."

"In that case," I said, the voice of reason speaking, "She needs to talk to the police."

Evelyn sighed. "I suggested that. But she insists she doesn't have any concrete evidence and that the police wouldn't take her seriously."

I tried a different tact. "Why would someone want to kill her?"

"Judith is a very wealthy woman. Very wealthy. She and her husband started and built up a major commercial construction company in the Richmond area. I'm sure you've seen signs for it on some of the university's building projects.

Her husband's dead now and Judith holds the purse strings. Except for gifts to charity, which have been very generous, she holds those strings very tightly indeed. She has two children and a goddaughter, all of whom expect to inherit fortunes when she passes away. Judith has been very clear that she wants them to make their own way in the world. She and her husband paid for their college educations, and she plans to do the same for her grandchildren. Other than that, however, they have largely been left to their own devices." She paused and thought for a moment. "That's not completely true. All of them other than her son-in-law have jobs at the company now. In fact, her son is running the day-to-day operations. Unlike in a lot of other rich families, however, there haven't been any large gifts, money to help with house purchases or graduate school. Judith and her husband have actually been less generous than a lot of les well-off parents I know. And although her heirs all work for the company, Judith still holds the majority of the stock and she's very involved in decision making."

That could be uncomfortable for a child, I thought. It was as though they were being given a chance at success but not the ability to truly reap the rewards of their labors. And if she was still the decision maker that could lead to a good deal of frustration on the part of the next generation.

"I still don't see…" Linda began.

"Oh, you will, if you talk with Judith and meet the family," Evelyn assured us.

"How does she get along with these people?" I asked.

"On the surface quite well," Judith said. "Of course, there are other players, like spouses and a grown grandson who has strong ideas as to what his position in the company should be. Recently there have been some unpleasant conversations, with the children and goddaughter implying that Judith should step aside and give the company to them."

"Is there anyone else who would benefit from her death?" Bernice asked.

Evelyn thought. "I haven't actually seen her will, but we've talked about it a bit. She's left some significant gifts to charities, particularly to the Virginia Museum of Fine Arts and the Richmond Symphony. She does have a long-time personal assistant. I believe she's left her a nice bequest. Nothing huge, but enough to enable her to travel and do some other things she might want to do."

"So, you're saying," Linda said slowly, "that any one of these people could be impatient and trying to hasten Judith's departure from the earth."

"Possibly," Evelyn agreed. "Or possibly not. The things that have happened could have been coincidences." She thought for a moment. "Except for the last one. That one really concerns me. I just can't see how it could have been accidental."

"What was it?" I asked.

"I'd rather you talk with Judith and let her tell you herself," Evelyn said.

"Evelyn," Marcia said, "This really sounds like something for the police to investigate. If she doesn't want to make a formal complaint, we know a police detective who's very good at his job. He might be willing to nose around informally."

For some reason my friends all looked at me. What? Count me out. I was *not* going to talk to Riley Furman about this. We had become acquainted with Riley while he was investigating my neighbor's murder. At the time he was a pain in a certain part of my anatomy. Many were the times I wished him gone,

26

permanently. Granted, that had changed gradually. We had started to see each other socially. We'd gone on some motorcycle rides and out to dinner. In fact, he was having dinner at my house on Friday. We were starting to develop what felt like a promising relationship, and I didn't want to jeopardize that by getting involved in another case, if indeed there was a case here at all. I remembered all too clearly how aggravated Riley had been with me when I kept poking my nose into the murder next door. His pet name for me was Miss Marple. It wasn't always said with affection. And I didn't always appreciate the tone of voice with which he said that name. Nope, I wasn't about to reopen that door. No way, no how.

"Jackie knows the detective really well," Marcia continued, seemingly oblivious to my consternation or the stubborn set of my mouth.

"I don't think that's a good idea," I protested, before this chain of thought progressed any further. "You know Riley has no patience for frivolous claims or for us nosing around where he doesn't think we should."

"At least talk to Judith," Evelyn pleaded. She lifted a cell phone that had been hidden in the pocket of her dress. "She's waiting for my call."

"It can't hurt to talk to her I guess," Bernice conceded.

"Wonderful!" Evelyn exclaimed. "And if you think she's exaggerating what's happened, tell her so. Maybe she'll be able to relax." She pointed past the koi pond. "Her house is just on the other side of the garden. We can walk from here." She took in Linda's stilettos. "Or maybe not," she muttered.

In the end we drove to Judith's house, arguing all the way. Of course, it wasn't very far so we didn't argue long, but things got pretty heated.

"This is a stupid idea," I said, backing out of our parking space. "We are not detectives. There's no way we'll know if this is just paranoia on the part of an old lady."

"We did pretty well solving Liz's murder," Marcia replied.

"Yeah, but we only got involved because one of our friends was looking at the inside of a jail cell," Linda said. "If this lady is as rich as Evelyn says, let her hire a private investigator. They know how to deal with things like this."

"I think we should at least listen," Bernice said. "Maybe we can make her feel better."

"I don't like this," I said, pulling into the driveway at the largest cottage we had seen. "We could make things worse, bumbling around like Clouseau in the Pink Panther. I agree with Linda. Let her hire a pro."

"Well, we're here," Marcia said, opening her door. "And Evelyn's parked behind us, so I'd say we're stuck."

"Come on," Bernice said. "Let's stick together. All for one and one for all." She also opened her door.

"I think we're more like the Summer Hill Irregulars than the Three Musketeers," Linda grumbled, likening us to Sherlock Holmes and his ragtag band of street urchins.

"Try the Four Stooges," I said. "There *was* a fourth brother, you know."

We joined Evelyn on the stoop of the house. Like most of the other houses, it had a deep porch. This one was decorated with wicker furniture and fall colored pillows. An assortment of chrysanthemums was arranged tastefully to one side of the front door. On the door hung a large wreath festooned with leaves and fall fruits.

The door opened as soon as we rang the bell. Obviously, Judith had been

28

waiting for us. I wasn't sure what I had expected, but she wasn't it. She was tall and slender, looking extremely fit in a pair of leggings and a fitted tunic. Her short gray hair curled charmingly around her face and her blue eyes shone with intelligence. "Please, come in," she said, moving aside.

"She doesn't look like a paranoid old lady to me," Marcia whispered as she passed me.

The door opened into an expansive space.. To the right was a dining alcove that held a long modern table and eight chairs. Straight ahead were couches sitting at right angles to one another, along with a wing back chair set next to a stone fireplace. An enormous kitchen with an island took up the right-hand side of the space. Bright modern art decorated the walls. The coffee and side tables held sculptures and art books. Family pictures dotted the built- in bookcases on both sides of the fireplace, tucked in among more books and art pieces.

"Please, sit down." Judith gestured toward the couches. "I so appreciate your agreeing to see me. I know you've just had tea, but I hope you'll join me in a glass of wine. Wine can make difficult conversations easier; don't you agree?" Indeed, we did.

"Mrs. Byrn," I started, having learned her last name from Evelyn.

She waved her hand "Please, call me Judith. I'm not much on formality, and your calling me Mrs. Byrn makes me feel ancient."

"Judith," I said obediently, "We're flattered that you seem to think we can help you with your situation, but we're just four ordinary women who somehow helped solve a murder case. And we only tried to do that because we were concerned for our friend and his daughter. It was pure luck."

"Was it?" Judith raised her eyebrows, handing me a glass of wine. "Or are you

29

good observers of human nature? Perhaps women who see more than anyone would suspect and are determined to get at the truth of a matter?"

"Why don't you tell us more about your situation?" Linda suggested, accepting her glass of wine.

"We're going to get sloshed," Marcia said. She glanced at me. "Remember that you're driving."

"We'll have coffee and a snack later" Judith assured us.

More food? Great. Just what my waistline needed.

Judith gave a long sigh and sat in the wingback chair. "Has Evelyn told you anything about me and my family?"

"A little bit," I replied.

"My husband and I raised good children," she said. "At least I have always thought so until now. But recently things seem to have changed a bit and I'm finding myself looking at them in a different way." She shook her head. "I don't want to do that. I love them all, including my in-laws. Well, with one exception. I'm not crazy about my son's wife. But that's nothing new. I try not to let it show, but I suspect she knows. After all these years I assume I've slipped up more than once." She gave a self-deprecating smile. "Bert, my husband, and I, always believed in giving children a strong start and then letting them have their heads. We didn't want to raise a bunch of entitled brats. As to my goddaughter, her mother died fairly young and I think of Emily as another daughter of mine, so I've treated her very much like the others."

"Why do you think things have changed?" Bernice asked.

"Oh, I don't think they have, I know they have," Judith replied. "My daughter has made some very unkind remarks recently about my holding the family

30

money over them and being unwilling to share. That's nonsense, of course. They all earn a good living from the company. I could have refused to let them join and made them earn their ways completely away from the family business had I chosen to do so."

"But you didn't?" I asked.

She shook her head. "No. One by one they have joined. For the most part they have performed well and, as I said, have been able to live quite comfortably." She took a sip of her wine. "But now they seem to be getting impatient. My son is pressing me to let him make more of the business decisions. And he keeps suggesting that for 'estate planning purposes' I gift them more of the stock. But if I followed his advice, he'd end up having control."

"What a surprise," Marcia muttered.

Judith smiled sardonically. "Exactly."

"At this point in your life would that be such a bad thing?" I asked.

Judith looked surprised. "My husband and, to a lesser extent, I, worked very hard to create this company. Parting with it would be like losing a child. And if the children didn't run it well it would break my heart."

"So, it sounds like your son hasn't proven himself to you," I said.

"No, he has. It comes back to that wife of his. She has a lot of power over him. I think if he controlled the company, she'd manage to suck it dry."

"Oh, my," Linda said.

"And now my grandson, who just graduated from college, is pushing for a place at the table. Like many of his generation, he seems to think he's entitled to start near the top, not work his way up like his father did. So far, I've encouraged him to get some experience elsewhere first. He hasn't taken that advice very

31

well. I'm afraid he's a lot like his mother when it comes to wanting things without working for them." Judith chewed her lip. "Against my wishes, my son offered Henry a job with our company. At least it's an entry level position; not what Henry or his mother wanted, but thank goodness my son has some common sense. Besides, he knows that giving Henry too much responsibility too soon could damage the company and that's not something Bert," she saw our puzzled faces, "that's my son, wants. He has great plans for the company, or so he tells me. He won't let Henry jeopardize that."

Wow. If Judith truly loved her family, I wasn't hearing it. She sounded like a tough, controlling lady.

She must have read my face. "I do love my family," she assured us. "I've provided very well for all of them in my will. And we can still have a great time when we're together doing what we love to do as a family. We love to cook together, ride horses, go to a good play or concert as a group, and even take some short trips. But in light of what's happened recently, I'm just not sure I can trust them all."

"What exactly has happened?" Bernice asked.

"It started a few months ago," Judith replied. "There's a metal plate on the step leading down to my garage. I caught my toe in it when it was loose and took a tumble. It was only one step and I didn't get hurt. I put it down to needing maintenance and had it fixed. Then around my birthday I received a big box of chocolates, supposedly from the family. I had a couple of pieces, as did the lady who cleans my house. We both got terribly sick. The doctor was suspicious about food poisoning, but the only thing we could remember eating in common was that candy. We had thrown the rest out, so the doctor couldn't have it tested."

I interrupted. "Who sent the candy?"

Judith frowned. "To this day I don't know. No one in the family took responsibility for the gift. My assistant, Veronica, received it at the door and it didn't have a tag."

"So theoretically it might not have come from the family," I said.

"I suppose that's true," Judith admitted. "I just can't think of anyone else who'd send me a gift like that."

"And just as theoretically, your assistant could have doctored the candy herself," Bernice said. "She even could have had it sent herself."

Evelyn clapped her hands. "See? I knew you were good at this."

"But why would she do that?" Judith asked.

"You tell us," I said bluntly. "Would she benefit from your death?"

"Yes," Judith said slowly, "She would. I've left her a nice bequest in my will. But I don't think she knows about it." She thought a while longer. "She's gone out with Henry a few times," she said. "They're not far apart in age. I guess she could want Henry to move up in the company and to attach herself to a wealthy young man." She shook her head. "When I say that out loud, it sounds absurd."

Did it? I wasn't so sure.

"She's your assistant,' I persisted, "Wouldn't she have access to your papers? She might have seen the will without your knowing."

"I suppose she might. I've tried to keep things like the will locked up separately. But I suppose I could have been careless at some point."

"Has anything else happened?" Marcia asked.

"There was one event that unnerved me, although it wasn't dangerous," Judith replied. "My dog went missing."

I look around for a dog and spotted a bed and toys in a corner of the living room. "Where is she now?" I asked.

"She's asleep in her crate in the bedroom," Judith replied. "I didn't want her to be underfoot."

"So how did she go missing?"

Judith shrugged. "That's the thing. I don't know. A few weeks ago, I came home from doing some shopping and I couldn't find her. I searched the entire house. There aren't that many places she can hide. I knew that she was in her bed over there when I left. She was chewing on her giraffe. That's her favorite toy. When I came back the giraffe was there and she was gone. She doesn't have a doggie door and all the house doors were closed and locked. I searched and searched for her. I canvassed the neighbors and walked all over the grounds looking for her. I was a mess." Her eyes teared up. "I love that little dog so much. Everyone around here knows it." She resumed her story. "I must have searched for well over an hour. When I came home and opened the door, there she was, sitting in her bed." She looked around the room "I don't understand it. For a moment I thought I was going crazy."

"Maybe someone was letting you know they had access to your house," Linda suggested.

Judith nodded. "I think that's very likely. All the family members have keys. So do my assistant and the housekeeper."

"The incident with the dog would have freaked me out," Bernice said. "It reminds me of the movie Gaslight. Does everyone remember that one? Charles Boyer was trying to make Ingrid Bergman believe she was going crazy."

"It's a classic, and very creepy," Judith said.

We all shuddered.

"Tell them about the most recent event," Evelyn urged.

"I often ride one of the horses here," Judith said. "Midnight is such a wonderful horse. He's so responsive and eager to please. Anyway, I have my own tack, which I keep in the community barn. Last Tuesday I was saddling him up. When I pulled the girth to tighten it something didn't feel right. I called the groom over. He ended up taking everything off. When he did, we saw that the strap was frayed. It easily could have broken while I was riding. The gear had been in perfect condition the last time I rode."

"When was that?" I asked.

"About a week ago."

"You could have been badly injured, if not killed," Bernice said.

"And if I'm badly injured my children have my power of attorney," Judith said softly. "Maybe they don't have to kill me to get what they want."

I admitted to myself that the series of events was alarming. As much as I hated to admit it, a conversation with Riley was starting to sound like a good idea.

"I still don't see what we can do," Marcia said.

"I agree. If I were you, I would definitely go to the police," Linda said. Once again, my friends looked at me.

"Maybe," I muttered. I wasn't sure Judith had anything concrete enough to support police interest. On the other hand, I didn't see what we could do. I wondered what Riley would say.

Judith leaned forward. "I don't want to raise suspicion if there shouldn't be any. Imagine how my family would react if the police suddenly appeared, asking all sorts of questions." She looked at us imploringly. "Can't you at least meet them? And meet my assistant also, now that you mention it. Just get a feel for them. If after you do that you think I need to consult the police I promise I'll do it."

I hesitated. "If someone really is trying to harm you, the police should be brought in sooner rather than later. This really is not our area of expertise."

"Besides," Bernice said, "How would we go about meeting these people? We can't exactly drop in to the company office and start asking questions."

"That's easy," Judith said. "I'm having a cocktail party in the main clubhouse in two weeks. Come as my guests. Bring your husbands. It's a large function. You'll fit right in."

"Absolutely," Evelyn said. She turned to me. "Bring your beau."

My what? Riley? My beau? No way. Nope. Not going to happen. I was not going to bring him. And I was not going to call him my beau.

# Chapter Four

"So, what do you think?" I asked as I drove us home. There was a strange noise from the back seat of the car. Linda and I looked at each other in alarm. "What was that?" I asked. It happened again. I was beginning to fear there was something really wrong with the rear end of my car and started to pull to the side of the road.

"That was a sucking sound," Marcia piped up.

I moved back onto the roadway. "A sucking sound?" I asked.

"The sound of our getting sucked into investigating whatever is happening to Judith Byrn."

"Oh, I don't know," I protested. "I still like Linda's idea of her hiring a private investigator."

"Why don't you at least talk this over with Riley?" Marcia said. "He probably knows of a reputable investigator who does more than chase cheating spouses around."

"I really don't want to get him involved," I said. "We're not on a footing where I'd feel comfortable dragging him into this. Besides, there must be dozens of regulations against his investigating anything other than what his boss tells him to investigate."

"I think you should reconsider, Jackie," Bernice said. "After hearing what Judith's been through, I'm truly afraid she may be in danger. How could it possibly hurt to tell Riley what Judith told us? We're not asking for him to investigate, just for his advice."

I remained silent. Of my friends, I tended to think of Bernice as being the most level headed. If she thought something was wrong, I needed to reconsider my position. In the back of my mind, however, I could hear that honey-smooth voice of Riley's saying, "Miss Marple, what are you getting yourself into?" As I said earlier, when Riley called me that, good things did not necessarily follow. I was certain I didn't want to take a big step backwards in our relationship, and discussing Judith could lead to that. Or worse, it could lead to no relationship at all. It was interesting that I didn't want to risk that. When I had time, I'd have to think about what that meant, but not now. The 'think about it later' pile grew again. When was I supposed to do all this thinking? And finish my book. The book. For a moment, I had forgotten all about it. 'Keep on trac, Jackie'. Focus. In the meantime, I was driving. And my friends were still talking.

"I know what we could do!" Linda said. "Riley's coming for dinner Friday, right?"

I nodded.

"Why don't we turn it into a group dinner? We could all come over and approach him as a group."

"That sounds romantic," Marcia muttered.

"Why not?" Linda persisted. "We've had dinner with him before."

"Was that the time he threatened to throw us all in jail for obstructing his investigation?" I asked darkly.

"There was that," Linda admitted.

"I could bring my famous wedge salad," Bernice said.

Tempting, but no.

"What were you planning on doing?" Marcia asked. "Unless it's X-rated, of course. In which case we don't need to know. But if it were, I could make some suggestions…"

"Stop right there." I said. "Keep it up and you'll walk home." I glanced in the mirror and saw her pouting.

Silence lingered. I thought about my upcoming date. What were we planning on doing? I knew from a conversation the day before that Riley was facing a tough week, being in charge of investigating a double homicide that had made all the local headlines. Two teenagers had been found shot to death in the boy's car. At least from the news clips, there seemed to be no suspects and no significant clues to help the investigation along. Riley had sounded frustrated and even a little angry at the senselessness of the killing when we talked. There! That alone should be reason not to drag him into Judith's troubles. He had enough on his plate without worrying about us.

"We were going to have a nice dinner and watch a movie," I said.

"What movie?" Linda asked.

"Incredibles II."

"Wow, that's really romantic." Marcia again.

"Riley's under a lot of stress. We decided to watch something lighthearted."

"How about Sleepless in Seattle?" Marcia asked. "At least that would be romantic."

"Would you cut it out?" Riley and I hadn't even reached the point of holding hands when we walked together. I liked him and, to be honest, I was quite attracted to him, but the ghost of my deceased husband kept making its presence known at inopportune times. Riley seemed to understand that and was amenable to taking things slowly, at least from what I could tell. I was determined to ignore Marcia's attempts to speed things up, even though I found most of them funny.

"Maybe we could help him with that double homicide in return for his help with Judith," Marcia said.

Where in the world did that come from? Sometimes I really did wonder if she were

alien life form. Her brain just seemed to work in a very wonky way and occasionally veer off into outer space.

"How in tarnation would we do that?" I asked.

"We have the inside track with the local teens. I mean, three of us have teenagers and Ray's the principal at the high school." Ray was Bernice's husband.

"Don't even go there," Bernice said firmly.

"No," Linda said, "I don't think I want anything to do with that case." She shuddered. "I can't imagine what those poor parents are going through."

"Drugs" Marcia said darkly. "I'll bet it had to do with drugs."

I couldn't disagree with that assumption. Opioid use was becoming a bigger and bigger problem in many areas of the country, including ours.

"Back to dinner with Riley," Linda urged.

I sighed. "I don't want to blindside him. Maybe he'll agree. He does actually seem to like all of you, in spite of what he's had to put up with. If he hesitates at all, though, I'm sticking to the original plan."

"That's fair," Linda said.

"What are you making?" Marcia asked.

I thought a moment. "I was going to make chicken cordon bleu, but if you all are coming over, I think I'll do my bacon wrapped tenderloin with the Madeira sauce."

"And stuffed potatoes?" Marcia asked hopefully.

"I'll bring the wine," Linda said. She was notorious for not cooking.

"I'll make my apple bread pudding," Marcia said.

"Wedge salad with lots of blue cheese," Bernice contributed.

Yum.

"In the meantime," Linda said. "Why don't we do some research?"

"What kind of research?" Bernice asked.

"Let's find out about all of the players in this game. You can find a lot of information on the internet these days."

"OK, let's divide up the names," Bernice said. "Do you have the list Judith gave you?"

"Yes." Linda fished around in her purse. "Here we go. The daughter is Ann Byrn Cunningham. Her husband's name is Steven. He's a surgeon in Norfolk. They have two younger children, Rachel and Walter. The son is Bertram, Jr. His wife is Elizabeth Waters Byrn. Their son is Henry. He just graduated from Boston University last year and moved back to Virginia. Then there's the assistant. Her name is Veronica Lake."

"Please tell me you're kidding," said Bernice, the old movie buff.

"Nope. Sorry. Let's see… Rosalinda Santos is the housekeeper. She's an employee of Woodford Hall but Judith says she does extra work for her and she'll be serving at the party."

"That's quite a few names," Marcia said. "How are we going to divide them up?"

"I'll take the daughter and her husband," Linda volunteered. "I have connections with the medical community in Norfolk."

41

"And I'll take the son and his family," Bernice said.

"That leaves us with the assistant and the housekeeper," Marcia said. "That doesn't sound too hard."

"Remember the goddaughter," I said. "Emily Johnston."

I stopped in front of Linda's house. "I'm still not sure about this," I said. "But I'll sound Riley out and let you know about Friday."

"That's all we can ask," Linda said. "But let's get together before then and go over what we've learned about this cast of characters. How about dinner at the pub on Thursday?"

"Works for me," Bernice said as Linda got out of the car and turned to say good night.

"Me too," said Marcia.

I suspected my reply was a bit less enthusiastic.

When I returned home, I found Nick and Max, Bernice's son, on the couch watching a ball game with Maggie sound asleep between them. Nick was balancing a bowl of popcorn on his knees and Max was sipping on a soda.

"We thought we'd order pizza," Nick said. "Do you want some?"

Suddenly the prospect of cooking seemed amazingly unattractive. "Sure," I said. "Pepperoni and mushrooms please. Order whatever kind you'd like for yourselves."

"Sounds like a plan," Nick said.

I poured myself a beer and settled down to watch whatever teams were beating each other up. After a moment I decided to take advantage of the commercial break.

"Say, did you guys know that couple who were killed on Wisdom Lane?" I asked nonchalantly.

Nick popped open a soda and shook his head. "No. They were a couple years ahead of us. Kelly did, though. Her older sister was on the homecoming court with the girl who was killed. Kelly said her sister was really shaken up." Nick had been dating Kelly since early summer.

"I didn't know them," Max volunteered, "but I remember them."

"Really?" I asked.

"Yeah. He almost ran me over when I was crossing the parking lot. He was on that big motorbike he rode. She saw it and really laid into him. After that, any time she'd see me she'd smile and say hi." He looked at me to emphasize what a big deal that was. "Most of the popular girls were stuck up. They wouldn't give a freshman the time of day."

Nick nodded. "I'd forgotten about that parking lot thing," he admitted.

"Why would someone murder them?" I asked. "I just don't understand the world anymore."

The boys just shook their heads.

"Riley's working that case, isn't he?" Nick asked.

I nodded.

"That would be gross, but it would also be really interesting to figure something like that out."

"I'm thinking about becoming a forensic scientist," Max said, grabbing a handful of popcorn. "Or a pathologist. I could work in the state lab in Richmond. That would be so cool."

Yuck.

"Riley has a fascinating job," Nick said thoughtfully. "I'm starting to think

43

about majoring in criminal justice instead of engineering."

I nearly spit out my beer. For as long as I could remember Nick had been set on studying engineering at one of the California power houses. I wasn't sure if this new thought train was good or bad. I'd need to think about it when I had some quiet time. Man, I had a lot of thinking to do. A whistle blew and the game was back on.

"Speaking of Riley, he called earlier." Nick told me. "He said to call if you had a chance." He paused. "He sounded really tired."

I picked up my beer and moved into my office. I closed the door and dialed Riley's number. Hmmm. I knew the number by heart. I wondered if that was significant.

"Furman."

"Olsen here."

Riley chuckled. "Hey, Jackie, I'm glad you called. How are you?" His voice had lowered into a soft, sexy growl. Oh, Jackie, look out.

"I'm fine," I said. "I just got back from tea at Woodford Hall."

"That's what Nick said. Is it as fancy as I hear?"

I filled him in on the menu and he groaned. "Please. I've been drinking vending machine coffee and eating stale sandwiches all day. I'm so hungry."

"We're ordering pizza in a little while if you'd like to come over."

He hesitated. "I'd love to but I don't think I'd be very good company. I'm pretty beat and this case has me climbing the wall."

"That's nothing a beer and some pepperoni can't cure," I said.

"Sausage and mushrooms too?"

I laughed. "The works."

"What's for dessert?"

"You never know." Oh my God, did I just say that?

He gave a full-throated laugh. "You've got a deal. How about if I stop by Mama Mia's and pick up some cannoli?"

"Be still my heart."

"I can be there in about an hour."

"That sounds good. There's something I'd like to talk to you about in any event."

His voice became serious. "Is anything wrong?"

"No, absolutely not. I just had an interesting conversation with a woman who lives at Woodford Hall and I wanted to run it by you." There, decision made. I was bringing Riley into our group.

"Am I going to enjoy this conversation?"

"Enjoy it? That's probably not the right word. Will you be intrigued? That's a possibility."

"Miss Marple," Riley said, "I have a bad feeling about this. What are you up to?"

"You'll see," I promised. "Pizza and mystery await."

# Chapter Five

Riley appeared at our door sporting a five o'clock shadow and bearing a brightly colored box from Mama Mia bakery. He leaned in and lightly brushed my cheek with his lips as he closed the door behind himself.

"C'mon Dude!" Nick called from his position on the couch. "You can do better than that!"

I felt a blush slowly work its way up from the base of my neck to my cheeks. The ends of Riley's mouth twitched up. He carefully placed the box on the table beside the door. He placed one arm around my waist and put his other hand behind my head, pulling me closer. He leaned forward and…wow! His lips met mine, gently at first, and then more insistently, the tip of his tongue teasing the end of mine. Nick and Max were whooping and hollering, pumping their fists in the air. Riley let me go and made a theatrical bow in their direction. He walked over to the couch and exchanged high fives with the boys. I picked up the box of cannoli, feeling a bit flustered and certain I had turned bright scarlet.

"Is it hot in here or is it me?" I muttered. Riley chuckled and followed me into the kitchen. He yanked off his tie, folding it and placing it into his jacket pocket. The jacket came next. He hung that neatly on the back of the chair. That left me with a sight I had yet to get used to, that of a handsome man wearing a shoulder holster standing in my kitchen.

In the bright light of the kitchen Riley looked tired. I spotted lines of tension around his eyes and mouth and his posture seemed a bit more slumped than his usual ramrod straight position. I handed him a beer and pointed him toward the family room. "Pizza should be here in about thirty minutes," I said. "Why don't you relax while I make a salad?"

He needed no more encouragement. Riley settled his long frame into a lounging chair, opened his beer and helped himself to some popcorn. Within minutes he was yelling along with the boys as whatever team they were supporting advanced or didn't. It always amazed me that all the men I knew could sink so quickly into a football game. It didn't seem to matter what team was playing. Any excuse to scream and holler and debate plays was welcome. And they claimed women were excitable.

The commotion was too much for Maggie. She jumped off the couch, stretched, gave Riley's hand a quick kiss, and retreated to her cozy bed in my office. Later we watched the game while we devoured pizza, along with Maggie's help. I noticed that she had settled by Riley's chair and that his hand kept dipping suspiciously over its arm. Maggie was enthralled with that hand. There was no doubt that Riley was making a friend for life with his offerings of sausage and pepperoni.

The last bite of cannoli coincided with the end of the game. Nick turned the television off and the room became mercifully quiet. The boys actually washed the dishes without being asked. "I'll walk Maggie before I go to bed," Nick offered.

"Yeah, I'd better go too before my dad comes pounding on the door telling me it's a school night. As if I didn't know that." Max snorted. The boys were both smirking suggestively at us. Were they match making? The idea came as something of a shock. On the other hand, the thought that Nick might welcome another man into our lives was encouraging. Affection toward my son washed over me in waves.

"Would you ask your father to call me tomorrow?" Riley said, handing Max a business card.

"Sure thing," Max replied. Both boys raised their eyebrows and whispered excitedly to each other as they left the house.

I turned on some light jazz and motioned for Riley to sit next to me on the couch. "Is that about the murder of those teenagers?" I asked.

"What makes you think that?" Riley said. I made a face at him. "Believe it or not, I don't live in a closet," I said. "I know you're heading up the team investigating the case. Everyone in town knows that. You've been all over television and radio with your 'no comments'."

Riley made a disgusted face.

I reached up and gently touched his beard. "You look tired and you seem a bit stressed. I just thought you might want to talk."

"What happened to my poker face?" he protested.

I laughed. When we first met, I had seen that face many times. That and a scowl were initially the only two expressions Riley had shown me. It was nice to know that he had others.

"You know I can't talk about an active case, Jackie." Now where had I heard that before?

"I'm not asking you to share anything you shouldn't," I assured him, "but it has to be hard when two people so young get killed. They should have had their whole lives ahead of them."

"Yes, they should have," Riley growled. "Hell, they weren't that much older than Nick or my niece. And now they're just bodies on a slab." He shook his head, his eyes clouding.

48

I don't know what made me do it, but I leaned over and kissed him. On the lips. Like I meant it. He pulled away and gazed into my eyes. Then he kissed me back. He was still kissing me when Nick and Maggie returned. Maggie immediately jumped on the couch and wiggled her way between us.

"Oh no you don't!" Nick said, scooping her up. "Time for bed."

I checked my watch. Really? So early? My son definitely was up to something. I watched as Nick and Maggie disappeared into his bedroom. A smile was tugging at the corner of Riley's mouth.

"He's talking about being a detective like you," I said.

Riley was surprised. "Are you kidding? What happened to engineering?"

I shrugged.

"Well, I'll have to talk him out of that idea," Riley said. "Besides, I'm starting law school pretty soon."

"Would you really talk him out of it?" I asked.

"No," Riley admitted. "It's a good career for the right person. Nick will just have to decide if it's a fit for him." He thought a moment. "I think I'll suggest that he do the ride along program the department has and go to their civilian academy if he's truly interested. He's old enough." He paused. "If that's all right with you, I mean."

"That's a great idea." Out of the corner of my eye I saw Nick sneak out of his room, open the refrigerator and then disappear with yet more food into his room. Where in the world did he put it all?

"Now, about talking to Ray?" I wanted to encourage Riley to share what he could, partly to try to relieve the burden he was feeling but also, I confess, out of good old-fashioned curiosity.

"I don't know Ray that well yet," Riley said. "But from everything I hear and see, he's good at his job. I'm willing to bet that he could give me some insight into these kids that I don't have. We're talking with their teachers and their friends too. So far other team members are doing that." He shook his head. "I don't know why, but I don't feel I'm getting a clear picture about them." He paused. "Nick's girlfriend said the girl was on the homecoming court at the high school."

"Yeah, she was one of the popular girls." I screwed up my face.

Riley laughed. "I remember how you feel about them."

"They're not always nice," I reminded him.

"So I've been told. I haven't figured out yet if that was true of her. In any event, these two were a study in contrasts. She was active socially, seemed to have a lot of friends. The boy was more of an outlier, barely made it through high school from what I understand. Her grades were pretty good and she was part of the "in crowd". She was going to the community college; he was working as a mechanic. He comes from a blue-collar family; she comes from a fairly wealthy one. On the surface I don't see what would have brought them together. That may be the key that will pull this all together, if only we could find someone who could explain the attraction to us."

"It could be good old-fashioned sex," I said.

Riley laughed. "You think?"

"Was he good looking?"

"What are you thinking?"

I pondered. "I'm thinking about all the movies where the society girl falls for the bad boy. Like Grease for example."

Riley wrinkled his brow. "You may have something there. At least you've given me something new to think about." He changed his position

50

to face me sideways, making it clear that he was also changing the subject. "Now, tell me about this mystery of yours." At least he didn't want to talk about sex. Or, even a scarier thought, do something about it. And now I was thinking about what sex might be like with Riley. How in the world did I get here? 'Back to reality, Jackie, and quickly'. I started to describe our meeting with Judith. When I told him about the metal plate in the garage being loosened, he shook his head. "But wait," I said, "here's the thing. She had it fixed. A few weeks later it was loose again." Riley frowned.

"Go on," he said.

I detailed the other events Judith had revealed. By the end of my story, he was leaning forward with his hands clasped together. "So, what do you think?" I asked.

"At first I was tempted to brush it all off," he admitted. "Now I'm not so sure." He searched my face. "Why are you getting involved in this again?"

"One of Judith's friends knows Marcia." Riley rolled his eyes. That wasn't an unusual reaction where Marcia was involved. "Stop that!" I swatted his hand playfully." "She may be a little nutty…"

"A little?" he asked.

"But she's also smart and has good people sense and besides, she's *my* nut and I love her."

"I know," he smiled. "I'm listening."

"Anyway, this lady, Evelyn, had heard about our involvement with the murder next door," I paused to look at him closely, afraid his temper would start to rise. Clearly, he was biting his tongue. I wondered if this would be a good time for another kiss. Riley seemed to read my mind.

"If you believe you can seduce me into not saying what I think…" he started. I kissed him. "Miss Marple," he whispered, "You're on shaky ground."

"Anyway," I proceeded. "Judith is very reluctant to go to the police. Before she does, she asked us to meet this cast of characters and see if we can figure out if she really is in danger or if everything is just coincidence."

"And what happened the last time you did something like that?" Riley asked sternly.

"You rescued me," I said sweetly.

The Riley Furman scowl was back. Oh dear.

"What would you suggest?" I asked.

He thought a moment. "I could send a uniformed officer out to take her statement," he said. "I could also send someone to talk to the family and the assistant."

"But then if someone *is* trying to hurt her, they'd be alerted to the fact the police are involved."

"Is that a bad thing?" Riley asked. "Maybe that's all it would take for that person to realize the effort isn't worth the risk."

I had to admit he had a point.

He studied my face. "You're not going to stop, are you?"

I sighed. "I honestly don't know. I like Judith, and it would be terrible if she were hurt or killed and we could have prevented it." I sighed again.

"Don't you have a book to write?" he reminded me. He gestured toward my office. "I don't hear it writing itself."

"I know, I know," I said. "Deadline's getting closer and closer and I'm still revising." I sat up straight. "You're right. I should just say no and let the others do whatever they want to do."

"Can't they get a non-lethal hobby, like basket weaving or something?"

I laughed. "You know this group. They're like a dog with a bone. Once they have it, they can't seem to let it go."

"Then what's the plan going forward? I assume you have one."

"We're all going to look into the family members, along with the assistant and staff." I saw his face and held up a hand. "We're just doing research on line. Certainly there's nothing dangerous about that."

"I suppose not. Go on."

I told him about the girls' plan to crash our Friday night dinner.

"Are Ray and Bob coming?" he asked.

I nodded.

"Maybe they'll put a damper on this then. I know they weren't thrilled with your sleuthing before."

Until they got sucked in and started helping. I decided not to remind Riley of that fact. "Friday night's fine," he said. "Why don't I think that's everything?"

"Judith's giving a cocktail party. Marcia suggested you come as my date." I scrunched my eyes closed, not wanting to see his reaction. The silence dragged on. Eventually I decided to open my eyes.

Riley shook his head again. "Miss Marple, Miss Marple," he said. He frowned and cocked his head to one side. "Do I have to wear a tux?"

I smiled at the idea of that delicious sight. Riley smiled in return. We leaned together. He kissed me. Or I kissed him. Or we kissed each other. Whatever.

# Chapter Six

I kept my nose to the grindstone until Thursday night. I wrote and re-wrote, conferred with my editor, re-wrote again, erased, inserted, tore up pages, tore out my hair and wrote some more. Except for regular walks with Maggie, dinners with Nick and occasional phone calls with Riley I ignored the outside world as well as the domestic one, which meant laundry piled up in the basket, dusting went undone and vacuuming was a non-event. I finally surfaced Thursday evening when I heard what I believed to be the clothes washer running. Puzzled, I wandered into the laundry room, where I found my sixteen-year-old son folding underwear.

"Hi," I said in what I hoped was a normal tone of voice.

"Hello," Nick replied. "Who are you? You look like my mother but I'm not really sure."

Oh, the guilt. "I'm so sorry, Honey," I said. "I've been meaning to do that."

"I hung your bras up," he said, pointing to a nearby rack. "I mean, I hung my mother's bras up. I'm pretty sure she'll be back soon."

"Ok, wise ass," I said, folding my arms. "I get it. I said I was sorry."

Nick grinned. "No problem, Mom. I know how you get when you're working. And since your work puts bread on the table, so to speak, I can do this every now and then. Anyway, Homecoming's almost here and I might need a small loan to take Kelly out to dinner."

Ah! I was being bribed. "Where are you going?" I asked.

"Humphrey's," he said, naming a very nice restaurant in town. "I know Kelly doesn't look like she eats much, but she does, and I need to be prepared if she orders the lobster." Nick's girlfriend, in addition to being a top scholar, was a gymnast who weighed about ten pounds.

I laughed. "And of course, there are flowers and pictures... Are you ordering a limo?"

"Naw. We're going with Max and Wendy. But there's the after-prom party at school, which they're charging for this year, and then breakfast, and I want to get her a nice present like a piece of jewelry..." He blushed.

I studied him. My son was growing up. He really liked this girl. He really, really liked her. I dreaded the heartache when one of them decided to end their relationship. But for now, all was good and I liked Kelly too.

"If you need some ideas for jewelry, I'm happy to help."

Nick's face lit up. "Thanks, Mom. That would be great."

"I'm going to the pub with the girls for dinner tonight. Do you want me to bring you something back?"

Nick shook his head. "No, thanks. You already told me you were going out." I had? When had I done that? My memory must really be going. Too much writing and not enough other stuff, I guess. "I made my patented meatloaf," Nick continued. "Max and his dad are coming for dinner and Mr. Bradley's going to help us with trigonometry."

I stared at him. "Who are you and what have you done with my son?"

"Right back at you, person who looks like my mom." Nick returned to folding laundry. I wandered down the hall to get ready for dinner with the girls.

The pub is one of my favorite restaurants in Summer Hill. The building itself dates to the late 1700's and bears a distinct resemblance to an English cottage. In the summer it sits in the middle of a wild cottage garden that delights the eye with its bright pinks, blues and yellows. Today, however, the weather was chilly and smoke from the wood fire in the fireplace was curling from the chimney. Light flickered through the multi-paned windows. Outside riotous combinations of pansies poured from old barrels. I love pansies. To me, with their combinations of purple, yellow and white they resemble smiling faces. I can't help smiling back when I see them. Near the pansies was stacked a variety of pumpkins and gourds. Corn shocks graced either side of the entrance doors. Seeing the autumnal display reminded me that Halloween would soon be upon us. Then would come Thanksgiving, then Christmas, then New Years. I cringed mentally. The idea of all the preparation around the holidays was mind boggling. Just thinking of cooking big dinners, making hundreds of Christmas cookies, wrapping presents and decorating seemed overwhelming. And I was having trouble just submitting my manuscript on time as it was. When book revisions coincide with holiday preparations things don't always go so well. I could imagine having a nervous breakdown over the task of writing Christmas cards, burned cookies, an undecorated tree and a myriad of other disasters. I shook my head slightly. It was way too early to start hyperventilating over everything coming my way. On the other hand, I needed to decide whether to invite Riley to Thanksgiving dinner, which I always shared with my neighborhood friends. Stop it! I admonished myself as I continued to fret. There was plenty of time to get organized…or as organized as I ever got.

 I looked for the gentle labrador who usually greeted pub patrons, but it must have been too cold for her to be in her normal place. Too bad. I missed her sweet face and wagging tail.

I opened the door and, as always, a smile crossed my face. The pub reminded me so much of the trip my cousin and I had taken to England after graduating from college. We had backpacked throughout the country, meeting cousins we had never before known existed, and sharing many a meal and a pint with our newly found relations. Entering the pub always brought back those wonderful memories. Some day I'd go back, but I certainly wouldn't be backpacking. Staying in beautiful inns and bed and breakfasts was much more my style these days. I wondered if Riley had ever been to England. Maybe we could go together. Oh, for Heaven's sake! Here I was thinking about a romantic trip and I hadn't even gotten up the courage to invite the man to holiday dinner, never mind go to bed with him, which, of course, I'd have to do if we were going to travel together. Unless we had separate rooms, which I doubted would happen. Obviously, my train of thought had derailed. Again. I pulled myself back to the present.

The wide plank floors in the restaurant gleamed and creaked slightly as I crossed them. Along one wall was a dark wood bar backed with a mirror. Three bartenders scurried to and fro, pulling pints, mixing drinks, and throwing insults at regular patrons. Set at a ninety- degree angle was the open kitchen, where you could see your food being prepared. Much of it was made on an open grill, and from time-to-time flames encouraged by grease would burst forth. On one wall was the huge wood fed fireplace. If the fire got going very brightly it burned so hot that it could chase away people sitting near it, but brave souls still requested the tables nearest to the fireplace, some of them wearing light weight summer clothing to counter the fireplace's heat. The tables in the restaurant of varying sizes were rustic. No white tablecloths and gleaming silverware here. A small dance floor was tucked into a corner, waiting for the local Celtic band to turn out its vibrant music.

I spotted the pub's labrador, wearing a vest that held jars of condiments such as chutney, mustard and ketchup, wandering from table to table, politely offering her fare and accepting a tidbit when it happened to fall her way. Behind her trailed a small puppy, trying to emulate its mother but instead falling over its oversized paws and enthusiastically licking any hand that came near it. I don't know how they skirted local health department rules, but no one ever complained and most people seemed happy to play with the friendly pups. I bent down and gave mama dog a scratch behind her ears. She wagged her entire behind. The puppy rewarded me by leaping up and planting a sloppy kiss right on my lips. Ugh. A laughing patron at a nearby table handed me a napkin. Laughing myself, I spotted a bottle of hand sanitizer tucked in among the condiments in the dog's vest pockets. I took a big squirt and swabbed some on my face for good measure.

I joined Marcia, Bernice and Linda at a rough-hewn table. Bernice and Linda had piles of paper in front of them. Marcia had a few sheets. I had nothing. Absolutely nothing. More guilt.

The pub offered what had to be the best fish and chips on the planet as one of its specialties. I didn't have to look at the menu to know what I wanted. My friends, on the other hand, were studying the menu as though they had never seen it before. I smiled. What they would order was completely predictable. Or, as it turned out, maybe not.

"Shepherd's pie," Marcia pronounced, slapping her menu on the table.

"Bacon cheese burger and fries," said Linda, doing the same.

Bernice was the wild card. She avoided fried foods, rarely ate meat, and usually had a salad or grilled chicken. "Fried pickles to start," she said. "And Irish nachos."

We all stared at her. Yet another person had been taken over by an alien.

Bernice smiled. "We're off on another adventure. What the heck?" We all clinked wine glasses, but I couldn't help but wonder what we were unleashing.

"I guess I should start," I said, dipping a pickle into a tasty remoulade sauce. "I couldn't find much about Rosalinda Santos." Three sets of eyes surveyed me. My friends apparently were uncertain I had even tried. "I did try," I said. More skeptical looks. I took a deep breath. "She's not on Facebook, Twitter, or any other social media site I tried." Nods around the table. That was probably not surprising for a middle-aged Hispanic woman. "Town records show that she is not registered to vote. She lives close to Woodford Hall with someone I think is her husband. I couldn't tell for sure, so it could be a brother or another relative. The person she lives with farms some of the Woodford Hall land. The house where she lives is in his name." I threw up my hands. "Give me some ideas. I don't know where else to look."

Linda shook her head. "I don't think she's important. I wouldn't worry about it."

Bernice bit into a pickle. "Maybe she's not a citizen. Or maybe she's here without permission."

"Someone could be holding that over her head so if she knows anything she won't talk," Marcia contributed.

That was an interesting idea. We'd have to see if Riley had a source that would tell us more about her.

"I don't think Veronica Lake exists." Marcia said, taking her turn.

"What do you mean?" I asked.

"Well," Marcia said. "She's all over social media now. But I couldn't find any trace of her until five years ago. I thought that was odd. And her Facebook page is pretty impersonal. She talks about where she's gone for dinner and things like that, but the only pictures are of things like food and her dog. Other postings are items like things she sees on Pinterest, and those are fairly infrequent. She doesn't comment on anything remotely controversial or political. In fact, she seems to avoid those things like the plague." She consulted her notes. "She bought a converted carriage house in town about two years ago. She has worked for Judith for four years but I couldn't find anything about employment before that." Marcia sat back. "Maybe she's in the witness protection program."

"Doubtful," I said, gesturing our waiter to bring another round of drinks.

"Maybe she's running from something," Bernice proposed. "Like a bad marriage or an abusive relationship…"

"Or something illegal," Linda contributed. "Maybe she was involved with drugs or something else that she wants to forget about. Maybe someone really nasty is looking for her."

"So how do we find more?" Marcia asked.

"I think we start by talking with Judith," I said, taking a sip of wine. "We need to find out what she knows about Veronica, how she came to employ her, if she came with references and who they were. Then we could track them down."

"Do you think it's worth all that work?" Marcia asked.

I nodded. "I think we need to look carefully at anyone who has big gaps in their background."

"On to the family," Linda said as the waitress placed her burger in front of her.

"After the meal," Bernice said, snagging a slice of potato loaded with cheese and chili off her plate. Right now, let's eat."

For the next several minutes we ate happily, talking desultorily about local events and gossip, simply enjoying good food and friendship. Finally, Linda swallowed her last French fry and sat back in her chair. "Here goes," she said. "To be honest, I chose Ann and her doctor husband because I have contacts at the hospital in Norfolk. I think I mentioned that. These contacts mean  I could try to go further than looking him up on the internet." We nodded in understanding although my stomach flipped at the idea of Linda sharing our investigation with outsiders. She seemed to read my mind.

"I told my contact we were setting up a committee to review some of our surgical procedures and were looking for a couple experienced surgeons to join it so we'd be sure to have input from someone outside our network." Linda smiled, looking like the cat that swallowed the canary. "She bought it, hook line and sinker. Even suggested some reciprocity. Actually, that might be a good idea. Every hospital has to continually reevaluate to make sure it's using the most recent techniques and tools. And our hospitals are far enough apart geographically that we aren't direct competitors…"

Bernice held up an apologetic hand. "You sound like you're pitching this to your executive committee."

Linda grimaced. "Sorry. I did actually get excited enough about the possibility to bring it up at the board meeting. Anyway…" She took a sip of wine "Let's start with the basic stuff on Steven Cunningham. He grew up in Maryland, graduated from the Naval Academy in Annapolis and then went to medical school. He served ten years in the Navy and is still in the reserves. He's been in private practice with two other surgeons for about eight years. There are no ethical or medical complaints against him that I can find. My contact said that he and his partners are all well respected and, moreover, they are well liked. It you know anything about medicine, you'll find that where surgeons are involved that's not necessarily the case. Their egos can be massive. Some of them are absolutely horrible to others on the operating team, even to other doctors. According to my friend, Steven treats nurses and other staff well and his office staff speaks highly of him. He and his partners do a fair amount of charity work, particularly with Operation Smile, with which one of his partners is very involved."

"Very admirable" Marcia said, looking a little disappointed.

Linda seemed to share her disappointment. "It's almost like the guy is vying for sainthood."

"I'll bet there's something less positive somewhere," Bernice said.

"Well…" Linda said, dragging out the word, "there have been rumors about a rough patch in his marriage a while ago and the possibility of his having an affair."

Marcia clapped her hands. "That's more like it."

I shook my head.

"I couldn't get much information on that," Linda confessed. "The person I was talking to isn't inclined to gossip,"

"Darn!" Bernice interjected.

"And she sort of let that slip," Linda continued. "She also was quick to say that the rumor died down pretty fast and that there has been no more talk about the doctor. It may have been just that - a rumor." Linda sighed. "In any event, he appears to be what everyone says he is – a good man and a good doctor."

"What about his wife?" I asked

Linda consulted her notes. "Ann Byrn Cunningham graduated from the University of Virginia with a degree in communications." She looked up briefly. "I'm never sure what that means."

Bernice laughed. "Theoretically it prepares you for work in the media, but I'm not convinced it gets many people very far."

"It's sort of like a degree in political science," Marcia commented. She smirked. "Would you like fries with that?"

"Well, Ann didn't even try to work anywhere other than with her family from what I can tell," Linda continued. "She immediately went to work for the family construction business after she graduated. She worked her way up from working in the accounting department to managing the human resources department." She studied her notes again. "I had to get some of the more personal information from Evelyn. Ann met Steven at a University of Virginia football game, where they were introduced by one of her sorority sisters. Steven's four year older than she is and was still in the Navy at the time. It was a whirlwind courtship and they were married within the year. Before Steven left the service, they were stationed for two years in Japan. They then came back to Norfolk. Ann returned to the family business and Steven opened his medical practice at the end of his enlistment."

"Sounds like a pretty standard story," I said.

Linda nodded. "According to Evelyn, Ann is very smart and good at her job. Evelyn says she's pleasant and well liked, but can be tough when she has to be. She and Steven have two children, one still in elementary school, and the other entering middle school. Ann is a skilled equestrienne and competes in the field of dressage. She volunteers with the Woodford Hall program that teaches handicapped children how to ride." She removed her glasses. "I didn't ask Evelyn about the rumors or marital strife. Somehow, I couldn't work it into the conversation."

"I don't know how you could have," Marcia said sympathetically. She grinned. "We'll just have to pay attention when we meet them and snoop around. I'll bet we'll find some clues."

We just looked at her and shook our heads.

"You know what I mean," Marcia protested. "Do they spend time together at the party or separate? Do they touch each other, stand close or far apart? That type of thing can tell you quite a bit about a relationship, if you're willing to pay attention."

I had to agree that she had a point.

"For example," she continued, "when you look at Bob and me you can tell we're really close and that we like each other. I mean, we really like each other." She looked around the table. "Do I need to spell it out?"

"Too much information," Linda said. "Please spare us the details."

Marcia put on her pouting face, but her eyes were laughing. She loved to get a rise out of us.

"OK, next," Bernice said, pulling her papers closer to her.

"Bertram, or Bert as he is known, is next." She paused to organize her thoughts. "Bert is a graduate of William and Mary. He received both his business and MBA degrees from that school. He apparently is very bright, having graduated *summa cum laude* as an undergraduate and with honors as a graduate."

"He's almost as smart as you," Linda laughed.

Bernice stuck out her tongue.

"He met his wife, Elizabeth, while they were both at William and Mary. They were married right after they graduated with their bachelor's degrees." She grinned. "From what I could find the wedding was quite the event with a lot of hoopla in the local newspapers and a roster of impressive guests. That seems to have largely been Elizabeth's doing. Her family in Richmond is very wealthy and very well connected. Elizabeth went to private school all the way through high school. Her debut was fawned over in the media, even in a time when debuts were less popular than in previous days." She passed around black and white photos of Elizabeth at her debutante ball and wedding.

"She is stunning," Linda said.

"These were taken years ago" Bernice replied, "and apparently she still is spectacular." She looked around the table. "Her kind of looks and grooming take a lot of money."

"Yours don't," I protested. "Why would hers?"

Bernice smiled. "Thank you, Sweetie. Remember I was in the fashion industry and I know a lot of tricks most people don't."

"Like what?" Marcia asked.

"Oh, Honey," Bernice said, "I could tell you but then I'd have to kill you."

Old line that it was, we still laughed.

"I've met a lot of women like Elizabeth during my career," Bernice said, "at least I think I have." She showed us a more recent picture. "See how everything looks perfect, how not a hair is out of place? We scrutinized the picture. 'That suit she's wearing cost a bundle. It takes a lot of money to look like that."

Brenda looked around the table. "Now, some of that may be supplied by Elizabeth's family. Even when Bert was in graduate school Elizabeth only held low level jobs. She clerked at a high-end fashion store in Williamsburg and then sold cosmetics at a department store. That's not the way to keep the household afloat when your husband is in school full time."

"Bert's family may have helped them," I contributed.

"That's true," Bernice conceded. "I don't think we'll know for sure unless someone tells us. But from what Evelyn said, it seems doubtful." She took a sip of water "Back to Bert. After his graduation he worked for about three years at Altria in Richmond. I guess he was getting his feet wet in the business world, because he went directly to the family business from there. He started out as his father's assistant and now, as we all know, ostensibly runs the company."

"With Judith's oversight," Marcia said.

Bernie nodded. "And as we've already heard, that oversight may be mighty uncomfortable for a man who is not only intelligent but has a wife who seems socially ambitious. Elizabeth is involved with several charitable causes, all of which are high profile and tend to get her a lot of recognition."

"There's a son, right?" I asked

"Yes, Henry. Henry just graduated from Boston University a year ago and, after a short stint elsewhere, is working with his father." Bernice looked around the table. "I haven't found out much about Henry yet. I looked at old high school yearbooks and didn't see anything that made him stand out. Frankly, that makes me wonder how he ever was accepted into Boston University. That's a very selective school and if you're not a top scholar and/or a standout athlete, it's unlikely they'll be interested in you."

66

"Then how do you think he made the cut?" Linda asked, frowning.

Bernice rubbed two fingers together. "I suspect someone made a very healthy donation. Elizabeth's father happens to be an alumnus of the school, and with his money and connections he could probably make it happen."

"That stinks," Marcia spouted. "Believing that someone like that could take a spot from someone who truly deserves it makes me furious."

Bernice smiled at her sadly. "It happens all the time, in a lot of schools. In our society money still talks."

Marcia crossed her arms over her chest. "Well, it still stinks."

"Agreed," Linda said. "You know, this information, along with Judith's attitude toward her daughter-in-law may give us a good picture of the family. And if Bert's really under his wife's thumb…"

"Hey," I said, holding up my hands, "Let's not jump to conclusions and judge this woman without even meeting her."

"Agreed," Bernice said, putting her notes away. "I'm going to look for more on Henry. I know Ray won't share anything he doesn't think he should, but I'm sure he'll give me a better picture of this young man."

We looked expectantly at Marcia.

"I'm on, I guess," she said with a smile. We waited while she collected her thoughts. "I confess I started my research about Emily Johnston by talking with Evelyn." She looked defensive. "Now, don't give me a hard time. I could find some information about Emily on the internet, but I wanted to know how she became so enmeshed in the Byrn family."

"That makes sense," Linda nodded.

"Emily's mother and Judith were close friends while they were growing up

67

and through college. They were even roommates during their last two years of school. After that, they kept in close contact. They were in each other's weddings and the women and their spouses remained close. Emily was born just about when Bert was and then…" her eyes clouded.

"Then what?" I asked.

"Emily's mother got breast cancer. Apparently, she fought hard, but it killed her when Emily was in middle school."

"Oh dear," Bernice breathed.

"Judith stepped in and took over the role of mother to a great extent. Emily's grandmother was already dead and Emily didn't have any close family members to help. From what Evelyn told me, Judith still is as close to being a mother as anyone has. Emily's father never remarried and he hasn't had any significant relationships with women since his wife died."

"Huh," said Bernice.

"Yes, well there may be a good reason for that," Marcia said.

"Is he gay?" Linda guessed.

"No. He became a Catholic priest." Marcia looked at our startled faces and laughed. "I knew you'd never guess!"

Linda shook her head. "Well, stranger things have happened I suppose."

"Maybe" Bernice muttered, "but this good old Baptist doesn't get it."

We laughed.

"Judith and her husband helped Emily get through school," Marcia said. "Like Ann, she graduated from the University of Virginia. She had a successful career as a financial advisor with a major firm, working her way into management. I have to guess from that fact that she was doing very well financially. Then

Bert senior died. It didn't take Judith long to realize she needed someone with Emily's expertise to help manage the company's finances. Emily ended up leaving her position and is now the Chief Financial Officer for the corporation."

"I bet she took a big cut in salary to do that," I commented

Linda nodded. "I'd bet on it. I wonder if she resents Judith for asking her for help." "And I wonder if Bert resents Judith for bringing in Emily instead of turning to him," I said.

Bernice shrugged. "Anything's possible. Is Emily married?"

Marcia shook her head. "No husband, no children, just a golden retriever."

We sat back in our chairs and pondered what we had learned.

"Well," Linda said finally. "We have a lot of information to sift through."

"And some background on our cast of characters." Bernice said.

"I guess we'll need to bring the guys up to date," Marcia said.

"Let's play that by ear," I said. "Maybe their meeting these people without all the information will let them draw conclusions different from ours. Now we're going in with preconceived notions and they aren't."

"You just don't want Riley to know what we've been up to." Linda teased.

Well, there *was* that too. I mean, he *did* know – sort of. He knew we were looking things up on line. What he didn't know (although he may have suspected it) was that we were unlikely to stop there, just because, well, just because of who we are. As we said earlier, once a dog gets a bone, he has to gnaw on it, doesn't he? Of course, he could bury it (i.e., we could look no further), but what's the fun in that? What Riley really, really didn't know was that my friends seemed determined to drag him along with us, wherever we were going. That could be a good thing. Or not.

# Chapter Seven

The doorbell rang just as I was putting my apple and sausage stuffed mushrooms into the oven to heat. Sure enough, it was Riley, holding a large bunch of flowers in one hand and a bottle of wine in the other. He looked incredibly handsome, dressed in a crisply creased pair of jeans and a pullover sweater in muted hues. Did the man iron his blue jeans? I certainly hoped not. I didn't think I could stand that much neatness. I put the thought aside for further consideration. I added it to the list of all the other things I needed to think about. That list was getting uncomfortably long.

"Welcome," I said, holding the door open. He grinned and kissed me gently on the lips. "Something smells good," he said. Behind him Marcia and Bob were crossing the street. I spied Linda walking in our direction as Bernice and Ray closed their front door and headed toward us.

Soon greetings had been performed, everyone had their beverage of choice, and we were attacking the appetizers as though we hadn't eaten in days. By silent agreement no one brought up Judith Byrn or teenaged murders. Apparently, we were saving those topics for after dessert. As I was putting the finishing touches on the main course, I overheard a spirited discussion concerning dry rubs, wet mops and combinations thereof. "We're having a barbecue throw down," announced Ray, who considered himself the African American community's answer to Bobby Flay. In reality he was an excellent cook and had won several awards for his ribs. Riley, who had enthusiastically joined the discussion, didn't know what he was in for.

"I still think my dry rub will beat your mop," he claimed. Ray just shook his head.

"I'm putting my money on my ribs," Bob proclaimed. "I do the dry rub and then the mop later."

"Next weekend at our house we'll find out who's the master," Ray proclaimed. I smiled, ridiculously happy that Riley was fitting in with this group of friends.

"Bring your baked beans," Marcia begged as we sat down. "Pretty pretty please." My beans, full of smoked sausage, bacon and secret spices were a prized recipe. I nodded.

"I'll bring the beer," Linda said. We all just rolled our eyes. Honestly, the woman was incorrigible. I couldn't understand why she didn't cook. Of course, I needed to acknowledge that many people didn't enjoy it like I did. And eating alone and then cleaning up without a companion probably was no fun. Linda would say she had mastered the art of dialing for take out. She saw no reason to master the appliances in her designer kitchen as well.

We finished our meal with Marcia's fabulous bread pudding and pushed back from the table. "I'm stuffed," Riley said. "I'm going to have to run a couple extra miles tomorrow." He glanced in my direction. "Do you want to come?" I shook my head emphatically.

"Jackie doesn't run," Bernice said. Riley looked disappointed. Uh oh. "I could ride my bike," I offered. He smiled. "That would work."

"I run," Ray said. The former professional football player was still a workout fanatic. "Mind if I come along?"

I could have sworn Bernice kicked him under the table.

"Sure," Riley said. "The more the merrier."

"Not romantic," Marcia muttered. I kicked *her.*

"Maybe I'll come too," Bob said. Marcia kicked *him.* Riley simply looked puzzled, probably wondering what was going on under the table.

"So," Riley said, sipping on a glass of brandy. "I've been thinking about Judith Byrn."

We all looked at him in anticipation.

"I'm sorry to say this," he said, not looking particularly sorry, "but do you realize that everything she told you about she could have done to herself?"

We pondered his statement.

"But why?" Bernice asked.

"It could be attention seeking behavior," he suggested. "She's getting older, the kids are running the company from day to day, and she doesn't feel needed or appreciated." He looked around the table. "Not everyone who has emotional problems or is mentally ill shows obvious signs. It's not like they wear on a sign on their forehead saying 'mental illness present'."

"I guess in your line of work you have to think like that," Marcia said. "But what about the dog?"

Riley shrugged. "What about it? For all we know it was sitting in the house all the time while she went from neighbor to neighbor building a story for sympathy."

"I'd hate to think that's true," I said. "She seems so credible."

"What about the girth?" Linda asked.

"She easily could have done that when the groom wasn't there. And if she had no intention of getting on the horse that day there was no possible harm."

We sat in solemn silence for a few minutes. "Does that mean that if Judith did ask you for help, you'd turn her away?" I asked.

"Not necessarily," Riley replied. "I might be skeptical but I'd probably still check her story out, just in case. It simply wouldn't go to the top of my case pile."

"Then what do you suggest we do?" Bob asked.

"You've already agreed to attend her cocktail party," Riley said. "Go. Check out the family members and the other people she mentioned. I suspect you'll be no further along, but on the other hand you may decide that Judith is a bit, shall we say, off kilter."

"And if we decide otherwise?" Linda challenged him.

"We'll cross that bridge when, or if, we get to it."

"Fair enough," Ray said.

"Are you still going to the party?" I asked.

Riley's grey eyes crinkled as he smiled at me. Where did he get those eyelashes? It wasn't fair. "Of course," he said. "I never turn down free food." He leaned toward me. "Or an opportunity to spend time with a beautiful woman," he whispered. Who? Me? Beautiful? I felt myself blushing again, something I seemed to be doing too often lately.

"Did he say something romantic?" Marcia asked, smiling.

"Marcia…" Bob cautioned her.

She moved out of kicking range, still smiling mischievously. Riley smiled back at her. "That's for us to know and for you not to find out." He said. She stuck out her tongue at him.

"Changing the subject," Ray said, "I brought you everything I could come up with on Lisa Jones and Bobby Wilson." Ray was referring to the teenagers who had recently been killed. He gestured toward a stack of folders on the sideboard.

"Can you share student information with the police?" Linda asked.

"It depends on the circumstances," Ray replied. "Certain records are considered private under federal law, but there are exceptions to that rule. Then on top of it you have to consider state law and constitutional law. In this case, however, there is no question but that we can give the police department information."

He turned to Riley. "After we spoke, I pulled together both Lisa and Bobby's academic and disciplinary records. Fortunately, we still had them. After students graduate or permanently leave for other reasons their records are ultimately stored with the county school department. We're behind on transferring those records, because the county is running out of space and taking its own sweet time to store them electronically. Anyway, I was able to pull out their files. Then I spoke to the teachers and counselors I knew had worked with them. Each of them gave me a written statement as to what they remembered."

"Thank you," Riley said.

Ray nodded. "After you read them, they may not seem valuable to you. Certainly nothing of importance struck me when I read them. All the people who wrote reports said they would talk with you personally also if you like."

"That's very helpful," Riley said.

Linda reached into her pocketbook and handed Riley a picture. We all leaned forward and looked. It was a photo of Henry and Lisa. Linda pointed to Henry's picture and named him for Riley. Riley's eyebrows rose.

"Where did you find that?" I asked.

Linda smiled, looking very proud of herself. "I went snooping on Facebook," she admitted. "Henry's not very particular about who he lets friend him." We looked at the picture again. "Did you realize these two were friends?" Linda

74

asked. "At least they seem to have been friends at one time."

"No, I didn't," Riley frowned. He studied the picture and then looked up at Ray. "What do you know about this?"

Ray could have been offended by Riley's tone of voice, but if that were true, he didn't indicate that he was. "Let me see." He leaned back in his chair and sipped his aperitif. "As I recall, Henry Byrn and Lisa Jones dated for a short while in high school. He was two years older than she was. I remember he wanted to bring her to the junior prom as his date, but we only allow juniors and seniors to attend." He chuckled. "Henry seemed to think we'd bend the rules just for him, but of course we didn't. He was a cocky kid."

"In what way?" I asked.

"He was one of those wealthy kids who thought his family name should bring him special privileges and open doors for him. It may have worked some places, but not in my school."

"Where *did* it work?" Bob asked.

"College," Ray replied promptly. "Henry was a decent student but he was lazy, so his grades, while above average, were not what I would normally think a college like Boston University would accept."

"Why did they?" I asked.

"Money," Ray replied, confirming our suspicion. "His grandfather was an alumnus of the college and left a very substantial gift to it in his will." He grimaced. It was just at Bernice had surmised.

Marcia was wearing her outraged face again. She crossed her arms tightly across her chest and angrily swung her leg back and forth. "It just isn't right," she muttered.

Bob patted her knee lovingly. "That's a battle for another day, Honey. You can't cure all the world's wrongs."

Marcia heaved a heavy sigh but patted him back.

"Tell me more about Henry and Lisa," Riley encouraged.

Ray thought. "There's not much more that I know. The families knew each other and may have been friends on some level. They belong to the same country club; probably travel in the same social circle." He reached out his hand. "Could I see that picture?" Riley handed it to him. "That looks like it was taken after they both graduated. Their faces are more mature and Henry's filled out a bit in this picture."

"Why did Lisa and Henry stop dating?" Riley asked.

"I'm not sure," Ray admitted, handing the picture back to him. "If I recall, her parents decided that Henry was too old for her and made her break it off. That's just a rumor, though. I don't know how credible it is. They could have simply stopped seeing each other once he left for college. That happens all the time."

"Not to us," Marcia said. She and Bob had been high school sweethearts.

"You're the exception to the rule," Bernice told her. "But apparently they were still friendly after graduation," Riley mused. "Ray, I know you've brought me a lot of material, but could you tell us in your own words what you remember about Lisa?"

Ray looked at the ceiling. "Obviously, Lisa was a real beauty. She was a cheerleader."

"Surprise, surprise," Bernice said.

"Don't be nasty, honey," Ray said, patting her hand.

"Sorry," Bernice replied, but her expression showed that she wasn't.

"What do you ladies have against cheerleaders?" Bob asked.

"It's not just cheerleaders," I said. "It's beauty queens and majorettes and the pretty, popular girls who ran the school. In my experience they were stuck up and sometimes downright nasty." Riley had heard this before. "I call them the mean girls."

"Hey," Marcia said. "I was a cheerleader. I wasn't stuck up or mean."

"Another rule to which you're the exception," Linda said.

"I don't think there are many rules that fit Marcia," Bob contributed.

Marcia eyed him suspiciously. "What is that supposed to mean?"

"I love the uniqueness of you," he answered.

Marcia kissed him and beamed. "Now that's romantic."

"There are always exceptions," I admitted, returning us to our original subject. "I shouldn't stereotype."

"Some of those popular girls were truly nasty to Lexie when her mother died," Bernice said, referring to the young woman who had lived next door. "They told everyone who would listen that Lexie's father was a murderer. Some of them even said Lexie did it. Then they had the nerve to show up at her mother's funeral and act so nice. No wonder Lexie and her father left town." She turned to her husband. "Was Lisa like that?"

Ray sighed. "Unfortunately, she could be. She knew she was gorgeous. How could she not? And her family was well off, so she always had nice clothes, a good car, special things others couldn't. Yeah, I'd say she could be mean from time to time, but most teenagers can."

"On the other hand, Max told me that she was always nice to him," I put in.

Ray looked surprised. "Really? I'm surprised. Given the age difference, I wouldn't have expected them to know each other. They certainly wouldn't

77

have shared classes."

I filled them in on Max's story about the parking lot incident.

Ray nodded. "Oh, yes, Bobby and that motorcycle. He could be a menace on wheels when he was in the mood."

"Why didn't Lisa go away to college?" I asked.

"She was a so-so student. Her grades weren't terrible, but nothing to get excited over either. She didn't have personal connections with a high-powered school like Henry did so no prestigious school would have accepted her. And she really didn't know what she wanted to do with her life. Therefore, she went to community college part time and worked part time. It was probably a good choice for her."

"What about Bobby?" Marcia asked.

Ray chuckled. "Bobby, Bobby, Bobby. Now there was a kid who marched to a different drummer. Although when I think about it, his older brother Tommy gave me far more trouble." He paused for a moment.

"What kind of trouble?" Riley asked.

"Oh, typical bad boy stuff. Fights. Skipping school. Smoking in the bathroom." We all smiled. Each of us had gone to school with a least one Tommy.

"Got caught with pot," Ray continued. "Used to drag race out on the highway. Darned fool was lucky he didn't get killed. As it was, he barely squeaked through graduation." Ray chuckled again. "Any time I get conceited and think I have teenagers all figured out, I think about Tommy Wilson. I was sure he'd come to a bad end."

"What happened to him?" I asked.

"He fell in love," Ray replied. "Married a girl from Portsmouth. I'll give her credit. She really turned him around. Refused to marry him until he proved to her that he could be a good husband and father. And he did it, by George. He trained as an electrician and has a good union job at the shipyard in Newport News. He and his wife have a lovely home and two of the cutest little kids you'll ever see. To top it off, he volunteers as a youth counselor at their church. He came by to see me not long ago. He wanted to apologize for all the trouble he caused and invite me to Sunday supper." He smiled at the memory. "Bernice and I went."

"It was a really nice afternoon," Bernice said softly.

"How was Bobby different?" Riley asked, clearly trying to get a handle on both of the murder victims.

"He was a quiet kid, unlike his brother. He was pretty smart. If he liked a subject, like math, he excelled. If it was something he didn't like, such as history, forget it. He was a loner. He rode a motorcycle and dressed in black. Bobby had this wavy hair that kind of swept over his face and big black eyes that looked like they belonged on a soulful spaniel. He reminded me of a modern James Dean."

"Did he spend any time with Lisa?" Riley asked.

Ray pursed his lips. "Not that I noticed. They were such different people and their backgrounds were different, too. She came from a successful family. On the other hand, rumors are that Bobby's grandfather was a bootlegger. His father isn't anything to brag about. He does odd jobs, seems to have trouble hanging onto a regular position. Tommy told me his father drinks a lot. I don't think the boys had much of a home life. Their mother walked out when Bobby was very young. Never made any effort to have a relationship with them from what I recall."

I sighed, feeling sorry for Bobby. "Bobby sounds like someone a lot of young women might find attractive. You know… a handsome, moody loner from a poor family, someone they might be able to 'save'."

"That's true," Linda agreed. "That plays into a lot of girls' fantasies, particularly when they're younger. Maybe that's why Lisa was with him."

"What's really interesting me right now is the connection between Henry and Lisa," Riley said. "May I keep this picture?" Linda nodded. "If I can find a connection among all three of them, I might get something to work with."

"Surely you don't think Henry was involved with the murders?" Marcia gasped.

"I have no reason to believe that right now," Riley admitted. "But any new connection is a new lead. The most logical explanation for this photo is that Lisa and he remained friends after high school. But this is the first time Henry Byrn's name has come up in my investigation. None of Lisa's friends mentioned him even though they look quite chummy in this photo." We were all staring at Riley.

"It's a very long shot," Riley said. "I shouldn't be thinking aloud. There's no evidence of any wrongdoing. I just can't figure out why I haven't heard Henry's name before. It probably means nothing. Nonetheless, this cocktail party suddenly sounds much more interesting." He smiled. Why did I think he looked like a wolf tracking its prey?

# *Chapter Eight*

The following morning Nick knocked on my bedroom door at some ungodly hour. "Mmmpph." I replied.

He opened the door and strode up to my bed. "Wake up, Mom," he said, shaking my shoulder. "We're going running with Riley."

"I don't run," I informed him, shoving my face into my pillow.

"You told him you'd ride your bike," my son said.

I opened one eye. "How do you know this?" I asked him.

"Neighborhood telegraph," he replied, pulling the covers off me. I grabbed them. "It was mistaken." I screwed my eyes shut.

Nick waved a cup filled with a steaming beverage under my nose. "Coffee…" he chanted, "Nice hot coffee."

I opened one eye. "No."

"Come on, Mom, it's a beautiful day."

"Good" I said. "Go enjoy it." I nestled deeper under my blanket.

My son sat on the edge of my bed, still holding the coffee mug. He surveyed me for a minute and then said "You've left me no choice but to bring out my secret weapon."

"Huh?" I muttered, putting my pillow over my head.

"Here, Maggie, come here girl!" he called.

Oh no. Maggie, wagging her entire body, jumped onto my bed and literally onto my stomach. Ouch. Her paws dug under the sheets and her little tongue frantically sought my face. "No, no, Maggie! "I cried, half laughing, half yelling. "Get off! You're too heavy! Oh, yuck! Stop kissing me. You have awful breath. What in the world have you been eating?" I pushed the puppy to one side where she sat wiggling frantically, grinning like a crazy person and still lunging to kiss my face.

"Are you up?" Nick asked, pulling the puppy off the bed.

"I don't want to be," I complained. He let go of Maggie's collar and she joyously jumped back onto the bed. "Ok, ok," I laughed, pushing her away, "Enough. I give up. Where's the coffee?"

Nick pointed to the cup steaming on my bedside table.

"You don't have to look cute, you know," he said. "We're just going to exercise. Throw on your sweats and meet me downstairs."

Fat chance. There was no way I was going to appear in public looking as though I'd just rolled out of bed. And I certainly wasn't ready to let Riley see me this way. Half an hour later I had showered, applied makeup (following Bernice's directive of more than mascara and lipstick), dried and styled my hair and, after much deliberation, chosen a pair of autumn hued leggings with a cropped top.

Nick smirked as I walked down the stairs. "At some point he's going to see you without your makeup, you know."

I scowled at him. "That point is far, far in the future. Like maybe never."

Nick laughed. "Mom, he likes you. Just relax and enjoy it."

I surveyed him for a moment. "You think that's what I should do?"

He was serious as he surveyed me back. "For now, yeah. It's cool that a good-looking dude thinks you're great. If it turns into something more, we'll talk, ok?"

"OK," I said meekly, wondering where my son had found this wisdom.

"Now come on," Nick said impatiently. "I bet everybody's waiting for us."

'Everybody' was definitely waiting for us. Riley, Ray and Bob were doing their warm up exercises at the end of the driveway. All three of Marcia and Bob's boys were doing stretches. Bernice and Linda were checking their bicycles. Always the individual, Marcia was doing figure eights on her in-line skates. Nick wheeled my bicycle over to me.

"You take Maggie, OK?" he said, handing me the boxer's leash.

Bernice's bichon was perched in a basket on the front of her bicycle. She was wearing something on her head. What was it? I wandered over to take a look. Oh no. It couldn't be. Yes, it was. The dog was wearing a tiny bicycle helmet.

"Really?" I whispered to Bernice.

"Isn't it cute?" she said enthusiastically. "It's a baby helmet. The smallest one I could find."

"I don't know why I'm doing this," Linda complained. Like the bichon, Miss Kitty was perched in a basket, but she was sitting regally tall and looking at us all disdainfully. She was attached to the basket by a pink leash that fastened onto a bejeweled collar. "Miss Kitty doesn't like morning," Linda said, smiling lovingly at the cat. As though to prove the statement, the cat pulled back her lips and hissed at Maggie.

"That makes two of us," I sighed. I'd be willing to bet Miss Kitty didn't appreciate being tethered to a bicycle much either.

Riley jogged over to pat Maggie and say a quick good morning. "Once around the lake, ok?" he said.

"Fine with me," I answered, thinking wistfully about my unmade bed upstairs.

We set out at a leisurely pace but Nick and Max soon broke away from the pack. The men ran at a steady pace while us ladies bicycled or skated nearby. Maggie trotted next to me on a loose leash, happily sniffing the fall air. Occasionally she tried to veer to one side or the other, almost upsetting my bicycle, but after a couple near disasters we settled into a rhythm.

"What a great way to start the weekend," Marcia enthused.

"Really?" I said through gritted teeth.

"Admit it, she said, turning a circle, "you're having a good time."

"It would be more fun if it were later," I groused, pulling once again on Maggie's leash.

Marcia laughed and skated around us, almost causing me to crash. I corrected my balance just in time.

"Sorry." Marcia said.

"Be careful," Bernice warned her.

Marcia obediently skated in a straight line. "What did you think about last night?" she finally asked.

"I thought it was great," Linda replied. "That tenderloin was to die for."

"That's not what I meant and you know it," Marcia chided her.

"I think it would be weird if those two murders and Judith's pranks were related," Bernice finally said.

"We're a long way from reaching that conclusion," I pointed out.

Marcia changed topics. "When we get to town, what are you going to look for at Esther's?"

Crap. I had hoped she had forgotten that we agreed to go shopping.

"Nothing," I said, my teeth once again clenching.

"Something sparkly," Linda supplied.

"I'd like a really simple dress," Bernice said, "but in a wonderful color."

Marcia did another circle, this time staying away from the bicycles. "I want something covered with sequins and incredibly slinky." She lifted an eyebrow at me. "Come on, Jackie, you need something that will make Riley sit up and take notice. What do you want?"

"Something on sale," I said.

"Not this time of year," Bernice replied.

Double crap.

We continued our journey around Summer Hill Lake. (Yes, I know, our founding fathers were not very original when it came to naming things.) The lake is the focal point of our parks and recreation system. It is a large lake, over a mile wide in parts and includes many inlets and coves that fishermen (fisher people?) and birders alike find inviting. On two sides thick stands of trees cozy up to its banks. On a day like this the bright yellows, oranges and reds of the maples, oaks and poplars created a cacophony of color that reached against a clear blue sky and reflected in the lake's shimmering surface. The entire area was replete with walking and biking trails. Some led to other attractions; some meandered in loops of varying lengths, returning eventually to the lake shore. When the town was first settled many wealthy families had built their homes on or near the lake. Unfortunately, some of those wonderful buildings had disappeared, but the ones that remained had gradually been repurposed to hold museums, restaurants and bed and breakfast inns. We glided past the Greek Revival home that now housed the town's art museum. A sign outside announced the presence of a visiting exhibit of Chinese porcelain. That sounded interesting. I made a mental note to return and take a look at it.

On the shore side we passed the public sandy beach, now closed for the season, where Nick had worked as a lifeguard the previous summer. The adjacent boat ramp and rental facility were still open and doing a brisk business. Several couples were putting rented kayaks or canoes into the water, while others launched their fishing boats. Riley dropped back for a moment. "How about taking a canoe out some afternoon?" he said.

"I'd love to," I agreed enthusiastically. "Canoeing is one of my favorite things to do in the fall."

He gave me a huge smile and picked up his speed to catch up with Ray and Bob.

Further along stood a large rustic house. When I say rustic, however, imagine something a Vanderbilt might have considered rustic. It was a rambling building that reminded me of a large Adirondack cottage, complete with twining wood railings and rockers on the porch. The house now contained our nature center, with hands-on activities for kids and more sophisticated classes for teenagers and adults. Its grounds held several picnic tables and built-in grills. Riley dropped back again. "Maybe we could take a picnic, too." He said. "We could get takeout from Betty's so you wouldn't have to cook." I grinned at him. That day was sounding better and better. Hopefully it would come soon. He slowed down again. "How about next Saturday if the weather's good?"

"You've got a deal," I said. Maggie barked her approval and Riley once again rejoined the other men.

We approached downtown and the path started to become more crowded. As we paralleled Main Street signs indicated the way to the university's science museum, complete with planetarium, and the performing arts center. Just before we reached the end of the downtown area Bob signaled for us to stop.

Betty's Restaurant, a favorite venue for breakfast and lunch, stood on the side of the path opposite the lake shore. We parked our bikes; Marcia took off her skates and we walked up to the deck where we found Nick and Max waiting for us. "What took you so long?" Nick complained. "We're starving." Max and Marcia's sons agreed in a noisy chorus.

Bernice, Marcia and I laughed. We had learned long ago not to underestimate the appetites of teenaged boys. The boys ordered breakfasts of three-egg omelets with plenty of bacon, cheese and other goodies. The rest of us had either coffee or something lighter. Having missed breakfast, I opted for a fresh fruit smoothie.

The temperature had warmed pleasantly and we basked in the sunshine, lazily talking about nothing.

"I guess we could walk to Esther's from here," Linda said.

"Are you kidding?" Bernice asked. "There's no way I'm going there until I've showered and changed. I'll bet Esther wouldn't even let us through the door looking like we do."

Marcia took a whiff of her husband. "Or smelling like this," she added.

"I think you look fine just the way you are," Riley said to me. He wrinkled his nose. "The smell, on the other hand, is another issue." I swatted at him.

"I bet I smell just fine. After all, I don't sweat."

"I know, you just perspire," he rejoined. We all laughed at the old joke.

Ray stood and stretched. "Onward," he said. "Things to do, people to see, etc."

"I hope things to do includes raking leaves," Bernice remarked. "Our yard is a disaster."

I caught Nick's eye. "Why are you looking at me like that?" he asked.

"You'll have a chance to try out our new leaf blower," I said. Yes, I had broken down and bought one.

Nick brightened. "That could be fun. I bet that thing really can blow things around."

Oh dear. Maybe I'd better be careful of what I wished for.

Upon returning to our street women and men parted ways, us women to shower and change, the men to do whatever it is that they do on a beautiful fall day.

"Leaves," Bernice murmured again to her husband.

Ray lifted an eyebrow. "I may try out that new leaf blower of Jackie's. I'll bet I could get the yard done in five minutes flat."

Bernice looked alarmed. "Maybe the kids could do the yard."

Ray smiled. "That's more like it." I noticed that Max wasn't looking particularly happy any longer.

An hour later Linda pulled into my driveway and tooted the horn. I joined the others in the car and the four of us were on our way to Esther's Boutique. Now don't get me wrong, the fact that I was complaining doesn't mean I don't like Esther's. In fact, I love the place. Esther's occupies a prime location with a double storefront on Main Street. The clothes in her windows, which range from casual to formal, often sing a siren song to me. I can always find something attractive and well made when I shop there. And therein lies the rub, as they say. Esther's is very bad for my budget. When I'm feeling particularly impecunious, I tend to walk on the other side of the street, shielding my eyes from whatever I might decide I needed if I looked in her windows. On this occasion, however, my credit card was handy and I was open to making a purchase, although I was still hoping there might be at least a small sale rack in sight.

Esther welcomed us to her store with open arms. She's a gracious, elegant woman in her mid-fifties who always looks stylish but never over the top outrageous. Needless to say, she has a great sense of fashion. One thing I like about her is that she would rather sell you nothing than let you leave the store with something that looks less than wonderful on you. Now that I think about it, that probably means she's a shrewd businesswoman. Seeing someone looking gorgeous wearing an outfit from Esther's is probably the best advertisement she could have.

"We're going to a cocktail party," Marcia informed her "and we all want to find something fabulous to wear."

"Whose party is it?" Esther asked.

"Judith Byrn's" Marcia answered.

Esther raised one perfectly arched eyebrow. "Oh, that will be special then" she said. "Judith's parties are *always* to die for."

Uh oh. I had the feeling the price of my dress had just quadrupled.

"Let me think," Esther said. "Ann, Elizabeth and Veronica Lake already came in to buy their dresses. So did Emily Johnston." She clapped her hands. "That's such good luck! Now you won't have to worry about wearing the same dress as any of them."

Really? Was it that important? I usually had a good laugh when I ran into someone wearing the same thing as I did. It just meant they had good taste, right?

Marcia pulled a cranberry dress with a drop waistline and pleated skirt of the rack. "All I'd need is a headband and I'd look like a flapper." Esther looked her over. "Actually, that chiffon drapes beautifully. Why don't you try it on? And I have the most wonderful pair of heels to go with it." She thought a moment. "If anyone could carry off a headband it would be you. Let me see what I can come up with." Marcia headed toward a dressing room.

Bernice, with her sure sense of style, had already chosen a few dresses and went in the same direction.

Linda was fingering a sequined grey dress. Esther shook her head. "With your hair, I think that would be too monochromatic. But look at this sky blue one with the pearls." Linda reached for it. "Oh, I like it," she said. Off she went.

That left me, thumbing through dresses and finding no inspiration. Esther frowned at me. Of course. There I was, the hopeless case who found herself pulling out yet another black dress. "No, no, no." Esther said. "Black is classic and it looks terrific on some women, but you need some color, some pizzazz, some bling." There was that word again. I seemed to hear it every time I went shopping with my friends. They all wanted to jazz me up. The word 'bling' actually made me nervous. I didn't like being the center of attention. Black was so serviceable that way. Esther took one look at my face and laughed. "Oh, Jackie, stop acting like an ugly duckling! You're so pretty. Let's see if we can turn you into a swan."

I peered into a mirror. Me? Pretty? A swan? Was it possible? I put my fate in her hands.

"If you insist on being unnoticeable, try this midnight blue sheath," she said. "It's simple but very elegant. And the blue is more flattering than black on you." Hmm. Maybe. Esther thumbed through the racks. "I have it!" She pulled out a rose-colored dress with a draping neckline. "This neckline is very flattering. It hints, but it doesn't show too much." That sounded good. She turned the dress around. "And look at this!" I looked at the back of the dress. Actually, I looked where the back should have been. It had no back. No back at all. "Ummm." Esther studied my face and sighed. "Too bold?"

"Try it on." Marcia, wearing her flapper style dress, appeared at my side. Esther had been right. The crepe fabric hung like a soft cloud. On Marcia's petite frame the dress looked wonderful. "Now for the shoes," Esther said. "Excuse me for a minute, Jackie."

I sighed and resumed my aimless search. Esther returned with shoes for Marcia and a fuchsia dress in her hand. "Now, look at this," she commanded. The dress featured a beaded bodice with three-quarter length sleeves and a gathered chiffon skirt. Esther held the dress in front of me and had me look in the mirror. "Just imagine, if you put your hair up," she used one hand to lift my hair to the top of my head, "and wore a spectacular necklace and earrings." Linda stopped admiring herself in the mirror. "Wear your diamond necklace and earrings," she said. "They'd be perfect."

I studied my reflection. Actually, I did look good. I grabbed the dress and walked toward the dressing area. I tried it on. It was perfect, the color, the fit, everything. I wondered what Riley would think.

By the time I had modeled the dress and changed back into my street clothes Bernice had chosen a fitted dress in a shade of coral that would have made me look like a corpse but looked fabulous on her. Esther talked me into a new pair of silver pumps and a clutch purse. Kaching! As I handed my credit card to her, I refused to think about Nick's car fund. I'd find a way to add to it later.

Linda gave me a quick hug. "Come on, lighten up!" she encouraged. "You can

91

afford this. You're going to be the richest woman in the graveyard if you don't loosen those purse strings a little."

I thought for a minute. She was right. Nick and I were comfortably off. And I had been very tight with money since my husband died. Probably too tight if I were to admit it. What the heck? It wasn't as though Nick's first car was going to be a Mercedes, anyway. More like a used car with lots and lots of safety features. He'd probably hate it. But beggars can 't be choosers, right?

"Let's get our hair and nails done for the party!" Marcia enthused as we left the store.

What? No! I was done. I could do my own hair and nails, thank you very much. I might loosen those purse strings a little, but I wasn't going to drop them. Besides, Esther had said I was pretty. That was good enough for me.

Linda tugged me across the street and we all entered Sylvester's Beauty Salon. Sylvester eyed me critically. "I think it's time for some highlights," he informed me. 'Nick's car, Nick's car', I said to myself. "OK" I heard somebody say. Who said that? I looked around. It couldn't possibly have been me. My friends were laughing. It *had* been me.

Have I said 'crap' recently? That word seems to cover a lot of situations. Two hours later I had highlights in my hair and red finger nails with little sequins in them. My toenails were red also, without sequins. After all, this girl can only take so much bling.

"All right," Bernice said as we settled our purchases into Linda's car. "We're ready for Judith's cocktail party."

"No matter what it brings," Marcia chimed in, "We're going to look fabulous, Darlings."

# Chapter Nine

Riley looked devastatingly handsome when I opened the door. He was wearing a dark charcoal suit with the jacket cut to emphasize his slender hips and broad shoulders, along with a blazingly white shirt and a tie in shades of gray and blue. His dark hair was tousled attractively and looked like it had recently been cut. The evening was chilly and he had thrown a full-length black wool coat over his suit. Honestly, the man looked like he belonged on the cover of a men's fashion magazine. He smiled and his dimples appeared, making him look even more attractive. Be still my heart!

"You look beautiful," he said as he helped me with my coat. He cast an appreciative glance over my ensemble and my heart fluttered. The new highlights seemed to give my hair more sheen and, although I hated to admit it, Sylvester had managed to style my hair in a sophisticated and attractive French twist I could never have managed myself. My red nails were newly polished and shiny. I had spent extra time applying my makeup and my eyes seemed to sparkle more than normal, although that could have been more the result of excitement than an expert application of eye shadow.

"This should be an interesting evening," Riley remarked, getting into the car after opening and closing my door. What a combination, handsome and a gentleman. I could get used to this.

We chatted as he drove toward Woodford Hall, for the most part avoiding our purpose for attending the party. As we drew closer, however, Riley brought up what was on both of our minds. "What exactly do you hope to accomplish here?" he asked.

"I guess we just want to get to know these people better and see if we can get a feel for their relationships." I could almost feel him smirking. "And, no, I don't expect anyone to try to poison Judith's cocktail or give her a deadly canapé. That would be too Agatha Christie."

He laughed.

"What about you?" I asked.

"I'm just looking forward to spending time with you," he said.

"Seriously? That's all?"

"I *am* curious about Henry," he admitted, "After seeing that picture of him and Lisa I've been trying to find out what I can and see if their connection leads me anywhere."

"No luck?"

"Not so far," he replied with a frown.

"It sounds as though you're having a terrible time trying to solve this murder."

"It's interesting" he said. "It almost feels as if this were a professional hit. But why in the world would anyone do that to two teenagers?"

My stomach turned over. "Maybe someone is very smart but also very crazy."

"Crazy like a fox," he muttered, turning onto the road leading to the Hall. "I have to be missing something." I could feel the frustration pouring off him and placed my hand on his knee briefly.

"You'll figure it out," I said confidently. "I know you will."

He snorted.

"Yes, you will. I've seen how you work. You're smart and you're persistent and you don't miss a trick."

"You didn't mention obnoxious in that list of attributes," he said, smiling.

"Don't tempt me," I said. "I hope I never see that side of you again." I shuddered, remembering our first encounters.

"Was I really that bad?" Riley slid his eyes in my direction.

Oh, dear. This was awkward. Should I be honest and direct? We were having a lovely evening and I didn't want to put a damper on it. On the other hand, lying was not my strong suit. I settled on diplomacy. "You were awful," I admitted, "and you scared me half to death. But you were just doing your job."

Riley raised on eyebrow. How did he do that anyway? I had tried, practicing in front of my mirror, but I just couldn't make my eyebrow move. "I was trying to hide the fact that I thought you were cute as a button," he said.

"Really?" I turned to stare at him.

"Really," he said.

Well, what do you know?

Riley pulled the car up in front of the hall. "Do you want me to drop you off? It's getting cold."

"No, thanks," I said. "A short walk won't kill me." I pointed ahead of us. "I think I see some spaces just ahead."

Light was pouring out of Woodford Hall's ballroom when we entered. The crystal chandeliers gleamed, their facets reflecting light in every direction. The room had a soaring ceiling surrounded by multiple layers of crown molding. The walls were painted a soft green and the room was carpeted with a flowered rug that repeated the green, along with rose, navy and gold. French doors opposite the entrance opened onto the Hall's garden. I caught a glimpse of the koi pond where we had learned of Judith's plight. Circular tables, some tall enough to stand at, others the correct height for sitting, dotted the room.

The tables had been covered with white tablecloths and overskirts of green. To the left stood a gleaming bar with two uniformed bartenders working hard to satisfy the requests of thirsty guests. Waiters and waitresses circulated bearing trays of wine and champagne. As I watched, a slender Hispanic woman backed through a swinging door carrying a loaded tray of appetizers. "I wonder if that's Rosalinda," I said.

"Easy enough to find out," Riley said. "Just ask her."

I sidled over to the woman and helped myself to an appetizer. "You must be Rosalinda," I said. "Judith has told me so many nice things about you."

A smile lit her face, white teeth flashing against her olive skin. "The senora has been very good to me," she replied.

"Judith was also telling my about some things that happened to her recently. They seem pretty frightening to me."

Rosalinda seemed a little confused. "Alarmante?" I tried, trotting out my college Spanish.

The maid nodded emphatically. "Si. I don't understand why anyone would try to hurt the senora. She is so good to everyone."

"Then you haven't seen anything suspicious?" I asked, snagging another nibble.

She shook her head violently. "No. Nothing." She started to turn away.

"What would you do if you did see something?"

"I would talk with my husband. He would know what to do."

"Would you talk to the police?"

Rosalinda frowned. "Si. If I knew something I would do so. I have no reason to be afraid of the policia." She looked at me suspiciously. "Why are you asking

96

these questions?" Darn. Why hadn't I foreseen her asking that? Fortunately, as I searched my mind frantically for a decent reply someone else called Rosalinda's name and she turned away.

At that moment I spotted Judith standing with a couple on the far side of the room. She noticed us and headed in our direction with the couple in tow.

Judith stopped by my side and gave me a quick hug and air kiss. She held out her hand to Riley. "This is my date, Riley Furman," I said, introducing them. Riley shook her hand warmly, using his dimples and beautiful eyes to great effect.

"Thank you so much for inviting us, Mrs. Byrn," he said. "We appreciate the invitation."

"You must call me Judith," she said. She turned slightly to the couple standing nearby. "Let me introduce you to my daughter and son-in-law." The introductions were quickly made.

Ann Byrn Cunningham was as attractive as her picture had indicated. She was a tall woman, not quite as tall as Bernice, and moved with the easy grace of an athlete. With her chiseled cheeks and straight nose, her resemblance to her mother was unmistakable. Her smile was warm, reaching her eyes. Not all people's smiles do that, you know. Steven Cunningham, her husband, had the erect posture of a military man. His hair, graying at the temples, was cropped short. Like his wife, his eyes exuded warmth that appeared genuine. I suspected that his appearance alone gave his patients great confidence in him.

"How do you know my mother?" Ann asked.

"Jackie's a writer," Judith said quickly. "She's going to give a talk to our women's group here." She smiled warmly. "And I'm hoping to talk her into

97

giving some classes on creative writing."

I was? She was? That was news to me, but I suspected her story was as good as any other cover would have been.

Ann's eyes sparkled. "I've never met a published author before." She hesitated. "You are published, aren't you?"

"Many times," Riley said firmly. "Jackie's very talented. You might enjoy her books."

"What type of books do you write, Jackie?" Steven asked with interest.

"Mysteries," I replied. Ann looked startled. "They're cozy mysteries, actually, No blood or gore, just a good puzzle." I shivered. "I don't do well around blood." Unbidden, the memory of finding my neighbor's blood- covered body came to mind. Riley grabbed a glass of wine from a passing waiter and handed it to me.

Ann seemed to have recovered from her surprise. "I've just started my daughter on Nancy Drew mysteries," she said, smiling. "I just loved them when I was her age."

"They were wonderful!" I enthused. "But don't forget the Hardy Boys. I read them too, along with Trixie Belden." Ann was leaning toward me now as though sharing a mutual memory. "I thought Trixie Belden was a little obnoxious, didn't you?"

"A bit," I laughed. "She certainly was a know-it-all."

Steven looked across the room, "Look, Elizabeth and Bert are here. We'd better go say hello."

Ann's smile wasn't as warm this time. "My sister-in-law doesn't like to be ignored," she said. She squeezed my arm. "Let's talk later. I was a communications major and that involved some writing, but I've always thought I'd like to branch out and do more. I might be interested in your writing classes. I think it might be fun to write an historical novel." She gave a self-deprecating shrug. "I don't mean a bodice ripper, but something less titillating. I've always enjoyed Phillipa Gregory's books, so those would be my model."

"First time I heard about that," Steven said, steering his wife toward their relatives. "There's Henry," he said, pointing toward his nephew, who stood at the entrance.

"Oh good," his wife replied. She didn't sound as though she really meant it.

"Are you ok?" Riley asked, his arm lightly wrapped around my waist. "I saw your face when you were talking about blood."

"I'm fine," I assured him. "Actually, it's throwing up that makes me ill. Even Maggie getting sick makes me gag."

"I'm not sure I wanted to know that," he said. He changed the subject. "Bernice and Ray just arrived. And I think Bob and Marcia are just behind them."

"Have you seen Linda?" I asked.

"She's talking to a handsome blonde man by the bar."

That was our Linda. She was like a male magnet, attracting the interest of any man who came into contact with her. It wasn't surprising, with her good looks, intelligence and quick wit. In fact, it was a bit surprising that Linda didn't have a date with her, but probably she thought she could circulate more successfully without one.

"What did you think of Ann and Steven?" I asked Riley as we made our way toward our friends.

He shrugged noncommittally. "They seem pleasant enough. I get the feeling there may be some friction between them and her brother's family, don't you? They didn't seem thrilled to see them."

"I agree. I got that feeling when Linda told us they weren't friends on social media, but I'd like to find out more."

Heads swiveled when Bernice and Ray entered the room. That didn't surprise me. I was used to it. Riley, on the other hand, seemed a bit taken aback, his pupils slightly dilating as he noticed people's reactions to them. The Bradleys had left their lives as a celebrity power couple years ago, although you wouldn't know it from people's reaction to them. She had been a supermodel. He had been a talented quarterback with a major football team. After much success, they both decided they wanted to settle somewhere quiet, devote themselves to education, and raise their brood of children. They had blended into Summer Hill well and after a while their fame was accepted as being only a small piece of who they were. Even though they were now firmly ensconced in our town's academic world, they still turned heads. To begin with, they still made a strikingly handsome couple. And they were well known in Summer Hill, both for their positions in education and for the literacy foundation they had spearheaded. Bernice's recent appearance on the Oprah Winfrey show had given their foundation a tremendous boost, and enhanced their position in our community even more.

As I watched, Elizabeth Waters Byrn detached herself from the group of people with whom she had been speaking and glided toward Bernice and Ray. Yes, glided was the word. She held herself very erect and walked on high heeled shoes with ease and grace. The expression on her face was a combination of ingratiating and calculating. Considering what Judith had told us about her daughter-in-law being a social climber, and what we had learned on the internet, I wasn't surprised at her reaction to the arrival of Bernice and Ray. Her husband and son trailed in her wake, Bert wearing a slightly amused expression and Henry looking unimpressed. Of course, Ray had been the principal at his high school, so Henry already knew him relatively well. We started toward Bernice and Ray. Judith also drifted in our direction. Linda moved toward us more slowly and Marcia and Bob, having stopped to relinquish their coats, moved slightly behind her.

Riley and I reached my friends first. I received enthusiastic hugs from both, while Bernice kissed Riley's cheek and my date and Ray exchanged cordial handshakes. From the corner of my eye, I noticed that Elizabeth's expression shifted slightly, showing surprise that ordinary seeming people like Riley and me could be close to these superstars.

Elizabeth smiled at us all, slightly tilting her head. "Principal Bradley, how nice to see you. And Mrs. Bradley. What a pleasure to meet you at long last."

"Please, it's Ray and Bernice," Ray interjected.

"Thank you," Elizabeth said. "I don't know if you know my husband and son?"

"I certainly know Henry," Ray said, uttering words that could mean anything. Henry ventured a smile.

"I didn't know you were friends of my mother," Bert said.

"Oh yes," Bernice responded. "Judith is going to be such a help with our literacy project."

Judith merely gave a nod.

Bernice turned to the rest of us. "Let me introduce you to our friends," she said. Introductions were made all around.

We talked idly for a few minutes, as Elizabeth and her family tried to gauge our relationships with Judith.

"You look familiar to me," Bert said to Riley. "Where did you go to college?" Not knowing the answer to that, I held my breath. I had a feeling pedigree mattered to this part of the Byrn family and that Riley would be snubbed if his school wasn't prestigious enough. It didn't occur to me that his profession would be sufficient grounds for that.

"University of Virginia," Riley replied smoothly.

"Then I don't know you from school," Bert said. "Say, what do you think of your school's chances this year?" Virginia Tech and the University of Virginia had a longstanding football rivalry. The men chatted idly for a few minutes, with Ray and Bob throwing in their opinions.

"You still look familiar to me," Elizabeth said, studying Riley's face.

"He should," Henry snorted. "His face has been all over television recently."

"It has?" his mother looked puzzled but definitely interested in learning more about this potential movie star.

"Of course," Henry said. "He's the detective leading the team investigating Lisa Jones' murder." You could have heard a pin drop, as they say, as the family members scrutinized Riley.

"I must say," Henry drawled, studying his fingernails, "I wouldn't expect to see a cop at a party like this."

His grandmother gasped. "Henry, that was incredibly rude. Apologize immediately."

Riley fixed Henry with a steely gaze. "Where would you expect to find a cop?"

102

he asked. "Swilling beer at the local pool hall?"

Henry held his ground for a moment. "Beat up any black people lately?" he asked.

Riley tensed, his gaze hardening as he surveyed the young man. "Excuse me?" he said, the softness of his voice indicating to me the level of his anger.

Ray stepped in. "I know some people like to disrespect the police these days, Henry," he said. "But I expected better of you."

Henry had the grace to blush. Steven and Ann were looking embarrassed, as was his father. Elizabeth looked unconcerned until she saw Bernice's expression.

"Henry," she urged her son.

"I didn't mean anything bad," Henry said. "I'm sorry."

"Are you?" Riley asked. He clearly was not accepting the apology. He continued to look challengingly at the young man.

"Lisa's death was such a horrible thing," Bert contributed. "I just can't imagine something like this happening in Summer Hill."

Like any other town, Summer Hill had its dark side, and the recent opioid epidemic only served to make things worse. But that wouldn't touch a family like the Byrns. Even drug addiction, if it existed in such a family, would be swept under the rug, to be treated very, very privately.

"Did you know Lisa Jones?" Riley already knew the answer to his question. It struck me that asking such a question was part of his overall investigation technique.

"We know her parents quite well," Elizabeth replied. "We belong to the same country club and Lisa's mother and I have been on some committees together." She frowned, allowing a small crease to form between her eyebrows. "I truly don't know what to say to them," she admitted. "I'd like to offer sympathy, but everything I think of sounds so trite."

"It's always hard to lose a child," Judith put in. "All you can do is let them know how badly you feel for them."

"I understand you knew Lisa fairly well," Riley said, focusing his attention on Henry.

Henry paled. "We went to high school together."

"Oh, for Heaven's sake, Henry," his grandmother said. "You were practically inseparable your senior year." She turned to Riley. "Lisa and Henry dated for a while."

"Yes, but that was years ago," Henry protested, his eyes darting around as though he was looking for an escape.

"We're talking to Lisa's friends," Riley said, taking out his wallet and removing a card. He handed it to Henry. "I'd appreciate your coming to the station and speaking with me personally."

Henry took the card reluctantly. "I don't have to, do I?" he asked. He straightened defiantly. "I mean, you can't make me."

"Not at this point," Riley agreed. "I'd be happy to come to your home or to your place of work if that would be more convenient."

"I'd rather not," Henry said.

Riley shrugged. "That's your choice." He gave Henry a thin smile, the one that made him look like a predator eying a scared rabbit. "There is one thing you might want to think about," he said.

"What's that?" Henry asked.

"It's something you see in police shows on television all the time. And, unlike most of their content, this one thing is true." He had the attention of the entire group. "When someone refuses to talk with us, we always wonder just why that is." He smiled again, a genuine smile, back to his charming and relaxed appearance.

Henry's eyes darted around the room. "Oh look, Veronica's talking to the banquet manager. I'll go see if she needs anything." He trotted to the other side of the room, where Veronica Lake, dressed in a bright red dress, was talking with a woman wearing a suit and sensible heels.

"I apologize for my son," Bert said.

"Don't apologize for him," Judith snapped. "He's an adult. He needs to start behaving like one."

Elizabeth glared at her mother-in-law. "It sounded to me like you were threatening Henry, Officer," she said.

"It's detective, ma'am," Riley replied. "Or lieutenant, if you prefer." He decided to lessen the tension. "I'd really prefer that you call me Riley while we're here. Otherwise, I'll be looking over my shoulder for someone else." The others issued forced laughs. "I didn't mean to seem threatening at all. To be honest, this case is proving itself to be very challenging. We're talking to as many people who knew Lisa as we can. In fact, since you know the family, I'd like to talk with you too." He spread his hands. "You'd be surprised to find out how often someone is unaware that they know something that helps us solve a case."

"We'll be happy to help, Riley," Bert said. "Just call my office to set up a time." Elizabeth gave him a frosty smile.

Linda decided to change the subject. "I was talking with Steven and Ann about some exciting changes coming to the hospital before Bernice and Ray arrived," she said. She turned to Steven and Ann. "I'd love to tell you more about it if you're interested."

Steven took Linda's arm. "We're very interested in the improved children's wing," he said. "Our son spent some time in the hospital when he was young and we'd like to learn more about what we might do to help the effort." He and Ann led Linda out of earshot. She glanced back at us and gave us quick thumbs up.

Elizabeth leaned closer to Bernice. "I'd like to learn more about your foundation," she said. "Why don't we chat?" Bernice also moved away with her, but I could tell from the set of her jaw that she wanted to give both Henry and Elizabeth a piece of her mind.

Judith heaved a sigh. "Well, there you have my family," she said. She looked around the room. "I can't imagine where Emily has gone. She's not big on these types of parties. In all likelihood she's sitting in the library with her head in a book."

She turned to Riley. "I really am sorry about my grandson's behavior."

Riley shook his head and smiled at her. "Don't be. A lot of people have low opinions of the police. Occasionally it's deserved. We need to work harder on improving our image."

"Still," she chewed on her lip. "That young man concerns me. I can't help but think that his attitude is going to get him in trouble one of these days. He's just so condescending to people outside his circle, even though he hasn't done anything that might support his feeling so superior. Not that anyone ever could justify feeling like that." She watched her son and daughter-in-law laughing with Ray. "I don't know how Bert could have let Henry get so spoiled." She sighed.

I noticed that Marcia, wearing her flapper dress and some type of headband, was chatting with Veronica Lake. Bob was standing nearby, studying his drink and listening with a faint smile.

As it drew close to eight o'clock the crowd started to thin. Waiters began to remove used dishes and glasses from tables and the bartenders signaled a final round. "They truly do such a nice job here," Judith commented. The slim woman I had noticed earlier approached her. Judith smiled. "Are you leaving, Rosalinda?"

"Si, Senora," she replied. "I don't want to keep Miguel waiting."

"Thank you so much for all your help, my dear," Judith said. "I'll see you Tuesday." Rosalinda dipped her head and departed. "Such a treasure," Judith murmured. "I'd be lost without her." She smiled again. "I'm a terrible housekeeper. It's just not my strong suit."

Veronica Lake drifted out of the room, talking once again with the banquet manager. Emily Johnston was still missing, having put in just a short appearance. Henry wandered down the hall toward the restrooms and the ladies in the family did the same. Riley and I stepped outside for some fresh air, although it was quite cold.

"What do you think?" he asked.

I shrugged. "I may have a slightly better handle on some of the characters here, but I don't think we've learned much, except that Henry seemed pretty squirrely when you asked to talk with him. It will be interesting to see what the others have found out." I shivered in the chill and we stepped back inside.

107

A slender Hispanic man stepped into the room and looked around.

"Miguel?" Judith said with surprise. "I didn't expect to see you tonight."

"Is Rosalinda here, senora?" the man asked.

"No," Judith replied. "She left a while ago. She didn't want you to have to wait for her."

"She's not where she usually is when I pick her up," Miguel said, frowning. "I thought since it was cold she might be up here at the hall, but I can't find her anywhere."

Riley walked over to the couple, his cop face on. "Is something wrong?" he asked.

Judith turned to him, her face troubled. "I don't know," she replied. "Rosalinda isn't where she normally waits for Miguel."

Bob glanced at his watch. "She left about thirty minutes ago," he said.

Miguel was beginning to look more anxious.

Steven and Bert had drifted nearer and overheard the conversation.

"She's probably fine," Bert said, "but why don't we fan out and look for her? She might have had an accident."

Riley nodded, moving into action. "We'll get some of the staff to help." He turned toward Miguel. "Show me where she normally waits for you." I moved toward the coat rack. Riley held up his hand. "Please, ladies," he said. "Stay here."

Elizabeth and Ann had joined our group, both wearing concerned expressions.

"Come on," Bert said to his son, who had re-entered the room.

Henry hesitated a moment, but responded to the serious expression on his father's face.

After the men left the rest of us waited restlessly in silence. There didn't seem to be any way to start a conversation, although we tried several times. After another thirty minutes Judith walked to the coat rack and grabbed her coat. "This is ridiculous," she said. "I'm going to help." We all put our coats on quickly and headed outside. We could see flashlights bobbing over the grounds and hear people crying Rosalinda's name. Judith started to shake, her eyes tearing. "Something's happened to her," she whispered. "I know it."

Almost immediately we heard a cry go up. "Here! Over here! Help! She's here!"

The voice was coming from the bushes at the far end of the parking lot. Riley burst past us, followed by Bob and Ray. Steven came running from the far end of the building followed by Miguel. Henry, Bert and some staff members came from the other side. All of us ladies hurried as quickly as we could, given our ridiculously high heeled shoes, toward the commotion. When we reached the other side of the parking lot, we saw a man frantically waving his flashlight. Rosalinda lay crumpled on the ground motionless. Miguel dropped to his knees beside his wife. Steven, in doctor mode, leaned over her. "My God," he said.

# Chapter Ten

Blood seeped from a wound on Rosalinda's head. Steven grabbed her wrist and counted. "She's alive, thank God," he said. "Her pulse is erratic, but at least it's still there."

He gently examined her head while Riley punched numbers into his phone and spoke softly but urgently. Miguel grabbed Rosalinda's hand and held it in both of his, trying unsuccessfully to choke back his tears.

Steven looked up from his examination. "I can't tell how bad the injury is," he said, taking a deep breath. He looked into Riley's eyes, communicating his sense of urgency.

Riley kneeled next to Rosalinda. "She was hit hard. When we get her to the emergency room and can see more, we may have a better idea of what did this," he said.

Steven looked up at the group surrounding Rosalinda's limp form. "Someone here hit her." His eyes surveyed the group. "I may be wrong, but I don't know who else it could have been." He checked Rosalinda's pulse again. "I've been a healer my entire career," Steven said softly. "It makes me sick, literally sick to my stomach, to think that someone I'm close to could have hurt this lovely lady." When he raised his head, is eyes were like granite. "If I'm right, and one of you did this," Steven declared, "I will do everything in my power to be sure you pay." He returned his focus to his patient.

Judith leaned heavily against her daughter. Marcia, Bernice, Linda and I huddled in a tight group, arms around each other. Ray and Bob stood on either side like bookends, while Riley continued to talk on his phone, standing a short distance away.

Veronica Lake stood next to Emily, who had finally made an appearance. Elizabeth, Bert and Henry stood in a family group, silent and staring at Rosalinda's form.

The faint wail of sirens grew louder and sharper as emergency personnel and police officers careened into Woodford's lot. Ambulance personnel ran over with a stretcher, consulted quickly with Steven and, after applying a neck brace and other stabilizing mechanisms, lifted Rosalinda into the vehicle. Miguel jumped in with his wife, as did Steven. He searched for Ann.

"I'll stay here with Mother," Ann said, seeming to hold up Judith's sagging form. "The sitter will stay with the kids. Don't worry about us." Emily moved to her godmother's side and took her other arm.

Steven gave a brief nod and the ambulance headed down the drive.

At a gesture from Riley a police officer began shepherding the rest of us inside. She managed to corral us into the room where the party had been held. Other officers joined us while still others roped off the area where Rosalinda had been found.

Riley reentered the room, his face grim. His tie was askew and he had clearly been running fingers through his hair. As soon as he appeared, the room exploded with questions. Riley held his hands up, trying to silence the cacophony. Gradually the noise dissipated and he was able to make himself heard.

"As I'm sure you know," he said, his gaze hitting everyone in the room, "Rosalinda has been assaulted. We won't know how serious her injuries are for quite a while. In the meantime, I'm going to ask everyone to give their contact information to Sergeant Williams," he gestured toward the female officer standing at the door "and to talk with her about what you may have noticed about Rosalinda's activities or anything else you think may be significant this evening. Any little thing you saw could be very helpful."

"When are you going to break out the lead pipes and the dogs?" called a voice. Henry was leaning against the wall, arms crossed, a lock of hair artfully falling over one eye. "Don't we have a right to an attorney before talking with the police?"

"Not at this time," Riley said, "You are not in custody."

"Then I can go," Henry said, pushing away from the wall. "I don't have to talk to any of you." He eyed the detective. "Especially you, Furman."

Out of the corner of my eye I saw Bernice stiffen. She drew herself up to her full height, already impressive without her stiletto heels, and walked toward Henry. For some reason she reminded me of a cat stalking its prey. He smirked at her, and then changed his mind and seemed to cower as she moved closer and closer. She must have been three inches taller than him in those shoes. "I have had it with you," Bernice said, her voice low and throbbing with emotion. She grabbed the collar of his shirt.

"Bernice" Ray said in alarm, starting toward his wife.

Bernice smoothed Henry's shirt and stepped back. We were all staring at her, not knowing what to expect.

Riley stepped forward. "Bernice," he said, whether in concern or warning I wasn't sure.

Bernice held up a hand. "That man," Bernice said, her voice quivering and her hand pointing toward Riley, "that good man, that kind man, has one of the hardest jobs in the world." Her arm sweep encompassed the other officers in the room. "And so do these officers. How dare you be disrespectful to them? How dare you be so horrible to people who want to do nothing but protect all of us?"

Henry stepped further back.

Bernice pointed to Riley again. "That man is my friend. You have been nothing but rude to him all night. You are no better than anyone else in this room, and the sooner you figure that out the happier life will be for you."

She turned to Elizabeth and Bert, who were watching with mouths open. "And you?" she spit. "With all your money and your position this is the best job you can do in raising your son? Well, it's not good enough."

"Honey," Ray protested.

"I'm not done, Ray," Bernice said. Marcia, Linda and I were both fascinated and aghast. Never had we seen this side of Bernice. "Don't send any money to our literacy fund. We will send it right back. I don't want to be associated with you unless you can be better than this." She sent a deprecating gesture toward Henry.

Bernice turned one more time. "I'm sorry, Judith," she said to the woman who was sagging even further against her daughter "I'm sorry," she said again, more softly, "I like you. I really do. But your grandson's behavior tonight is unacceptable." She lasered Henry one more time with an ice-cold glare. "Maybe it's time someone let him know that.' She looked Henry up and down. "And for Heaven's sake get your hair out of your face. You look ridiculous." She turned on her heel, stuck her elegant nose in the air, and marched from the room. Henry unconsciously shoved his hair back.

113

"Well, I never!" Elizabeth turned a furious glare on Ray. He met it unwaveringly. "When Henry was in high school," he said, "I told him that he would benefit from an attitude adjustment." He turned toward Henry. "That advice still stands." He nodded to the rest of us in the room and followed in Bernice's wake.

You could have heard a pin drop, as they say. "Wow!" Marcia whispered.

After a few more moments of silence, we heard rhythmic clapping. The clapping noise approached Elizabeth and Bert. There stood Ann Byrn Cunningham, applauding the Bradleys. "It's about time," she said. "It's about time someone let you know that you are not royalty. You're behaving like a bunch of jerks and I for one have had enough of Elizabeth's and Henry's attitudes. Good grief, Bert, man up. You wonder why Mother won't let go of the company? Look around you. She doesn't want either of them within a mile of what she and Dad built."

By this time, Judith, though still pale and upset, was standing on her own, regaining her usual regal posture. "That's enough. We will not air our dirty laundry in public. I for one am far more concerned with Rosalinda and want to do anything I can to find out what happened to her." She eyed her grandson. "What do you say, Henry?"

"Yes, Grandmother," he said, studying his shoes. He looked up at Riley, who, while he was trying to keep his policeman face in place looked a bit bemused. "I'm sorry, Detective," he said. "I don't know why I said the things I did this evening. I sincerely apologize."

Riley nodded but said nothing.

"How would you like us to proceed, Detective Furman?" Judith asked.

114

"Sergeant Williams," Riley said.

"Sir!" I thought the officer was going to salute.

"Please get contact information from everyone remaining and take down any details about this evening, particularly after Rosalinda left, that they are able to share."

"Yes, Sir." She began assigning tasks to the other officers in the room and settled at a table in the corner.

"I'm sorry you had to see that." I heard a soft voice at my elbow and turned to see Judith's goddaughter, Emily, standing by my side.

I offered a vague smile.

"I'd like to say Henry's a good kid at heart," she continued, "but I'm not sure I can."

I raised an eyebrow.

"I know his feelings about the police are quite popular among his generation and his going to a liberal college in New England has probably reinforced those leanings. But there's always been a core that's hard to reach. He's a lot like his mother. Elizabeth's not a bad person, but her entitled attitude can be hard to take and unfortunately that entitlement has rubbed off on Henry." She gave a short laugh. "You can probably see it rubs Ann the wrong way. She's never said anything before. But it's hard when you've been required to work for things and you're constantly thrown together with someone who has had everything given to her on a silver platter and likes to flaunt it."

Having been a worker bee all my life I could identify with Ann. "How do you manage, working and living with this conflict?"

Emily smiled. "Nose to the grindstone, avoid taking sides, and have a wonderfully loving dog and good friends who don't even know my family for the most part. It's not too bad, and I really love Judith. Besides, running the financial side of the business is a challenge I enjoy."

"I understand you were a financial advisor."

She nodded. "I was. And in a way I still am. In my old world I was accountable to a lot more people – clients, staff, management. Here, I just keep the company on the straight and narrow and moving forward."

"I heard that Bert does a good job as president."

"He does. And he has some very good ideas about shaping the future." She sighed. "I do wish Judith would give him a little more leeway. Change can be a good thing."

"What kind of change is he proposing?"

"Moving more into the area of green building."

"Do you agree?" I asked.

Emily nodded enthusiastically. "Absolutely. It's the wave of the future. Judith is concerned because we'd have to invest quite a bit of money into education and training, and eventually into some new equipment. But the company can stand that financially. It might cut into profits while we get up to speed, but I think the result could be even more business." Her eyes followed Judith, who was rising from a chair after speaking with the sergeant. She smiled fondly. "I think Judith is coming around, albeit slowly. She tends to let all the family issues get in the way of clear thinking. After tonight, you can understand why." The sergeant waved in our direction. "I guess it's my turn," Emily said. "Thanks for talking to me."

It had been more listening in actuality, but I had learned some valuable information. Emily appeared to be satisfied with her current role in the company and looking forward to the future. There were some major divisions between Bert's family and the remaining members. Judith's personal fears were impacting the future of the company and Bert's plans. With a little push from his wife and son, would Bert actually try to do something about that?

# Chapter Eleven

I tried to be helpful when it was my turn to talk with Sergeant Williams, but I feared I didn't contribute much to her information gathering efforts. I relayed my conversation with Rosalinda, but if the officer found that information valuable, she didn't show it. I wasn't sure if that meant it was worthless or if, like Riley, she played her cards very close to the vest. "Well, thank you," she said after I had recounted my version of the party, with an emphasis on from where I had seen people appear when Rosalinda was found. "I have your address and phone number, but I'm sure Detective Furman knows how to get in touch with you in any event." She raised one eyebrow (how do people do that anyway?) and gave me a crooked smile. The rumors would be flying around the department after tonight. I debated whether I should fuel those rumors by giving Riley a kiss when I left or whether I should just say a staid good night. Being the coward that I am, the second choice won out. I found my friends waiting for me in the Woodford Hall lobby. Bernice was looking a little worse for wear, chewing on her lower lip and gazing blankly into the distance.

"I'm so sorry," she said immediately upon my arrival. "I don't know what got into me."

I hugged her. "It's perfectly all right. That kid had it coming to him."

"Now I've blown our investigation," she murmured. "There's no way we're going to get anything out of Bert and his family."

"We'll see," I replied. "Emily was pretty forthcoming just now, and Ann is clearly fed up. We may be able to get in through a back door."

"I could have been more helpful," Ray confessed. "Probably I could have smoothed things over a bit if I hadn't laid into Henry also." He smiled at his wife. "I could simply have told them that you are emotionally unstable and that you would regret everything you said in the morning." He kissed her on the cheek.

"As if," Bernice said, laughing. "I get so sick of these college kids, acting like they know everything when they've barely begun to live. Some of it is natural and I understand that, but this hatred of our institutions and our way of life is unnerving. Surely we can fix what needs fixing without tearing each other apart."

"I'm sure we were less than perfect when we were in college," Linda contributed.

Bernice nodded. "Of course, we were. But we were nothing like today's kids."

"Personally, I was perfect," Marcia said, executing a quick pirouette and a curtsy.

"I'm sure," Bernice said.

"I would have liked to be a fly following you around and observing," Linda said.

"It was different," Bob admitted. Now there was a surprise. How could it not have been 'different'? We *were* talking about Marcia, after all, and she was nothing if not entertaining, always following the different drummer marching around in her head. Bob had a dry sense of humor and I had no doubt that his tales of his early days with Marcia would be wildly amusing. I'd only heard a few, but I remembered laughing so hard at her antics that I could barely catch my breath. I made a mental note to drag some more stories out of Bob at a more appropriate time.

"I guess what really bothered me was the way Henry attacked Riley. He's such a sweet man..." Bernice began.

"Who is?" asked a voice behind her.

She spun around and found herself face to face with Riley Furman. "You're eavesdropping."

"Professional habit," Riley said with a smile. "By the way, thank you for sticking up for me."

"Happy to do it," she returned.

Riley turned to me. "I need to stay for a while."

"I understand. Linda already volunteered to drive me home."

"I'll see you later, then." He hesitated. I suspected he was wondering about sharing a kiss, just as I had been. With him also, discretion won out. He bade us farewell and turned on his heel.

"What now?" Marcia asked.

"Now we all go home," Bob said, taking her arm. "We stop sticking our noses where they don't belong and let Riley do his job."

Marcia made a face at him. "That doesn't sound like fun."

"I'm going to check in with Judith tomorrow," I said. "She looked awful when we left."

"And I'll see what I can find out about Rosalinda when I'm at work," Linda volunteered. "But I'm not going to share anything confidential," she cautioned us.

"Let's compare notes on what we saw this evening," I suggested. "People seemed to come running from a lot of different directions when Rosalinda was found. Seems to me a lot of people had the opportunity to conk her on the head."

"But why?" Ray wondered. "She must know something even if she doesn't know she knows it."

We took that in.

"Good thing you never taught English," Bob said. Ray punched him in the arm.

"My, that turned into quite a night," Linda said as we drove home.

I chewed on my thumbnail.

"Don't do that," she directed. "You'll ruin your manicure."

I dropped my hand into my lap. "I keep thinking about the last thing Ray said. Someone at that party has to be spooked. And Rosalinda has to be a key to the identity of the person who's been scaring Judith."

"I'll see if her husband knows anything," Linda said. "I assume he'll be at the hospital."

"When I talked with her, I got the impression she hadn't consulted with him." I gave a deep sigh. "Right now, and most importantly, I hope Rosalinda will be all right. Maybe she'll remember who hit her."

"If she wakes up," Linda said grimly.

I sent up a short but heartfelt prayer.

When I got home, I found a note from Nick saying that he had gone to Kelly's house to prepare for a test. I knew that Nick would be in good hands. Kelly's parents were probably both in the same room as the kids while they studied, making sure no parts of their bodies touched. Nothing to worry about on that score. Her parents were so strict that they made my own parents' behavior

121

during my high school years seem liberal. Nothing could be further from the truth. I'm sure my father would have locked me in a chastity belt had they still been available. As it was, he always met my dates and gave them the third degree, insisted they come to the front door every time they picked me up as opposed to beeping the horn and was always waiting up when I came home. How I ever found a boyfriend and actually got married remains a mystery. In my memory my dad was everywhere, driving my crazy, but I guess he really wasn't. Kelly's parents, however, came pretty close. Nick joked that he expected them to pop up in the back seat while he was on a date with Kelly.

Suddenly I was exhausted. I took Maggie out for one last potty break, washed my face, brushed my teeth and fell into bed. Sleep came, but it was far from restful. My dreams were filled with pictures of Rosalinda's limp body, her husband's anguished face, Henry's scowling visage and the sound of Ann Byrn Cunningham clapping her hands over and over. I woke up anxious and unrefreshed, with the beginnings of a terrible headache. Nonetheless, I crawled out of bed, took some aspirin, made coffee and headed off to work. Of course, that meant walking all the way to the back of the house, but it was work nonetheless.

That morning I was scheduled to talk with my editor, going over her suggested revisions for my book, and work we did. I am blessed with a wonderful editor. She is talented, creative, and, best of all, she can tell whether I'm digging in my heels or likely to come around to her way of thinking. We sync so well that I can't imagine having to work with someone else, although that day may come as she is much older than I.

Even though we worked together well, my editor could tell that my mind was only partially on the task at hand. Finally, she changed direction and managed to worm all the details of the previous night out of me.

"Well," she finally said in her typical measured way, "That mother and son are peas in a pod, aren't they?"

"What do you mean?"

"They expect things to be given to them without their working, their values, or rather lack thereof, seem closely aligned, so they're peas in a pod."

"Yes, that's true, but how does that help us?"

"Possibly it doesn't, but it seems to me there could be something important there. How far would one go to help the other get what he or she wanted? Would they cover for each other if they knew one was doing something wrong? You know what the term 'enable' means. I suspect there is something of that in their relationship. I would try to find out more about them, if I were you." She cleared her throat. "On the other hand, I might just finish my darned book."

"Very funny," I replied. "After last night, how in the world can we get close to them?"

"Do you have anything they want?" my editor asked.

"No." I said. "Bernice did, but that's off the table, I'm sure."

"Hmmm. Maybe you'll think of something else. In the meantime…" (Hint, hint hint.) Back to the book we went.

In the end she advised me to make a nice cup of tea (did I mention that she's from England?), put my feet up and then, naturally, get back to work. "Sometimes answers come when you're busy thinking about something else." I happen to dislike tea, but I did grab a diet soda from the refrigerator, put my feet up, and try to think. Of course, I fell asleep.

The buzzing of Flight of the Bumblebee jerked me awake. When I chose that ring tone for my cell phone, I thought it was quite cheery and amusing. Now I realize it is just plain annoying. One of these days I will change it. To my son's amazement, I actually know how to do that. The problem is I think of doing it when my phone is not with me, like when I'm in the shower. Showering with your phone would be a really dumb idea, so there you are, with an idea and no way to act upon it. Unless, of course, you want to step out of the shower dripping wet and search for your stupid phone and by the time you find it you can't remember what you were thinking anyway. Someday I'll think about changing the ring tone when my phone is in my hand and I'll change it. Really, I will. Maybe to one of those restful tones. But then I probably wouldn't hear it when it rang, which can be a good thing sometimes anyway. I am not one of those people who needs to be super connected. Except I really need to hear the phone if Nick needs me. That means a restful tone is not a good idea. As you can see, there are many reasons Flight of the Bumblebee keeps flying. All this ran through my mind while I searched for my phone which, amazingly enough, was on my desk.

"Rosalinda's still unconscious," Linda said in my ear.

"That's not encouraging," I said.

Linda sighed. "No, it isn't. Her poor husband is just devastated. I feel helpless."

"Right now, the best we can do is make sure he's getting enough to eat and drink. We can  work on finding the person who did this without bothering him."

"Riley was here this morning," Linda said. "He saw me and sort of gave me the evil eye."

"Uh oh, I know that look."

"I pretended I was busy at the nurse's station," Linda said. "I don't know whether he bought it or not."

"Probably not," I said glumly.

"In any event," Linda continued, "I did ask Miguel if he knew of any reason Rosalinda would be attacked. He claimed he couldn't think of one. She hadn't said anything to make him worry. He did say that she'd been preoccupied recently, but that when he asked her what was bothering her, she told him she didn't want to get anyone in trouble."

"Well, that's not helpful," I said. "It indicates that Rosalinda saw something or someone she wondered about. Something must have felt out of place. And I guess she wasn't telling me the complete truth last night. In any event, if she doesn't wake up, we're no further ahead than we were."

"The doctor did say that even if she regains consciousness, she may have a big hole in her memory," Linda said.

"Terrific." I thought a moment. "Keep us posted. I'm going to check on Judith. She must be a wreck." We disconnected, feeling despondent.

After a few moments I gathered up my nerve and called Judith. She answered the phone immediately. "Oh, Jackie, I'm so glad you called. I just talked to Miguel about Rosalinda. He told me it doesn't look promising." A sob caught in her throat. "Who could have done this to her?" "I don't know," I admitted. "It has to have been someone who was at the party last night," Judith continued. "Probably," I said. "I guess there's an outside chance it wasn't one of your guests or a person who works at Woodford Hall, but I wouldn't bet money on it."

"What are you going to do?"

What was I going to do? What was *I* going to do? What *was* I going to do? I thought a moment. "Why don't I come see you? I suspect you could use some company and maybe we can work our way through what you know of Rosalinda's movements over the last few days."

"That sounds like a good idea." Judith sounded slightly more cheerful. "Come for lunch around 1:00. And don't dress up. I do some of my best thinking when I'm walking. We can take a stroll after lunch."

I must have driven more quickly than I realized, because I was early for our lunch date. When I arrived a sporty Mercedes convertible was parked in Judith's driveway. I hesitated, wondering if she had invited other company. If so, it wasn't anyone in my circle. No one I knew drove such a jaunty car. Even Linda, single, very well paid and with no dependents other than a cat, drove a small SUV and it wasn't a luxury model. I approached the door, raised my hand to knock, and heard a raised voice. Because of the glass panels beside the door, I could hear quite clearly. I stepped back quietly and positioned myself so I couldn't be seen if anyone glanced outside.

"I don't understand why you have to be so stubborn, Mother!" It was Ann's voice. I leaned forward slightly. "It really is time for you to let us run the company on our own."

I couldn't make out Judith's reply.

"Why do you care if Bert lets Elizabeth spend his earnings on clothes or jewelry or spa treatments? And Henry…who cares if he buys a stable of race horses or dates a stripper or snorts his money up his nose?"

Another reply, slightly louder. Judith sounded upset.

126

"Of course, I'm exaggerating, Mother. But the bottom line is that, so long as Bert does a good job and you get your quarterly dividends, how they spend their money shouldn't matter! How Steven and I choose to spend our money isn't any of your business, either. Bert and I have worked hard to keep the company successful. Emily too. And Bert has some terrific ideas. So do I. You have to stop holding us back."

I heard Judith's voice once more.

Footsteps approached the door rapidly. "Think about it, Mother! You are being very unfair!" I stepped back and raised my hand to knock just as Ann jerked the door open, almost causing me to fall on my face.

"Oh, hello," she said in surprise.

I attempted what I hoped was a normal smile. "Hello, there," I said cheerily. "Judith invited me to lunch. I didn't realize you were coming too. It's nice to see you." Ann tried to smile, but failed. "I'm just leaving," she said, stepping through the doorway. "I need to get back to the office. It's good of you to spend time with Mother. She's very upset about what happened last night." Without a backward look she trotted across the driveway to her car.

I watched her back up. 'Well,' I thought. 'That was certainly interesting.' After the previous night I had assumed Ann was the golden child. Maybe not.

Judith came to the door, her cheeks flushed and eyes flashing. "Welcome, Jackie," she said, giving me a brief hug. "I'm so looking forward to our time together." I glanced over my shoulder as Ann steered her car away from the house. She cast an intense glance over her shoulder as her car picked up speed. From the expression on her face, she didn't seem very happy to see me.

Curiouser and curiouser.

# Chapter Twelve

Lunch turned out to be a flavorful vegetable soup accompanied by a Greek salad and fresh rolls.

"I tend to chop when I'm agitated, and I've been chopping a lot recently," Judith said with a wan smile.

"It's wonderful," I said sincerely. "What herbs are in your soup?" We chatted for a few minutes about culinary matters.

Judith finally leaned back in her seat. "I thought Veronica might join us, but she begged off," Judith said. "She said she had some errands to do."

Ah, yes, the mysterious Veronica. "What exactly does she do for you?" I asked.

"She essentially keeps me straight," Judith replied. "I think you know that I'm very active with the symphony and the art museum. Veronica keeps my schedule, handles my correspondence, organizes social and charitable events, acts as my personal shopper and does whatever other tasks I need her to. She put together last night's party."

"She did a very nice job," I said.

"Yes, it would have been a very pleasant evening except for…" Judith sighed.

"I know," I said. "Poor Rosalinda."

"I still can't believe it," Judith said. "I talked with Miguel shortly before you arrived. He said there's been no change. I offered to sit with him, but he said their priest was there and that he was expecting his brother and sister-in-law to come later."

"At least he has some support," I said. I decided to change the subject. "Where did you find Veronica?"

"She worked for a friend of mine," Judith said. "My friend is slowing down and decided she no longer needed an assistant. When she heard I was looking for one, she recommended Veronica."

"Did Veronica give you a resume or anything?" I asked.

"Yes," Judith replied. "Do you want to see it?" I responded in the affirmative.

"Let's see," I said, spreading the resume out on the table. "This says she graduated from the Cornell hospitality program. Let's see who she says she worked for." We scanned the list. "Whose name do you recognize?'

"Let's see. There's my friend. And I know Elaine Porter, but not well. There's no other name I know."

"Did you check any of these references?" I asked.

"No, I didn't," Judith admitted. "Since my friend thought so highly of her, I didn't think it necessary." She looked up. "Do you think that was a mistake?" I shrugged "I don't know. How about if we see what Cornell University says." It seemed to take a century before Judith reached someone who could give her the information we needed. After a short conversation she hung up, a stunned look on her face. "According to the woman I spoke with, Veronica did not attend Cornell."

I took a deep breath and thought.

"You're not surprised, are you?" Judith asked.

I shook my head and explained our failure to find any significant presence on social media. "For someone older, that wouldn't be unusual," I said, "but for someone Veronica's age, it seems pretty strange."

"Let me see if I can get hold of my friend," Judith said, dialing her phone. "She didn't check her references either," she said a few minutes later, "because she knew Elaine Porter, and Elaine vouched for Veronica."

129

"Let's think a minute before we do anything rash," I said, sensing that Judith was prepared to fire Veronica as soon as she walked in the door. "For all we know, Lake could be a married name and her record could be under her maiden name. Or she could have changed her name for any of several reasons." I thought a moment. "Marcia thinks she's in witness protection." We both laughed. But in the back of my brain, something was setting off an alarm. What if it wasn't witness protection, but another reason Veronica was trying to hide her true identity? Like she was a criminal. Or she was running from someone. Or maybe both. As much as that idea was niggling at me, I decided not to share it with Judith.

Judith relaxed a bit. "Obviously I have some questions to ask of Veronica. I'll also try to get hold of Elaine, although that isn't an easy thing to do. She's always off galivanting somewhere. What else do you think I should do?"

"Do you have any reason to believe she's doing anything wrong? Has anything gone missing? Is money gone from any of your accounts? Has she done anything to make you think she's been snooping?"

"No, on all accounts," Judith replied.

"Can you act as though nothing's wrong when she returns?" I asked.

Judith nodded. "And then she'll have two days off. I can try to contact some of her other references while she's gone."

"That sounds like a plan," I said. "If I hear from Riley, I'll see if he has any other ideas. Do you have anything with her birthdate or Social Security number on it?"

Judith rose and walked toward the den. "I made a copy of her driver's license." She came back and held out a piece of paper. "That must mean she exists,

130

mustn't it?"

"Either that or she's gone to extraordinary lengths to hide her real identity," I said, folding the paper and putting it in my purse.

"Are you up for a walk?" Judith asked. "I need to get rid of this nervous energy. There's a lovely nature trail near here."

"Sure, let's go," I said, reaching for my jacket. "I'm always up for a little exercise." Actually, that wasn't true, as I have definite couch potato traits, but it was a lovely day and I sensed Judith needed some company along with the release that exercise can bring.

We walked the winding trail, which started at the end of her street, for a short while paralleling pasture fence. "There's Midnight," Judith said with pleasure. "Isn't he beautiful?" Indeed, he was. He was a large horse with a broad chest and muscular legs. Judith let out a piercing whistle. Midnight raised his head and ambled over to her. He came to the fence and thrust his head over it, nuzzling her jacket breast pocket. "You are such a greedy boy," she said, stroking him and removing a small carrot. The horse took it gently, gazing at her with his soft dark eyes. "I just love this horse," she said, smiling.

"It looks like the feeling is mutual," I said.

"Give him a pat," Judith said, finding another carrot.

I approached the horse gingerly, and patted the front of his head. He shook it and I jumped back.

Judith laughed. "He likes to have the side of his neck rubbed," she said. "Try it."

I reached again for the huge animal. To my delight he stood quietly, seeming to enjoy my touch.

"You should come riding one day," Judith suggested.

"I don't know," I demurred. "He seems awfully big and I've never been a horse person."

"Really?" Judith looked at me like I came from another planet. "It's never too late to try. There are smaller horses here. Winnie would probably be a good fit for you."

"Linda loves to ride," I said. "Maybe I'll come with her." There. That should appease Judith for a while.

She looked at me knowingly and laughed. "And I suppose pigs will be flying sometime soon," she said .I joined in her laughter and we headed away from the pasture. "Rosalinda used to love to walk this path on her lunch," Judith reminisced. "She told me she grew up on a farm and she enjoyed seeing the horses. Of course, she and Miguel live nearby and still farm, but they only have goats."

The path began to climb. From time to time, I caught glimpses of a bridle path weaving through the trees. We reached a clearing and had a view looking down onto a narrow river and a country road. In the clearing were three picnic benches. "Isn't this a lovely spot?" Judith asked. "Rosalinda often had lunch here in good weather. And I like riding this path and then just taking in the view.' I walked closer to the crest of the hill. The land undulated lazily, hazy foothills in the distance, the river and roadway sharper in contrast. A tractor slowly made its way along the road. The driver pulled onto a cleared area to let a faster vehicle pass. "Is this County Road 61?" I asked, an uncomfortable thought lodging itself in my mind.

Judith nodded. "It is indeed. It's a popular road for weekend wanderers." She chuckled. "That area down there is a favorite spot of kids who want to do a bit of necking. There's even a path that leads to the river. I've seen more than one person skinny dipping down there." She laughed. "It really is true that most of us look much better with our clothes on."

"I think that's where that young couple was murdered," I said.

Judith frowned. "Are you sure?"

"Not 100 percent, but it's easy enough to find out."

We watched the farmer pull back onto the road.

"What are you thinking?" Judith asked.

"I don't know why, but my instinct keeps telling me that there's some connection between those murders and what has been happening to you."

Judith stared at me. "How in the world could that be?"

I shrugged. "I'm not sure yet." I thought a bit longer. "What if," I finally said, "Rosalinda saw something connected with those murders when she was up here? Maybe she didn't realize it at the time." Judith was silent. "Maybe she saw someone or something at your cottage that tied them together in her mind."

"What could she have seen?" Judith asked. "I don't know. A person? An object?" I turned to Judith. "You said you ride that path frequently." She nodded. "What if it was *you* ? *You* saw something and someone decided you needed to be stopped from revealing what it was you saw. Then Rosalinda figured out who was trying to stop you, and she was the next person who was in the way." Judith turned a puzzled face to me. "But what did I see?"

"I don't know," I said, staring down at the road. "But I have a feeling that if we can figure that out, we'll have the answers to not one but two puzzles."

# *Chapter Thirteen*

"I'm positive that Riley's murder case and what has happened to Judith and Rosalinda are related," I said, jamming my finger onto the table, pointing at the paperwork laid out in neat piles. It contained every article we could find about the murder as well as the information we had gathered on all the people we had investigated.

"Have you talked to Riley?" Bernice asked.

"No."

Has he called you?" she asked.

"No."

"Have you called him?" Linda queried.

"No."

Marcia cradled her head in her hands and shook it. "How are you EVER going to get laid?"

Excuse me?

She raised her head. "Don't you WANT to get laid?"

"Um, no?" I replied.

They all stared at me.

"Well, of course, some day, at some time, maybe." I expanded my answer.

Silence.

"Sex is not the foundation of a healthy relationship," I said. I gazed pleadingly at Linda. She held up her hands. "I'm just a spectator here. I have no input."

"Have you broken up without your knowing it?" Marcia asked.

"How can we break up when we're not even together?" I replied.

"That has to be the dumbest thing you've ever said," Marcia replied, putting her head back into her hands.

I looked around the table. Things had obviously gotten out of control. I shot Bernice a beseeching glance.

"Girl," she said, shaking her head.

"Help me out here," I said. "What am I missing?"

"You have this wonderful, gorgeous guy who's crazy about you and you don't think you're together?" Marcia said. "Are we back in grade school?"

"Calm down, ladies," Bernice said. "You do know this is none of our business."

Linda and Marcia maintained a stony silence, arms crossed over their chests.

She smiled at me and put her hand on my arm. "None of our business, but we see how you guys click. Would it be such a bad idea for you to call him? I'll bet he's frustrated and tired and would love to hear your voice."

I tried to digest what she was telling me.

"Call him. Feed him a good meal," Linda said.

"And then ask him every question on this list," Marcia said, pushing over two pages of handwritten notes.

I thought about what they were saying. I supposed it wouldn't hurt to call him and offer him a home-cooked dinner. About asking all of those questions, only time would tell.

After my friends left, I settled down to read Marcia's questions. Obviously, she had been thinking a lot about not only Judith but Lisa and Bobby's murders. A lot of her questions had to do with the crime scene. Some dealt with the teenagers' backgrounds. I shook my head. Chances were that Riley wouldn't answer her questions, even if he were allowed to. I squinted at a question half

135

way down the first page. "What would be your perfect date?" it read. What in the world? It was followed by several questions about Lisa, Bobby and Henry. Then "How do you feel about being in a committed relationship?" Huh? I found several more similar questions. That little rascal. I tossed the papers to one side. There was no way I was going to let Riley see these. My nosy little friend would just have to stop poking into my affairs. I had to chuckle, though. Marcia was nothing if not persistent. Maybe she *would* make a good detective. She certainly was curious enough and she wasn't afraid to go where most people would fear to tread. I reached for the phone.

"Furman." The voice that came through sounded tired and irritable. Uh oh. Maybe this was not such a great idea. I almost hung up. "Jackie?" Riley's voice mellowed.

"Hi," I said. What a great start to a phone call.

"Hi, yourself."

"How are you?" I asked, being a creative conversationalist.

"I'm tired and irritated and frustrated," Riley replied. "How are you?"

I swallowed hard. "Actually, I'm good. I was thinking of you and know that you've been working really hard and that you probably haven't had a chance to unwind and that you're also probably exhausted and just want to go home and sleep for a week…"

Now he was laughing, a soft, sexy sound. "Is this sentence going anywhere?" he asked.

"Would you like to come for dinner tomorrow night?"

There was a short silence. That didn't bode well, I thought. Maybe he didn't want to see me. Maybe that's why he hadn't called. Maybe we were actually breaking up before we were even were a couple. Maybe I should apologize and hang up. "I'd love to," he said.

His reply caught me a bit off guard. "That's great," I said. "And I promise there will be no hangers-on this time. Just you and me and Nick. Probably. I mean Nick will probably be home. You never know with teenagers."

"I should be able to make it by 6:30. Will that work?" Riley asked.

"Absolutely. Is there anything in particular you'd like to eat?"

I mustn't have been hearing clearly. I could have sworn he said, "Just you."

"What was that?" I asked.

"Nothing," he said hastily. "Everything you make is good."

"OK, we'll see you tomorrow, then," I said, preparing to disconnect.

"You haven't been getting into trouble, have you, Miss Marple?" he asked.

"Absolutely not," I said, crossing my fingers. In reality I hadn't been getting into trouble, but I had been poking around where he would prefer I not. So that wasn't really a lie, right?

After we disconnected, I decided to take Maggie for a walk. As usual, she jumped and danced and turned circles and did everything but sit so I could hook her leash to her collar. "For goodness' sake," I muttered, puffing frustrated air into my bangs. Suddenly her little behind hit the floor and she sat looking up at me, a perfect boxer puppy. Before she could change her mind, I harnessed her up and, after putting some training treats in my pocket, headed out the door.

It was a lovely fall afternoon and, as we often did, Maggie and I headed to the lake. Once again, I heard someone running behind me and stepped to one side. Ray pulled up next to me and jogged in place.

"How ya doing?" he puffed.

"Fine," I said, pulling Maggie away from Ray before she wrapped her leash around his moving feet. "How are you?"

"Good," Ray replied. "Looking forward to Thanksgiving. I'm going to barbecue the turkey this year. That OK with you?"

"Sure. Sounds scrumptious." Thanksgiving was well over a month away. Who in the world could be thinking of his menu already?

"Are you going to make your corn pudding?"

"If you want me to." This year we were celebrating at the Bradley's house. I would happily bring whatever Ray wanted me to.

"Please. And your green beans. And your pumpkin ice cream pie with the gingersnap crust if that's not too much."

I surveyed him. "Did you by any chance miss lunch?"

"No," he said, "I just love Thanksgiving and I have to think about something when I run."

I laughed and tugged on Maggie's leash again. She had found something very tasty on the side of the path. I shuddered to think what it might be.

"Bring Riley," Ray said, still bopping up and down.

"I'll see," I said hesitantly. "He might want to celebrate with his sister and her family."

"Whatever works," Ray said. He took a deep breath. "Speaking of Riley…"

I hoped he wasn't about to give me relationship advice. I'd enough of that recently.

"Tommy Jones, Bobby's brother, called me today. Riley has asked him to come into the station. Tommy sounded a little worried."

"If he's the good person you say he is, everything should be fine." Now Maggie

138

was rolling around in the leaves. What else was she rolling in? It was going to be bath time when we got home. Again. That was always an interesting struggle that ended with not only Maggie and me being wet, but every surface n the bathroom being soaked. Why couldn't she just stay clean? Oh, yeah – she was a puppy.

"He wanted to know if I would go with him. What do you think Riley would say?"

I hesitated. "If he's not a suspect, I doubt he would mind, but obviously I can't speak for him. There may be all sorts of rules about interviewing that we don't know."

"Understood." Ray pumped his arms up and down. "I was thinking that instead of going to the station, Riley might be willing to meet somewhere less threatening."

"Like your house?" I asked.

"More like yours," he replied.

I blinked.

"With all the kids and the dog coming and going at our place I thought it might be a little too hectic. You could ship Nick and Maggie off somewhere and it would be just the three of us."

Jogging turned into jumping jacks. Didn't the man ever stop?

"I don't know what Riley would say. That certainly isn't standard procedure. Why don't you ask him and, if he agrees, it's fine with me."

Ray was eying me. "You want me to ask him, don't you?" I said. He nodded his head, still jumping. I decided he was moving so I couldn't strangle him. "*You* ask him," I said firmly. "I'll go along with whatever he says."

139

Ray sighed. "Deal." His arms started pumping again. "I want to make it around the lake before dusk," he said. "See you."

I brushed leaves off Maggie, who was now sitting with a goofy grin on her face. I would remain strong and make sure Ray asked Riley for this favor. There was no way I was going to start using our relationship as leverage for my friends. Nope, I was not going to ask. This time I really meant it.

Nick insisted on making his patented meatloaf for dinner the following evening. "Riley's going to be tired," he argued. "He needs real food, not that fancy stuff that disappears in two bites." Forget the fact that I had planned on making braised short ribs with mashed potatoes. I gave in, because Nick's meatloaf is truly fabulous. He makes it with three kinds of ground meat, sautéed onions and peppers, secret spices, and wraps it in bacon. When he moves out, he'll at least be able to cook that dish for himself, assuming he can afford the ingredients. I stuck with my side dishes of garlic mashed potatoes and roasted asparagus, and added an apple cranberry tart now that I wouldn't spend time making the main dish. I was looking forward to them meal, and not just because Riley would be there. The menu was a perfect fall feast, and that's my favorite season. Well, it's one of them. Just not winter, remember?

Riley did indeed look exhausted when he arrived on our doorstep. He followed his now-familiar routine of hanging his jacket on a chair and putting his folded tie into a pocket. "When do you get time off?" I asked, studying his tired face. "Tomorrow," he replied. "I need to crash or I'm not going to be good for anything."

"How many cases are you working?" Nick asked, opening a beer and handing it to him.

"I don't know," Riley replied, sinking onto the couch. "Four? Five?" He stopped and counted. "Five."

"Don't you get any help?" Nick asked, helping himself to a slice of cheese and a cracker.

"Of course, I do," Riley replied. "I don't know what I would do without my team. But I still need to review everything they do and sometimes they don't talk to the people I would, or ask the questions I'd like to be asked, or they come back with ideas we hadn't considered before." He sighed, leaning back. "It works. I just need a few hours off." His eyes closed.

I snuggled next to him for a moment. A wet nose and two paws appeared between us. "Does she like me or want my cheese?" Riley asked, smiling.

"I think it's some of both," I said.

Maggie covered his face with sloppy kisses.

"Oh, gross," he said, sputtering. "She stuck her tongue in my mouth."

"She likes to do that," Nick said, bringing him another beer.

"When I think of a female who I'd like to do that," Riley commented, sliding his eyes in my direction, "Maggie would not be my first choice."

Nick turned red. "I'll check on the meatloaf. Dinner shouldn't be long."

"You did that on purpose," I said.

"Did I?" Riley asked. Now it was my turn to blush.

Dinner was a leisurely affair, with good conversation and equally good food. Riley and I did the dishes together and Nick headed to his room, ostensibly to study, but probably to talk to Kelly before her parents cut off her phone privileges at nine o'clock.

"Five cases seem to be a lot," I said, shoving Maggie to one side and curling up next to Riley on the couch.

He shrugged. "One of them is pretty straight forward. In fact, the guy we suspect has probably already been arrested. The rest of them…" he shrugged, "It varies."

"I guess the homicide is still taking most of your time."

Riley's frustration resurfaced. "Things seem to be cooling down. It's been over a week now. Leads are already getting cold."

I wasn't sure if it was time to bring up my ideas about Judith's problems and the murder being connected. After all, I had nothing but conjecture.

Riley put his feet on the coffee table. There was a rustling noise. "Oh, sorry," he said. "What was that?" He held up a wad of papers.

Oh, crap. I had forgotten to put Marcia's questions away.

"Nothing important," I said, reaching for the pages.

He eyed me suspiciously and took a quick glance at the writing on the pages. "Tire tracks?" he asked. "Finger prints? Witnesses? What the Hell?" He didn't look happy. "What would be your perfect date? Jackie, what in the world is this?"

"It's Marcia," I said, grabbing the papers. "She was just thinking out loud, sort of."

He snorted. "I should have known." He narrowed his eyes. "You ladies are trying to solve my case, aren't you?"

I cringed. "Not exactly," I said, "but I just can't get over the idea that your case and Judith's case are connected."

"It's not a case," he corrected me.

"It could be" I argued.

Riley heaved a huge sigh. "I think I'd better head home." He started to rise. I put a hand on his shoulder. "Please don't. You're exhausted. We have plenty of space for you to stay."

"Jackie," he protested, his grey eyes boring into mine. "Miss Marple, please don't give me anything more to worry about."

"I'm sorry. I won't," I said, kissing him lightly. "Let's just put these away."

"Maybe I'll go over these in the morning," he said, reaching for the papers. "Sometimes Marcia has a good idea in spite of herself." His eyes searched mine. "Like that perfect date question. How about right here and right now?"

I melted.

# Chapter Fourteen

I started the coffeemaker when I heard the water in the guest shower running. Yes, Riley had spent the night. No, we hadn't slept together, not that the thought hadn't crossed my mind. The poor man had been so tired that he dozed off on the couch. I convinced him that he had no business driving himself home across town, supplied him with a new toothbrush and other necessities and pointed him toward the guest room. Now I pulled out eggs, bacon and grated cheese, getting started on breakfast.

Riley wandered into the kitchen and walked up to me. He smelled freshly laundered, the scents of soap, shampoo and deodorant mingling pleasantly. His hair was still damp from the shower and curled appealing on his forehead and the nape of his neck. Riley was wearing one of Nick's T-shirts, and it clung to his form, showing off his muscled chest and flat abdomen. I felt a wave of heat run through me just looking at him. He smiled lazily and kissed me on the check. "Thanks for last night," he said. "I feel so much better."

He looked better, too. His eyes had regained their sparkle and his straight posture had returned.

"I'm so glad," I said, popping a canister of coffee into the machine on the counter.

"Morning," Nick said, cruising in from the porch with Maggie at his heels. Maggie gave an excited leap when she saw Riley.

I gazed at the trio, Riley by the coffee maker, Nick with his head in the refrigerator and Maggie trying to trip them both. This felt so comfortable, so natural, all of us being together like this on a Saturday morning. Uh oh. Was I falling for Riley? Was I ready for this? Was Nick ready? What about Riley?

144

I pushed these questions into the back of my brain, knowing I would need to bring them out and think hard about the answers sometime in the near future. There grew that pile of things to think about again.

The Flight of the Bumblebee sounded.

"What in the world is that?" Riley asked.

"Mom, I thought you were going to change that ringtone," Nick said.

"I am," I replied. "Soon." I found my phone hidden under the morning paper.

"There's a strange car in your driveway," a voice sang out. It was Marcia.

"Yes, there is," I said.

"Finally! This is so exciting."

"Nothing happened," I told her. "Don't you dare start spreading rumors."

"How could nothing have happened?" Marcia asked, nonplussed.

"It just didn't. Riley was so tired that I didn't want him to drive home. That's all," I said firmly.

"Well, you know the street gossip line is already lit up. Why don't you do something to justify all that speculation? You know, if you just…"

"Is that Marcia?" Riley asked, reaching for the phone. I nodded but held the instrument out of his reach. He cocked an eyebrow at me and wiggled his fingers. I handed him the phone.

"Good morning, Marcia," Riley said. "How are you?"

I heard squawking coming from my friend.

"Yes, it's true," he said, grinning at me. He listened for a moment. "No, I don't need suggestions, thank you anyway." I reached for the phone but he danced away from me, still listening to that squawking noise.

"Yes, I read your questions."

Squawk.

"Some of them I can answer, some I could answer but won't, some of them I can't answer and a few of them I will never answer, no matter how long I know you."

He pulled a funny face as the noise from the phone picked up again.

"Tire tracks?" he asked. "Of course, we check, but the truth is that only very rarely is that kind of information useful. Most car tires are standardized these days, particularly when people have replaced the ones from the car manufacturer." A pause.

"Footprints? Same answer. Unless we know a suspect has very unusual feet or footwear, they're usually useless." He chuckled. "These are interesting ideas, but all the CSI shows have given people a lot of false impressions."

He listened further, pouring creamer into both our coffees. He already knew how I took my coffee. Was that significant?

"Witnesses? We're unaware of any. We don't know of any to Rosalinda's assault or the incidents that happened to Judith either. In any event, eye witness testimony is notoriously untrustworthy. People don't see what you think they should, or they see incorrectly, or memory is inaccurate. You've probably read some of the literature on this, since you're obviously thinking very hard about the cases."

Squawk.

"What hill?" Riley frowned at me. "Where? Who do you think could have seen Lisa and Bobby?" The subject hadn't come up last night, so I hadn't told Riley about my venturing to the county road overlook. "Yes, I'll look into that. It's an interesting theory." Riley started to hand me the phone but Marcia

146

apparently kept going. "Breakfast? Jackie was just starting to make some. Extra eggs? Does she need extra eggs? For what?" Now the poor man looked terribly puzzled. "You're coming over? Who exactly is coming? When? Now?" Puzzled had turned to terrified. "OK, I'll tell her." He disconnected.

Nick was laughing and had already turned to the freezer to take out one of the pans of sweet rolls I always kept on hand.

Riley headed toward the guest room. "I have to see how bad my shirt smells." He grimaced. "On the other hand, maybe I'll just climb out the window." Nick continued laughing. "Dude, you look fine. Besides, that window's painted shut. One of these days we'll get around to fixing it but for now, you're stuck." Riley sighed. "What can I do to help?"

"Why don't you start the bacon?" I suggested as the doorbell rang.

"I'll show you Mom's brown sugar trick," Nick added, joining Riley at the stove.

"Hold that thought," Riley said. "There's one thing I want to do before the mob descends on us." He grabbed his phone and headed toward my office.

The front door burst open and my friends tumbled in. No surprise, the whole gang was here; Ray and Bernice, Linda, Marcia and Bob.

"So?" Linda said, giving me a quick hug. "Where's the man?"

"Hiding," I said grimly. "I can't believe you guys are doing this to us. He'll never come back at this rate."

"If he wants to be part of your life, he needs to take the bad with the good," Bernice said, handing me a bottle of orange juice.

I shook my head. "Was it this crazy when Lars was here?"

"You know it was," Linda said, "and he loved every minute of it."

147

Marcia rummaged through my cupboards, pulling out dishes and utensils. "I did bring some more eggs," she said. "Do you need them?" She handed the dishes to Linda, who started setting the table.

"I brought nothing other than my cheerful disposition," Linda informed me. Now there was a surprise.

Nick popped the rolls into the oven.

Marcia swiveled her head, looking for Riley. "I think we scared him off," she declared.

"He went to make a phone call," I said.

"He didn't seem to think much of my questions" Marcia said, disappointed.

"Maybe he'll appreciate us a bit more when I tell him I may have a couple leads for him," Ray said. "I've been digging around my old files at school, the personal ones with notes on kids that I don't want to go into their permanent files."

"Why do you do that?" Bob asked, pouring himself a cup of coffee.

"Keep a separate file?" Ray asked. Bob nodded. "Lots of kids make mistakes," Ray said. "If everything goes into their school file, that mistake may prevent them from getting into the college of their dreams, or getting a scholarship. Not every poor decision should derail you forever."

"Agreed," Bob said. "But why do you keep those private files? Why write down anything at all?"

"They can remind me to be looking for a developing pattern of behavior. Or they can key me in to relationships I wouldn't otherwise expect. In other words, they can identify things that could develop into a problem if not addressed I don't always want to rely on my memory when it comes to those things."

148

"Like what?" Marcia asked.

"Such as a good kid starting to spend too much time with the wrong crowd, which could result in a mistake that *would* be life altering."

"Such as hanging out with someone you think might be using or dealing drugs?" Riley asked from the living room.

"Good example," Ray said.

My friends all made 'good morning' noises. Riley made appropriate noises back. He moved to the stove to help Nick finish off the bacon while I whisked eggs and cream together.

After breakfast Nick left for Kelly's house and the rest of us took our coffee onto the front porch. The initial chill of the morning had lessened, but we could smell whiffs of smoke curling from some of the chimneys in the neighborhood. The leaves seemed even brighter against a crystal blue sky, and the sun shone high above, creating the illusion of late summer. Riley sat next to me on a loveseat and put his arm around my shoulders.

"Ray," Bernice prompted him, "Tell Riley what you've been thinking about."

Ray took a slow mouthful of coffee. "I simply can't get Lisa and Bobby's deaths off my mind," he said, "so I decided, like I said, to go back to my private files during their years at the high school. On top of that, I decided to take another look at anything I had made note of where Henry Byrn was concerned."

"Did you find anything significant?" Riley asked.

"Well, I guess that will be for you to determine," Ray said, "but one name came up in both Henry's and Bobby's files. I don't know why it didn't occur to me earlier."

"Who was that?" Riley asked.

"A kid by the name of Alan Wallace."

"What's important about that, Honey?" Bernice prompted him.

"I had made notes that both Henry and Bobby spent time with him. He was sandwiched between their grades in school."

"Was there something about this Alan that concerned you?" I asked.

"That's the thing. I never could put my finger on it. And I never caught him in any trouble, although something about him made me suspicious."

"Suspicious of what?" Marcia asked, leaning forward.

Ray took his time in responding. "Alan was a smart kid, from a decent middle-class family. But, sort of like Henry and Bobby, he was one to cut corners. He liked nice things, he liked dating pretty girls. He always seemed to have something going that was going to make him money."

"What kind of things?" I asked, stealing a glance in Riley's direction. He was quiet, but something in his body language told me that Ray's information felt important to him.

"He organized poker games with some of the kids," Ray said, "Surprise, surprise, he won a lot more than he lost. Occasionally he would have a bunch of video games, or maybe some popular jewelry and would sort of run a store out of the trunk of his car. He claimed he bought things in bulk on eBay and re-sold them." Ray shrugged. "For all I know, that was true."

"But you suspected him of something else, didn't you?" Bob asked.

Ray nodded. "I always suspected him of selling drugs. Never could catch him, though. I never heard a thing against him, never a whisper on the grapevine. I never saw anything, either, except that he always seemed to be flush with cash.

150

I would swear he didn't use drugs. He was always neat and clean, oriented to his surroundings. I never saw him lethargic or overly hyper, which could be indications of drug use."

"The most successful dealers don't touch the stuff," Riley contributed. "They know exactly what it does to those who do."

"What was the connection to Henry and Bobby?" Linda asked.

"Henry went to several of the card games," Ray said. "I remember hearing him rant and rave one day about how much he had lost. Also, I suspected Henry dabbled with drugs. He didn't get hooked, from what I saw, but I heard rumors about some parties he went to. And guess who was usually there?"

"Alan Wallace," I said.

"Bingo," Ray replied.

"What about Bobby?" Marcia asked.

"Bobby never seemed to have any money. Understandable, considering his family background. The only time he had any was after he started working part time in an autobody shop, and even then, it wasn't much. He did spend time with Alan. Sometimes he seemed to be helping run that business out of his car."

"What happened to Alan after graduation?" I asked.

"He said he didn't know what he wanted to do as a career, so he went to community college."

Marcia sat up straight. "That could be a connection with Lisa!"

"I hadn't thought of that," Ray said.

Riley was staring into his empty cup.

"What do you think?" I asked him.

Deep in thought, he started at the sound of my voice.

"Don't you dare say you can't tell us," Marcia said, wagging her finger in his direction.

Riley smiled crookedly. "Let me simply say, Ray, that this has been very interesting."

"That's not enough!" Linda protested.

He held up his hand. "I'll admit that the name Alan Wallace is ringing a bell. A very faint bell, but a bell nonetheless. I'm going to talk with my colleague on the drug squad. I'm not certain, but I think, Ray, that your instincts were correct and that Alan Wallace is very good at what he does."

Marcia clapped her hands. "Finally! A clue."

"Maybe," Riley said. "I certainly appreciate your work, Ray."

Ray cleared his throat. "Maybe this is a good time to ask a favor of you, then."

'Here we go,' I thought, recalling my earlier conversation with Ray.

"Tommy Jones, Bobby's brother, called me the other day. He told me that you asked him to come in to meet with you."

Riley nodded, his cop face returning.

"Should he bring a lawyer with him?"

"That's up to him," Riley said.

"Does he need to bring one?"

"That's up to him," Riley repeated.

"You're not being very helpful," Bernice said softly.

"I understand that," Riley replied. "For the third time, it's up to him, but at this point it's not necessary."

"Could I come with him?" Ray asked.

"If he would like you to," Riley said, "you may. However, be aware that at any time during our meeting I could ask you to leave."

"And give him the opportunity to call a lawyer?"

Riley shrugged.

Marcia grimaced. "Boy, you do this cop thing awfully well. Can you tell us if Tommy's a suspect?"

"No," Riley replied.

Marcia groaned. "No, you can't tell us, or no, he's not a suspect?"

Riley remained silent, but his lips twitched. He was enjoying tormenting Marcia. "Could we meet somewhere other than in your office?" Ray asked.

Riley narrowed his eyes. "What did you have in mind?"

"Here," Ray said.

Riley looked around. "Here? As in here on this porch?" He raised his eyebrows. "Don't tell me you *all* want to be present?"

It broke the tension, and we all laughed.

"I just think Tommy might be more relaxed in this environment. Frankly, I think you might get more information in this kind of setting. It would be just the three of us, unless you think Jackie should be here."

Riley gave me his patented stare. "Is this your idea?"

"Absolutely not!" Ray and I said simultaneously.

Riley relaxed. I took a deep breath. He squeezed me around the shoulders.

"I can be anywhere else," I said. "If you want to use the house, you can."

"We'll see what we can work out, but I make no promises," Riley said. "If we do meet here, no food!" He was focused on me.

"Drinks?" I asked meekly. "You know, like soda or seltzer…" My voice trailed off as everyone seemed to be staring at me.

"Here's one thing I can tell you," Riley said. Everyone edged forward on their seats. "Rosalinda seems to be regaining consciousness."

Marcia jumped to her feet and shouted. The others cheered and clapped each other on their backs. Riley held up a cautionary hand. "This doesn't mean she'll remember anything. It doesn't even mean she'll ever function as she did before." "But it's a step in the right direction," Linda said. "I'll check on her when I go to work on Monday."

Riley turned to Marcia. "Tell me more about this lookout near Judith's house."

"It's really Jackie's story to tell," Marcia responded.

I told him about my walk with Judith, the fact that both she and Rosalinda went to the lookout regularly, and the fact that it had a bird's eye view of the turnout where Bobby and Lisa were murdered.

"Do you think we could go there today?" Riley asked. "It's private property and I'd prefer to have permission, although I probably don't need it."

"Let me call Judith," I said. I left the porch to talk with her in private. "She said that's fine," I told Riley, poking me head out of the door. "She'll be home all day." I still held my phone, Judith waiting to hear our plans. "Oh, and she asked whether you wanted to go by horseback or on foot?"

"On horseback," Riley said. "It's one of my favorite modes of transportation."

"Darn!" said Linda. "I wish I could go."

Riley must have noticed that my face had lost all its color. "Miss Marple," he said, "You're going to learn to ride."

Great. Just great.

# *Chapter Fifteen*

Like the last time I visited Judith, there were additional cars in Judith's driveway when we arrived. One was a snazzy red BMW two-seater, the other a sensible Toyota SUV.

As we got out of the car, her daughter-in-law, Elizabeth, exited the house and walked toward us. I half expected her to stick her elegant nose in the air when she saw us, and I wasn't disappointed. Her chin lifted, and so did mine. I was totally prepared to face her. The problem is that I immediately tripped over my own feet, while she continued to glide gracefully across the driveway. Riley grabbed my elbow to prevent me from falling. From the corner of my eye, I could see him fighting to hold back a smile.

Elizabeth stopped a few feet from us, sweeping her eyes up and down over our entire bodies. I'm sure she wasn't pleased with what she saw. I was wearing a much-loved pair of blue jeans and my favorite cowboy boots, which I usually wore when I went line dancing, together with a flannel shirt that had seen a good number of washings and a leather jacket (not designer). Riley also wore jeans, but his were pressed. We really were going to have to talk about that.

"Oh, Detective Furman," Elizabeth purred, pasting a tiny smile on her face. And…uhm?"

"Jackie Olsen," Riley said, before I could open my mouth. "You remember? The author? You met at Judith's party?" I shot him a surprised glance.

"I'm sorry," Elizabeth said. "I didn't remember your name. I suppose I'm not familiar with your books." Meow. Claws out.

"Even if you don't read mysteries, I'm sure you've seen Jackie's work. In fact, one of her books is on the front display of Barnes and Noble right now," Riley informed her.

Elizabeth blinked. So did I. It was? Really? After we left, I was going to make Riley run by the store so I could take a picture.

"You'll see her books on Amazon, too," Riley said. He shrugged. "I understand, however, that reading may not be your thing." I wondered; did men have claws also? It sure seemed like *this* man did. Had he been looking at my books? I knew he had read one and that his niece was a fan, but this was beyond surprising.

Suddenly, Elizabeth seemed to collapse into herself. "I'm sorry," she said to me, holding out her hand, "I was being a snob, wasn't I?"

I shook her hand briefly but couldn't think of anything to say. 'You betcha!' seemed a bit over the top.

Tears appeared in her eyes. "Ever since that horrible night, I've been hearing from everyone in the family how awful I am, how stuck up I am, how spoiled I am. Even my husband thinks I'm terrible. My sister-in-law won't speak to me. Do you know what it's like to be shunned by your own family?"

Thankfully, for me at least, the answer to that was 'no'. I had wonderful relationships with my parents, siblings and their offspring. In addition, Lars' family still regarded me as one of theirs. I had always taken this for granted, but as I listened to Elizabeth, I sent up a short prayer of thanks.

To my horror and Riley's embarrassment she began to cry. "I know I've spoiled Henry," she confessed. "He's the only child I have. I never could have more. But I think I've created a monster." She began to sob in earnest. I saw Riley desperately seeking an escape route. I approached Elizabeth and awkwardly put my arms around her, gently patting her back. The door opened again.

"Oh, dear," Judith said. She gently pushed me aside, took Elizabeth by the waist and led her inside. As we entered, Veronica Lake crossed from the kitchen toward the office, an undecipherable expression on her face. She truly was a beautiful woman, tall and slim, but curved in the right places. Her blonde hair was parted to one side and hung to her shoulders, imitating the actress' style. I wondered if she did that on purpose. She acknowledged Riley and me with a small nod, gave Elizabeth a disconcerted glance and continued her progress into the office, shutting door behind her.

Judith eased her daughter-in-law, who by now was heaving huge hiccups, onto the couch. I brought a glass of water from the kitchen, while Riley stood near the door, trying unsuccessfully to disappear. Why is it that even the strongest, macho man tends to fall apart when a woman cries? Crying is an essential weapon in a woman's arsenal but still, you'd think a hunky detective would have seen a woman cry before.

"What's this about?" Judith asked, folding Elizabeth's hands around the glass.

"You all hate me!" she sobbed.

Judith frowned. "Nonsense. We don't hate you."

"Yes, you do," Elizabeth gasped. "You never liked me. You think I'm stuck up and useless and...and... you think I'm a terrible mother!"

Oh, dear. Judith *had* confessed to not caring for her daughter-in-law. She caught my eye and grimaced.

"Now, Dear," she said, "That's not true." She glanced at me again and I made a face that I hoped said 'don't hurt her feelings any more than you already have."

"The night of the party was rather horrible," Judith said softly. "After what happened to Rosalinda…"

Elizabeth nodded and blew her nose on a napkin Judith handed her.

"Henry was rather awful, wasn't he?" Elizabeth asked, finally looking her mother-in-law in the eye.

"Yes, he was," Judith said. Oh, my, there was nothing warm and fuzzy about the woman. I put that into my mental file to ponder. In all likelihood, this contributed to the difficulties she was encountering with her family members.

"It's all my fault!" Elizabeth wailed, starting to cry again.

"Nonsense." Judith said sharply.

Elizabeth jerked her face out of the now shredded napkin.

"I blame all of us for Henry's behavior," Judith said firmly. "Never have we spoken against it. And I blame Bert."

Elizabeth looked surprised.

"I blame him whole heartedly. He could have stepped in, tried to be more active with Henry, but he was totally focused on his career."

"It was because of the miscarriages," Elizabeth whispered. "He thought they were my fault."

"What in the world?" Judith looked genuinely shocked.

Elizabeth met her mother-in-law's eyes. "I know I coddled Henry. Bert let me. He let me because he didn't want to talk about the others. He thought if he let me concentrate on Henry, the others would go away, but they never did. They never will! Never!" She was sobbing again and Riley was trying to slip out the front door. I glared at him and shook my head. He stopped in his tracks.

Judith seemed to collect her thoughts. "Elizabeth," she said. "I didn't know about any miscarriages. I had no idea how you felt. I had no idea what my son felt. I am so, so sorry. Why didn't you tell me?" Now I thought she would cry.

"What am I going to do?" Elizabeth asked, avoiding the question. "Ann won't even talk to me."

"Well, that has to stop," Judith said crisply. "It's juvenile and unkind, and I won't tolerate it." She took Elizabeth's hands in her own. "Henry needs your guidance. Can you and Bert talk about what steps you might take to help him?"

"I think so," Elizabeth said softly. "But it's too late."

"I don't think so," Judith said. "There's a good young man in there, someone who just needs some direction and some consequences. Principal Bradley was right. You need to help Henry with that attitude correction he mentioned."

"Consequences?" Elizabeth asked.

"Yes," Judith replied firmly. "For example, he's earning a decent salary with the firm. I dare say he's earning more than many of his college classmates."

"Really?"

Judith nodded. "Absolutely," She patted Elizabeth's hand. "Cut off his allowance."

Elizabeth gasped. "Are you sure?"

"It's up to you and Bert to decide, but it makes sense to me."

"OK," Elizabeth said uncertainly.

"Then, once he gets used to that, make him move out or pay room and board." Elizabeth gasped again.

Judith stiffened her spine. "I am going to be very frank with you, Elizabeth, and you won't like it." Elizabeth almost cringed. "Your parents did you no favors, bringing you up the way they did. They love you, but they never required anything from you. I am quite different from them and may be too hard on

159

my children from time to time, but I think that is preferable." She squeezed her daughter-in-law's hand. "No parent is perfect. Your parents probably think I'm a bitch and I'd be willing to bet you think the same thing." She laughed at the expression she saw on Elizabeth's face. "That's all right. We can agree to disagree when it comes to parenting, or anything else, for that matter. Disagreement doesn't mean we don't care about each other."

She helped Elizabeth to her feet. "Now, you and Bert talk things over. Have a quiet dinner at a nice restaurant and be kind to one another." She smiled. "When you think you have a plan for dealing with Henry, we'll have a family meeting. In the meantime, I'll talk with Ann. Do we have an agreement?" Elizabeth nodded.

"Good. Now, Riley and Jackie are waiting to go riding. I don't want to hold them up any longer." I noticed she gave no indication that we might be poking our noses into their family's affairs. Obviously, she didn't want to make Elizabeth suspicious, in case she was involved in any of the recent events.

The two women hugged and Elizabeth left. Judith looked stricken. "I have been such a fool," she said to herself. "How that child has been hurting, and I had no idea. Shame on me. And shame on my son. To let a young wife be burdened with that kind of guilt... I'd like to slap him silly."

Judith seemed wrapped up in her thoughts as we headed toward the barn. "It's at times like these I wish my husband were still alive," she said. "He was so much more sensitive than I seem to be." She smiled faintly. "My father was a military man and my mother was British. The family motto was something like 'Suck it up. Who said life is fair'? I guess I largely inflicted that on my own children."

Riley laughed. "That sounds a lot like my father. We turned out all right," he said. "And I think my nieces and nephews got the same message. It doesn't seem to have hurt them either. If anything, it's made them less tolerant of all the whining one hears these days."

"I see that Veronica is still with you," I said, changing the subject.

Judith nodded. "I talked to two other former employers. Both were pleased with her and let her go for reasons other than Veronica's performance. One hired a niece who needed event planning experience before she could land a job with a high profile company she had her heart set on. The other said her life simply took her in a direction where she no longer needed an assistant."

"What about Cornell?"

"No one had checked that reference. It was all word of mouth and personal referral."

Riley was looking puzzled. We explained that Cornell had no record of Veronica graduating from the school.

"I have a crazy suggestion," he said. We looked at him expectantly. "Ask her."

'Ask her?' That was it?

"I know you like all this cloak and dagger stuff, Jackie," he said, "but sometimes the most direct approach is the best."

He made sense. Marcia would be disappointed not to play detective, but she'd get over it. There were times when my friends and I made things much more complicated than they needed to be. Direct and to the point. That's how we would be when it came to Veronica. Maybe.

We stopped at the barn and a groom came out to meet us. "Mrs. Byrn, Midnight is all ready for you. I checked all the tack really carefully. Everything looks

161

fine."

"Thank you, Dennis," Judith said. She indicated the groom with a nod of her head. "Dennis was with me when we discovered the cut girth," she said. "If it hadn't been for him, I could have missed it."

The groom shook his head. "No way. You're too careful and you know what you're doing. That sure was odd, though." He shook his head. "No matter how hard I try, I can't think who could have done that damage. Or who would want to hurt Ms. Byrn."

"Did you see anyone you didn't recognize near the barn that day?" Riley asked. Dennis shook his head again.

"Any strangers around between Ms. Byrn's previous ride and that day?"

Once again, Dennis responded in the negative.

He stepped back to survey us. "How much riding have you done?" he asked.

"I've done quite a bit," Riley said. "My grandparents had a small farm and they always had horses."

"All right, then. Let's introduce you to Caesar and see how that goes." Dennis looked at me.

"What about you?"

"I've never been on a horse in my life," I admitted. "In fact," I added, looking toward Midnight, huge and black and stamping a back hoof, "I could walk up to the overlook and meet you there. Yep, I think that's just what I'll do." I turned toward the footpath.

"Come on, Jackie," Riley coaxed. "I'll bet you'll love it. If you do, it's something you, Nick and I could do together."

That stopped me in my tracks. It sounded like Riley intended to be around for

162

a while. I contemplated how I felt about that and decided that I felt good. I wasn't ready to say he was the man for me definitely, although that was feeling more and more like a possibility. But there was so much I didn't know about him. I didn't even know his political affiliations, or the names of all his siblings and their children, or…the list went on and on. I had to admit, however, that I liked Riley a lot. As to physical attraction? Wow! Whenever I spent time with Riley, I seemed to have X-rated thoughts. A new idea struck me. Would I remember what to do if we actually went to bed together? I chewed that thought over. Maybe I should watch a pornographic movie or two first. Or I could just consult Marcia. Oh, that was ridiculous. Having sex was like getting back on a bicycle, wasn't it? I suddenly realized that, for the first time since my husband had died, I was contemplating a future with another man filling the space Lars held for so many years. I cast a glance Heavenward. Was God sending me a message? My friends had been encouraging me to be open to romance for a while now. Maybe they were right.

The groom's next remarks brought me back down to earth. "I have just the horse for you, ma'am. First, though, let's have a look at Caesar" Like Midnight, the horse was huge. He had a reddish-brown coat and black mane. Riley informed me that he was what is called a bay. Riley walked over to the horse and for a few minutes stood and quietly talked to him. The horse stared at him and gave a toss of his head. Riley accepted a carrot from the groom and fed it to the horse, starting to stroke his neck and then move his hands over more of Caesar's body. The horse turned its head and butted Riley gently on the chest. Riley laughed and gave him another carrot. "I think you two are going to be good buddies," Dennis said, pulling out a saddle. "Let's get him ready and then I'll get Minnie."

Minnie? Like Minnie Mouse? Well, I guessed that name sounded non-threatening. Names could be deceiving, though. With my luck the horse should have a name like Killer.

Riley vaulted easily onto the horse's back. "Why don't you take him around the paddock a few times, let him get used to you, while I saddle Minnie?" Dennis suggested. Riley nodded and urged the horse forward.

Then it was my turn. Dennis disappeared and returned leading a beige horse with a brown mane. She wasn't gigantic, but she still was big. Minnie tossed her head and eyed me. I couldn't read the expression on her face, but I hoped it was friendly. Dennis handed me a carrot. "Minnie loves her carrots," he said. "Give her a couple and don't be afraid, she won't bite you." I flinched as her soft lips grazed the palm of my hand. Dennis started to saddle the horse. "Minnie is a good girl," he said. I wasn't sure if he was trying to convince me or the horse. "She wants to please, and she'll probably just follow along behind the other two. Now, before you get on, let me give you a quick lesson on using the reins and commands."

Judith had climbed onto a box and eased herself into Midnight's saddle. He started to do a little dance. Judith stroked his neck. "When was the last time someone rode him?"

"Mr. Jones took him out this morning," Dennis said. "He got a fair amount of exercise. I don't think he'll want to have his head, probably just go for a nice walk." She nodded and joined Riley in the paddock.

Finally, Dennis moved the box into place next to Minnie. She stood still while he helped me into the saddle. Unlike Riley, I did not vault. It took an effort to reach my leg up and over the horse. Dennis gave me a slight push to help. Apparently, I wasn't in as good shape as I thought I was. I looked down. Oh boy, the ground looked far away. I grabbed the reins in a death grip. Minnie looked curiously over her shoulder.

"Try to relax," Dennis said.

Easier said than done. By now Riley had returned with Caesar. He looked like he was one with the animal. "He's a wonderful boy," Riley said, grinning. "What a great gait. Nice and smooth. And he responds really well."

"All the horses we have here are carefully chosen for their temperaments," Dennis said, letting go of Minnie's bridle. "Some are more spirited than others, but I've been here five years and I've never seen one misbehave."

That was encouraging. However, there was a first time for everything. I hoped this wouldn't be it. I held the reins like Dennis had shown me. "You're going to be fine," he assured me. "Have fun."

Have fun? Any second I could tumble to my death. I took a deep breath and off the three of us went, heading to the overlook where, if we were lucky, Judith might remember seeing something that had set off the events she had told us about. Maybe she would even help solve a murder.

# Chapter Sixteen

After we had been riding for a while, I started to become more comfortable astride Minnie's broad back. I was actually beginning to enjoy the soft rocking motion. The view truly was different from up here. The trees seemed closer together and shorter. I could swear the call of birds was sharper and the sun more intense when we rode through an un-treed patch of ground. I began to relax. Riley, still looking as though he were glued to Caesar, was directly in front of me. I was enjoying the view of his broad shoulders and firm posterior when Midnight decided to pick up the pace and Minnie did the same. I panicked, my first impulse to pull sharply back on the reins to stop her. I don't know why, but I didn't act on that impulse. Minnie's gait seemed longer and even smoother and the trees definitely disappeared from behind us more quickly than before. I felt jittery, but I managed to hang on, letting the horse decide our speed.

Judith was in the lead, oblivious to my anxiety. Riley, however, slowed his horse to walk beside me. "I'm proud of you for not panicking back there," he said.

"Oh, I panicked," I assured him. "I just didn't give in to it."

He urged Caesar to go slightly faster, and I allowed Minnie to follow his lead. Riley looked me up and down. "You have a good seat," he said, sounding surprised.

"What do you mean?" I asked.

"You sit well in the saddle, you're holding the reins correctly, and your heels are tilted down. I think you're a natural, Jackie."

Me? A natural? Seriously? I was the person who was always chosen last for

166

any sports team, who managed to fall down during a run-walk exercise, who got tangled up in the jump rope, who couldn't hit a moving ball to save her soul and was, in one word, a klutz.

"What do you think of horseback riding so far?" he asked.

"I think I like it so far," I said.

Minnie snorted.

"That's your opinion," I told her, feeling brave enough to lean forward and pat her broad neck.

Judith looked over her shoulder. "Midnight may have been exercised already today, but he wants more. I'm going to let him canter. See you at the overlook." She took off, looking incredibly graceful on top of her steed.

I prepared for Minnie to follow him, but she kept on pace with Caesar, who seemed uninterested in more vigorous exercise.

"Judith was saying that we could ride here if she gave permission. Two of the grooms, including Dennis, give lessons on the side. She said they're very good teachers and very patient." Riley slid his eyes in my direction, seeming genuinely interested in my reply.

"I've always heard that horseback riding is an expensive hobby," I objected.

"It's owning a horse that's expensive," Riley corrected me. "From what Judith told me, the prices here are quite reasonable."

"It's something to think about," I said, not sure I wanted to commit to another hobby.

"Fair enough," Riley said. "Just think about it."

"You love it, don't you?" I asked, taking in his relaxed posture and happy face.

He nodded. "I'd forgotten how much. It brings back fond memories of summers spent on my grandparents' farm."

"Where was it?" I asked.

"Near Staunton," he replied, naming a town toward the western border of Virginia. "They worked us like dogs, but then we'd go riding, or drive over to a lake for swimming and a picnic. My grandfather had a small flock of sheep and two border collies." He smiled. "Those dogs could make those sheep do anything. They always amazed me. Grandpa used to shear the sheep and Grandma would spin the wool into yarn and knit the most beautiful sweaters…" He seemed far away.

"Would you like to live in the country some day?" I asked.

He looked askance. "Are you kidding? It was fun as a kid, but a heck of a lot of work and the social isolation would drive me nuts. I'm happy right where I am."

Well, I had learned a little more about my "beau". The best part was that I liked what I had learned.

In front of us Judith had dismounted and was letting Midnight munch happily on some particularly tasty grass. Riley slipped off Caesar. Judith held Minnie still as Riley helped me down. Judith grinned. "Are you hooked yet?"

"I might be," I admitted, looking at the tranquil scene of three majestic animals resting under the bright autumn sun.

We strolled past the picnic area and stood at the overlook.

"You're right," Riley said to Judith, "This is a beautiful view." We stared over the river to the rolling hills beyond. The turnout where Lisa and Bobby had been murdered was empty.

She crossed her arms over her chest. "What do you think I might have seen?" she asked without turning her head.

"I don't know," Riley admitted. "Possibly a car, maybe a group of people?"

"When were these young people murdered exactly?" Judith asked.

"A week ago, Tuesday," Riley replied. I could hear the frustration in his voice. "The medical examiner estimates that they were shot sometime in the late afternoon or early evening."

"Hmmm," Judith said. "That may narrow things down a bit. I tend to go riding in the morning, but I've been out later a few times in the past month." She closed her eyes. Riley and I stood as still as statues, not wanting to intrude on her concentration.

"What kind of car were they in?" Judith asked.

"A blue Honda Civic," Riley responded.

Judith opened her eyes, stared at the county road, then closed them again. Finally, she sighed deeply. "I'm not remembering any specific cars," she said. She shook her head. "I just wouldn't have been looking for one, so it could have completely slipped my mind, even if I was here at the time."

Riley's expression was dejected. "I appreciate your trying," he said.

"There was one thing I *did* notice," Judith said excitedly. "It may not mean anything."

"What is it?" I asked, keeping my fingers crossed.

"There was a motorcycle," she said slowly. "Not that parking a motorcycle there would be unusual, particularly with the path to the river starting at the turn off. But I saw it there more than once." She appeared to think some more. "A couple times there was a car there at the same time. I didn't think anything of it, but I remember it clearly now."

"Do you know what kind of motorcycle it was?" Riley asked hopefully.

"No, but I know what kind it *wasn't*."

"What do you mean?" I asked.

"It wasn't one of those big touring bikes," Judith replied. "And I don't think it was a Harley Davidson. It pulled out when I was here on the hill one time and it didn't sound like one. You know how they make that rumbling noise. It was painted and didn't have a lot of chrome either." She shrugged. "That about exhausts my knowledge of motorcycles," she said apologetically. She turned to Riley. "Does that help at all?"

"It might," he said thoughtfully. "We did take some tire casts, and a couple were of motorcycles. Those tires tend to be easier to identify than car tires." Maybe Marcia's ideas hadn 't been so far-fetched after all.

"What good will checking prints do?" I asked. Before he could answer, I snapped my fingers. "If you suspect someone, you could find out if they drive a motorcycle!" I was getting excited. "And then if they do you could question them or check their movements and see if they have an alibi…"

Riley gave me a half smile. "Calm down, Miss Marple. You're on the right track." He took me by the shoulders. "But note that this is something *I* can do. Not you and your neighborhood spy network."

I started to retort but bit my tongue. He was right. Besides, we didn't know anyone to question, did we? I thought a moment. Or *did* we? I gave myself a mental slap. Riley was right. This kind of work was for him and his team to do. The ladies and I needed to focus on who had tried to hurt Judith. Maybe we were jumping the gun when we thought the two incidents (three, including

170

Rosalinda's attack) were connected. After all, Judith hadn't received any threats about keeping quiet about anything, had she? Had we ever asked that question?

I turned to speak to Judith and noticed that Riley was eying me intently. I suspected he was trying to read my mind, all the while wondering if something ridiculous or something enlightening was going to come out of my mouth. It could go either way.

Judith had turned to look once again toward the river.

"Judith, has anyone actually threatened you or sent you a warning?"

She started. Riley and I exchanged glances.

"Actually…" Judith said. I think Riley and I held our breaths. "I did find a note on my car one morning."

I stared at her, feeling an emotion that was halfway between frustration and annoyance. "What did it say?" I asked, trying to hide what I was feeling.

"Mind your own business," Judith replied.

"When did you get this?" Riley snapped, one hundred percent in cop mode.

Judith had the grace to blush. "A couple days after the incident with Midnight."

"And you didn't think it important enough to mention?" I said incredulously.

Riley laid his hand on my arm, a signal to calm down.

"I should have," Judith said, concentrating on picking at a cuticle. "But it didn't occur to me that the two could be related." She lifted her head, "You see, I had also had quite a quarrel with one of my neighbors around the same time."

"What was the argument about?" Riley asked.

"It was stupid, really," Judith admitted. "One of her relatives had visited her and managed to cut his …" she gasped "*motorcycle* through the corner of my lawn. He ran right over some of my plantings. It wasn't the first time he had done it. I complained. When she wouldn't even apologize or let me talk to him, I complained to management. My neighbor was furious."

"What kind of motorcycle was it?" Riley asked.

"I don't know," Judith said. "I think it was one of those Japanese ones you see all over the road. A Kawasaki, or something."

I turned to Riley. "What are you going to do?"

Riley frowned. "I'll find out who this guy is and get more information from him. It's possible he's the person you saw down there."

"And then he wouldn't have anything to do with Lisa and Bobby," I said.

"Highly unlikely. I don't believe in coincidences, but I'll check it out."

I turned back to Judith. "Did you keep the note?" I asked.

She nodded. "I was furious with my neighbor and thought if I had any more trouble with her, I would show it to our manager. I assumed the note came from her."

"What did you do with the note?" Riley asked.

"I put it in my desk drawer," she replied.

"That could be a clue!" I explained. "There could be fingerprints! Or maybe a handwriting expert could identify the handwriting!"

"Or it could have been typed on a 1960 Remington typewriter that the culprit inherited from his grandmother, and we could identify the typeface," Riley said, clearly poking fun at me.

I pouted. "It could still be important."

"But how could it tie in with Rosalinda?" Riley asked, playing Devil's advocate.

I couldn't come up with an answer to that. Unless…unless Rosalinda had seen

172

the same thing.

Riley turned back to Judith. "Do you lock your doors when you're not at home?"

"Not always," she admitted. "It's not as though we're close to town or any other place where people just drive through for no reason. When I'm riding or taking a walk, I often leave the door unlocked."

"Then your neighbor could have played all those tricks on you," I said.

"Well, yes," Judith admitted, "But…"

"And the neighbor could have hit Rosalinda over her head?" Riley asked skeptically. "All that over a gardening dispute? Really, Jackie?"

"Well, no," I admitted. "Not unless she's a real sociopath."

"Which she is not," Judith said. "After we both calmed down, she said she was sorry and paid to replace the plants."

I sighed and returned my thoughts to the mysterious motorcycle. "I wonder if Rosalinda could have seen the same motorcycle you did?"

"It's possible," Judith said. "I don't think she would have been attacked just because she saw a bike, do you?" She asked this question of Riley.

He shook his head. "It's highly unlikely. If she saw anything, she must have seen something related to either your near accident with Midnight or the murder on the turn out. I'll check again with the hospital and see how she's doing. I'm glad she's coming back to life, but I hold out little hope for her being able to tell us anything helpful."

The horses were still grazing peacefully. Judith mounted Midnight, Riley gave me a boost onto Minnie and flung his leg over Caesar's back. The horses seemed content to take a leisurely stroll back to the barn, enabling me to become more comfortable in the saddle. Dennis the groom was waiting for us when we returned. He let us help give the horses water and curry their coats before leading them to stalls. Minnie seemed to love the attention, nudging me with her head when I was brushing her neck and leaning slightly toward me as I worked my way along her sides. Before Dennis led her away, I fed her another carrot from his seemingly endless stash. "You're a good girl," I told her. "I hope I see you again soon."

"I'll be happy to ride with you whenever you like," Judith assured me. "And Dennis and I will give you some lessons if you want."

"I want," I said, grinning like a lunatic. Riley looked happy too. Maybe this *would* give us something we'd enjoy doing together.

"You know," Judith said as we walked back toward her house, "This would be a good time for me to ask Veronica about her college education. Having the two of you with me will give me courage. I don't know why, but I'm nervous about how she might react when I ask her."

We turned a corner and Judith paused. "Oh dear," she said, staring at her driveway. "She's gone."

Indeed, Veronica's car was nowhere in sight.

"Is that a surprise?" Riley asked.

Judith shook her head. "No, not really. She doesn't often work on Saturday. We just needed to put the finishing touches on a project. She probably got her work done and left." She thrust her shoulders back. "I'll ask her when I see her next week. I know I have to get to the bottom of this puzzle. I need to know why she lied on her resume."

"Assuming she did," Riley said.

"Assuming she did," Judith agreed.

"Before you go, I'd like to take that note with me," Riley said.

"Really?" I said. "Why?"

"Any little piece of information I can gather might help us figure out all these cases," he said.

"Am I a case now?" Judith asked.

"Not officially," Riley said, "However, I have an open mind when it comes to everything being connected."

Judith opened the door to her house. Sure enough, it wasn't locked. "Let me get you some water, unless you'd like something stronger?" We both accepted water and followed her into the office. Judith opened her desk drawer and reached in. "That's funny," she said.

"What is?" I asked, watching her rummage around.

"It's not here," she said, puzzled.

"Are you sure?" I asked, moving to her side of the desk.

Judith felt around the drawer, looking into the file folders inside and around the edges of the drawer. I could see that the contents were well organized, in stark contrast to my desk at home. Judith ran her fingers around the back of the drawer, frowning. "It's absolutely not here," she declared after a moment.

"Are you certain this is where you left it?" Riley asked.

"Completely," Judith replied. "I have a lot of faults, but absentmindedness is not one of them."

Now Riley was frowning.

"What are you thinking?" I asked.

"Remember what I said about coincidences?" Riley asked. Judith and I both nodded. "I really don't like them."

Shortly after we took our leave of Judith and headed back to town.

"Something's on your mind," I said. "Spill."

"That note bothers me," Riled said. "Why would Judith not have mentioned it earlier? She's an intelligent woman. Surely it should have occurred to her that the note could be important. At the very least, it could have backed up her claim that someone was harassing her."

I had to admit that I agreed with him. In fact, I had been quietly seething, and I was building up a head of steam. "How could she not have told us about the note?" I asked, slamming my fists repeatedly into the car seats. "I mean, could anything be more important?" I started to bounce up and down.

Riley put a gentle hand on my k nee, but I kept going.

"Maybe you were right from the beginning. Maybe this whole thing  is a terrible hoax." I slammed my fist and bounced.

Riley took a deep breath. "Jackie, you're going to destroy my car. I just paid it off."

I sat back, hands in my lap. "Sorry."

"Who has access to that desk?" Riley asked, thinking out loud.

"Well, Judith, of course," I replied. "I guess her family could go into it, as well as Rosalinda, and certainly Veronica," my voice trailed off. Veronica who conveniently left before we returned from riding.  Riley glanced at me. I wondered if he was thinking the same thing.

I gazed out the window as the scenery flew by.

"Penny for your thoughts," Riley said.

"Barnes and Noble," I said promptly. "Is my book really at the front of the store?" Talk about a change of subject.

"It was the last time I saw it," Riley said. "I put it there myself."

I slapped his arm. "That's not funny!" I waited a moment. "Did you really?" I asked softly, disappointed if he had been teasing me all along.

Riley glanced over and saw my crestfallen face. He reached for my hand. "I'm sorry, Jackie. I know your work is important to you. I shouldn't tease you about it."

I sat silently on my side of the car.

"It truly is there," Riley said reassuringly. "Give me fifteen minutes and I'll show you." My fingers curled around his.

# Chapter Seventeen

There it was! My latest book was standing prominently in a large bookcase cubbyhole toward the front of Barnes and Noble. Riley had been telling the truth all along.

"GET A CLUE" read a sign on the top of the bookcase. "MYSTERIES FOR EVERY TASTE". Indeed, the books seemed to cover the gamut. There were classics by Agatha Christie and Arthur Conan Doyle, hard boiled detective/ thrillers by Harlen Coben and Tami Hoag, historic tomes by Anne Perry, humorous books by Elizabeth Peters and Joan Hess, cozy mysteries by Laura Childs and Ellery Adams, books featuring food by Diane Mott Davidson, paranormal novels by Victoria Laurie and Charlaine Harris and there, under a label that said 'local author' stood my book. I gave a little jump of joy. Grabbing my phone, I took a picture of the display, then zoomed in on my contribution. My agent was going to love this!

"Let me take your picture with the books," Riley offered, reaching for my phone. I posed in my old jeans and boots, hair messy from a windy horseback ride.

"Wait a minute!" I opened my purse. "Let me comb my hair. And I need to put on some lipstick. Maybe there's some powder in here..." I searched through the satchel.

"Jackie," Riley said laughing. "You look fine."

I found a brush and ran it through my locks. Ahhah! Lipstick. There, that was better. I stepped next to the bookcase and flashed my best smile.

"Would you like me to take a picture of both of you?" someone asked.

"No, that's OK, thanks," Riley demurred.

"That would be awfully nice of you," I said at the same time. Riley gave a sigh and moved to stand beside me. I handed my phone to the photographer, who said the normal things, including "cheese!" before snapping the picture. She looked at me quizzically.

"Is this your first time in a Barnes and Noble?" she asked. Apparently, having one's picture taken in front of a book display was not something one usually did.

"No," I said. I gestured to the bookcase. "That's my book." I think I was blushing.

"Really?" She took a copy off the shelf and looked at my picture on the back cover. I looked far better in that photo than I did in real life, believe me. In the snapshot my hair was flawlessly smooth, my makeup professionally done, the lighting perfect. It looked nothing like me. And now…I took a small sniff. Oh great! On top of my appearance, I smelled like a horse.

"I read this," our inquisitor who, I noticed, was wearing a Barnes and Noble name tag informed me. "I enjoyed it. In fact, I picked up another one in your series." She held the book out to me. "Would you sign this for me?" She handed me a pen. "I promise I'll buy it," she said. "I won't put it back on the shelf. I'm Jennifer," she said, offering me her hand. "I'm the assistant manager. We were planning on reaching out to your agent to see if you'd do a book signing. Maybe you could even do a reading?" She looked hopeful.

"That would be great!" I enthused. We exchanged information and she trotted off, holding her book to her chest. I turned to leave and bumped, literally, into Emily, Judith's goddaughter.

"Oh!" she exclaimed, reaching out to prevent me from falling, "I'm so sorry." She took a second look. "It's Jackie Olsen, isn't it?" She spied Riley standing a short distance away. "And Detective Furman."

"Riley," he said with a smile.

"Riley," she repeated. Emily glanced at the display of mystery novels. "Oh, this is one of your books, isn't it?" she asked, taking it off the shelf. "Ann was just telling me that she had read the first one in this series and thought it was quite good." I felt a little burse of pride. "Her birthday's coming up and I always pick up a few things for her. I think I'll give her this." She opened her purse and took out a pen. "Would you sign this?" Unlike my bag, which was designed to hold not only my wallet and keys but hair implements, makeup, an appointment book, a novel or two, a bottle of water, doggie treats and anything else you could imagine, her pocketbook was neat and compact.

"Hey, would you two like to grab a cup of coffee?" Without waiting for a reply, she said, "I'll just trot over and buy these books (she was holding several other weightier looking titles) and then I'll meet you in the café."

"I feel like I've been run over by a steamroller," Riley said as we made our way past stacks of books and found a table. "People seem to love your books." He grinned and moved to the counter to buy drinks, something simple for him and something with loads of sugar, whipped cream and other bad things for me. I had reason to celebrate, I thought. And besides, horseback riding burned calories, didn't it?

Emily joined us, lugging a large shopping bag. "I really shouldn't go into book stores," she admitted. "I buy for my electronic reader, I buy on line, but all of a sudden, I see a book store and voila! "She gestured toward her bag. "Here I am." She laughed. "I grabbed one of yours for myself at the last minute," she said. "Would you sign this one too?"

Elizabeth allowed Riley to buy her a cup of coffee and we chatted about local events, the weather, anything that wasn't personal. Finally, she put her cup down and leaned forward, hands folded on the table. "That was quite a night at Judith's, wasn't it?" We nodded. "Poor Rosalinda. Do you know how she's doing?" She focused on Riley.

He chose his words carefully. "She's regained consciousness. The doctors are keeping her heavily sedated. They don't want her to be agitated by anything."

"Which would include your questioning her?"

"For now," Riley said. "Only her family members and close friends are able to visit. We do have an officer stationed outside the room, and he checks her periodically."

"A guard?" Emily said, surprised. "That sounds pretty drastic."

Riley shrugged, watching her carefully. I watched him in turn. His was squinting slightly, something he did when he was thinking hard or when he was observing a suspect. "It was a vicious attack. Until we've figured out more about who struck her and why I'd rather be safe than sorry."

"I certainly agree with that," Emily said. "Rosalinda is so sweet. She's worked for Judith for several years now and I've seen her at all kinds of functions, everything from small dinner parties to big parties like the one the other night."

Judith needed help at dinner parties? She said she loved to cook, and I had seen evidence she was good at it. Maybe having someone like Rosalinda serve and clean up was something rich people did as a matter of course. In any event, I would never know through personal experience. I was making a decent living, but unless I sold a blockbuster or two or three or more my parties would be served by me, myself and I. And, at least for a couple more years, Nick.

Emily must have seen my quizzical expression. "Judith is a very good cook," she said, "but Rosalinda is a great one. If you'd ever had her roasted pork with mole, or her adobo chicken you'd know why Judith sometimes likes her to make the meal. And even if Judith can cook, she's not a baker. I've even seen her throw what was supposed to be crust across the kitchen and then curse the entire time she was cleaning it up." She chuckled. "But Rosalinda's desserts are fabulous. I know Judith has offered more than once to send her to culinary school." She stared into her cup. "I guess that will never happen now."

"You never know," I said encouragingly. "Just keep praying for her," I hesitated, knowing that not everyone prayed and not wanting to offend her. "Or keep hoping, whatever it is that you do."

"I pray," Emily said fervently. "I haven't stopped since the party. Rosalinda's name is on the prayer chain at my church. I'm only afraid for her because I know God doesn't always say yes." Tears appeared in her eyes and I squeezed her hand.

Emily drew a series of circles on the table. I searched for a topic of conversation. Riley sipped his coffee and watched both of us.

"So," I said, deciding that I would breach the silence with any inane topic I could think of. Emily jumped in before I could come up with a safe topic.

"Work has been so weird," she said. Clearly, this woman needed someone to talk to.

"It's like walking on eggshells. Bert and Henry are barely speaking. Bert took Henry out of accounting and sent him to the estimating department."

182

"Is that some kind of demotion?" I asked.

Emily shook her head. "Not necessarily. It's something that Henry needs to understand if he's going to rise in the company. But it's not glamorous. You spend a lot of time outside getting dirty and cold or hot, depending on the season. The guy Henry's working with is a nice person, but he's a stickler for accuracy and has no patience for slackers. I think Henry's having a rude awakening. It may not be a demotion, but I bet it feels like one to him."

"That may not be the worst thing that could happen to him," I said.

"I'm sure it isn't," Emily agreed. "And the only alternative is that Henry looks for another job, which might be good for him in the long run."

"Would he do that?" I asked.

Emily laughed. "Very doubtful. He knows what side his bread is buttered on. He probably thinks his father will relent in a month or two and he'll be back in air conditioned and heated comfort with a supervisor who's not as demanding. Besides, he doesn't have to wear a tie every day now and for some jobs he can actually ride his motorcycle to the job site."

Riley and I exchanged quick glances.

"Henry has a motorcycle?" I asked, hoping I sounded nonchalant.

"Yes," Emily replied. "He drives a Lexus convertible, but he loves his motorcycle. He and his parents each have one."

Riley nudged me under the table.

"Well," I said, looking for any kind of signal that I was going in the right direction, "I guess the family that rides together stays together."

Emily looked at me as though that was a strange comment, which it was, and Riley kicked my ankle. "What kind of motorcycles do they drive?" I asked.

"Bert has a big road bike, a Harley," Emily said. "I've been on the back of it. It almost feels like a car." She thought a moment. "Elizabeth has an Indian, a real antique. It's beautiful. Henry's bike isn't anything special. From what I've heard it's built for speed, not looks."

"Maybe one of the Japanese motorcycles we see so many of," I said, glancing at Riley. He nodded.

Emily looked puzzled. "Why are you interested in motorcycles?"

"I ride," Riley said smoothly. "I have a Harley that Jackie is just getting used to." I smiled faintly. Riley kicked me again. I thought hard. What else did I want to know?

"Does Judith know they have motorcycles?" I asked. Riley gave me a very slight nod. Emily raised an inquisitive eyebrow. "Some parents are so afraid of them that their children don't tell them they have one," I adlibbed.

"Of course, she knows," Emily said. "She goes riding with Bert all the time."

Riley caught my eye. I did a mental sigh. Yet another thing Judith had not told us about.

# *Chapter Eighteen*

"There are too many motorcycles," Marcia complained. "Even Riley rides one."

"I'm more worried about the fact that Judith didn't tell us about the threatening note or seeing a motorcycle more than once in the turnout," Linda said, frowning. "It makes me wonder how much we can trust what she says."

"I agree." Bernice helped herself to a scone.

I took a long sip of coffee. "Do you think she's started to realize that someone close to her is creating this chaos and she's now trying to protect that person?"

We all sipped and chewed for a while.

"Let's think this through," Linda said, reaching for a piece of paper. She drew two lines. "When we first met Judith, we assumed, based on what she told us, that someone was trying to frighten her into loosening her control of the family business. Agreed?" We all nodded.

"Does that really make sense?" she asked, surveying our group.

"What do you mean?" Bernice said.

"It's the incident with the dog that doesn't fit that scenario," Linda said, circling the picture of a dog she had drawn on the paper.

"Why not?" I asked.

"The other incidents could have injured, possibly killed Judith." Linda hesitated as she tried to explain her reasoning. "Having her dog disappear would have frightened her, but it wouldn't impact her ability to control the business."

Marcia nodded vigorously. "I like your thinking." She grabbed a pencil and sketched a picture of the note supposedly left for Judith. "The note could tie in better with Judith having seen something she shouldn't have. And taking her dog would let her know someone was watching her and could do her harm."

"So, your idea is," Bernice contributed, "that the attacks on Judith were not related to her business but to some outside event."

"I disagree," I said. Linda raised her eyebrows. "If you want to convince someone it's time to retire, what better way than to convince them they are slipping mentally? Losing your dog and then finding her again where she was to begin with could certainly do that." Maggie, who had been dozing at my feet, woofed softly in agreement. I reached down and scratched her behind her ears.

More chewing and sipping except for Maggie, who went back to sleep.

"Let's think about the connections among the people we've heard about," I suggested, grabbing another piece of paper. "Here are the family members: Elizabeth, Bert, Henry, Ann and Steven. Over to this side, a little tangential, is Emily. And slightly further away is Veronica."

"I still don't think that's her real name," Marcia muttered.

"Agreed," I said. "We know that no one by that name graduated from Cornell, so chances are that somewhere along the way she adopted another identity."

"The question is why," Bernice said. "We really need to work on the answer to that question."

"I agree with Riley," Linda said. "Just ask her." They all looked at me. Oh, terrific. I was on the hot seat again. Why did this keep happening?

"Okay," I muttered. "I'll do it."

Marcia shot me a smile and a thumbs up. I considered for a moment. Maybe I'd take her along for protection when I talked to Veronica. I looked across the table at her. Today her hair was striped blue and green. I had no idea what

186

that meant, but it went nicely with the top she was wearing. Marcia would be a terrific shield if I needed her. No one other than her friends and family would take her seriously until they discovered that she knew karate and also could scream so loudly the entire state would hear her. There, it was settled. Marcia and I would tackle this task together. Just in case Veronica was a serial killer or something.

"Then there's Rosalinda," I said, adding a semicircle that included her with all the people already mentioned. "Everyone we've talked about knows her well. They all seem to think highly of her, but she didn't hit herself over the head. One of them did it, or has a good idea of who the culprit is."

"I really wish the doctors would let Riley or someone talk to her," Linda said. "I can't help but believe she knows something important, or at least suspects it."

Nick strolled in and grabbed a scone. "I love these," he said, eating one in two bites and taking another. He studied our papers. "Are you guys crime solving?" he asked with a smile. We explained what we were working on. Nick tapped his finger on Henry's name. "I don't know him, but from what I've heard, he's always up for a good time." He studied the papers further. "Who's Veronica?"

"She's Judith's assistant," I said.

"Is she pretty?" Nick asked.

"I'd say so," Bernice answered. "Why does it matter?"

"She's too old for you," I said.

"Mom." Nick rolled his eyes, turning that word into three syllables. "Kelly and I are cool, OK?"

That was more than OK as far as I was concerned, but I didn't want him to know it. "Fine," I said, taking a long drink of coffee.

"I'm asking," Nick said, taking yet another scone (thank goodness I had made two batches) "because the grapevine says that Henry has been taking a gorgeous blonde to some of the local parties. It sounds like she's older, not anyone my friends or I would know."

"What kind of parties?" I asked, always on alert.

"You know, parties," he responded. "Dancing, drinking…" his voice trailed off.

"Drugs?" Bernice asked sharply.

Nick was starting to look unhappy that he had opened this line of conversation. "Probably," he admitted. "I mean, there are drugs at most parties these days." Now all of our eyes were drilling into him and he was beginning to squirm. "Well, not the ones that Max and I go to." Here he looked at Bernice. He held up his hands "I swear."

"That's why you only go to chaperoned parties," I said, hoping that was true. Nick looked at all of us in alarm. "Honestly, Max and Marcia's boys and I would never do drugs." He stared at me. "You believe me, Mom, don't you?"

I considered for half a second. "Yes, I do," I said. "But tell us more."

Nick relaxed a bit. His hand snaked out for another scone. "Enough." I said firmly. He sighed.

"Kids talk, you know?" he said. "And there are some kids at our school who go to these parties with older people," he slid his eyes toward Bernice, "and some of them talk. Please don't tell Principal Bradley," he begged my friend. "I don't want to get anyone in trouble."

"He already knows," Bernice assured him. "And he knows that you and our

188

sons are not part of that crowd." Bernice included Marcia, who was looking serious for once in her life, in an encompassing gesture. She narrowed her eyes. "But if you so much as think of it, you will be grounded for life."

Nick gulped and slid his eyes toward me. "You'd better believe it, buddy," I said firmly.

"Anyway," Nick said sidling out of the door, "maybe you should look into that mystery woman." He made a hasty exit.

Linda was frowning thoughtfully.

"What's up?" Marcia asked.

"This is bringing to mind something I saw at Judith's party," she said slowly. "When Henry and Judith's assistant were close to one another, I saw them brush hands. It happened more than once."

It was Bernice's turn to grab a pencil. She drew a heavy line connecting Henry and Veronica. "I do declare," she said, batting her eyelashes, "we may have a romance to investigate."

"How likely do you think that is?" Marcia protested. "Veronica's older than Henry and she's a family employee. I would think that in itself would make dating taboo."

I shook my head. "If we believe her resume..." groans ensued from everyone else at the table, "if we believe *part* of her resume," I continued, "she's only a few years older than Henry. I don't think the age difference counts for anything. And from what we've seen of Henry, he'd ignore any prohibition against dating a family minion, particularly one as pretty as Veronica."

"I think you're right," Bernice said. "It's probably another red herring, but if we can find out more about their relationship it won't hurt."

189

"It seems like we have more red herrings than anything else," Marcia complained. "There are motorcycles everywhere and now a forbidden romance, but I don't see how it's getting us anywhere."

"I agree with you," I said. "Let's look at Riley's case." I took another piece of paper from the pile on the table. "We have Lisa and Bobby, who were high school classmates and were currently dating." I wrote down their names. "We have our friend Henry, who dated Lisa in high school. It's not a big school, so it's fair to assume he knew Bobby also."

"Then there's this mystery man, Alan Wallace," Bernice said, adding his name to our list. "Bobby used to help him with his 'trunk sales', so to speak. He and Henry went to the same parties. And he very well may be a drug dealer, at least from what Ray suspected."

"And," Marcia added, drawing another line, "He and Lisa went to the community college together."

Linda leaned forward, frowning. "If we try to connect Judith and the dead teenagers directly, our only link is Henry."

"Henry, Henry, Henry," Linda said, "Why do we keep coming back to you?"

Nick darted back into the dining room "Incoming!" he announced.

What in the world? I rose to my feet just before I heard a woman's voice penetrate our cozy space.

Veronica Lake stormed up to the table. "You!" she shouted, pointing at me. "You are ruining my life! Why are you harassing me? Why are you making Judith harass me? I'm going to sue you! I'm going to make your life miserable. Leave me alone, you f...ing b..."

My friends stood up beside me, Bernice drawing herself up to her almost six-foot height. Linda was standing ramrod straight and looking ready to do battle. Tiny Marcia had managed to grab the rolling pin from my kitchen counter and was smacking it against her palm.

"How dare you?" Bernice said, showing her most regal side. "You have no right to barge in here, calling one of us (of course it was me) a disgusting name and threatening her. You need to leave. Now."

Marcia advanced, continuing to hit her hand with the rolling pin. She stopped and held it over her head menacingly.

Nick brandished his phone. "I've called the cops!" he announced. He positioned himself between Veronica and me.

The police? Oh dear. Why did I suspect that meant Riley? I thought I heard a faint siren and decided that if anyone could deescalate the situation it would be me.

"Veronica," I said, in what I hoped was a soothing tone, "help me understand why you're upset."

My friends all cast disparaging glances in my direction.

"Really?" Marcia said out of the corner of her mouth. "That's the best you can do?"

Outside the siren got louder, tires screeched to a halt and heavy feet ran up our stairs. I couldn't imagine what the tableau would look like when the police appeared. In one corner was Bernice, looking like an African warrior princess and holding, what was that? my favorite water pitcher? over her head, Linda was crouched in some martial arts stance, Marcia was still wafting the rolling pin, Nick was frantically filming everything and there I was in the center of it all, looking like a total dweeb, hands stretched out beseechingly toward

Veronica.

"Judith's been checking my records!" Veronica screeched. "She called Cornell! She said it was all your idea!" She lunged in my direction but Linda cut her off.

"She should have done that before she hired you," I said. "That's what any responsible employer should do." Everyone stopped. The police officers had run into my entrance hall and were surveying the scene, hands on their holsters. I heard other footsteps behind them. All eyes suddenly seemed focused on me.

"Excuse me?" Veronica asked, looking nonplussed.

"If you lied on your resume," I said, trying to sound reasonable, "She needs to know it and decide whether to continue your employment."

Riley tore into the dining room and skidded to a halt.

"Oh, my God," Linda hissed, "Are you really going to talk about this now?"

"Well, did you?" I asked Veronica.

"Did I what?" she responded, finally realizing the police presence.

"Lie on your resume."

Veronica seemed to deflate. "No, I didn't."

"But Cornell didn't have a record of you," I said.

"Because I changed my name," she said, sinking into a chair, head in hands. "It was because of my boyfriend." She was crying now. Out of the corner of my eye I saw Riley motion the uniformed officers back. "It was awful. He hit me. And when I broke up with him, he kept stalking me, showing up wherever I went, going to my parents' home and threatening them." She was sobbing in earnest now. "I couldn't even go home because I was afraid of what he might do to them." She raised a tear-stained face. All of us were riveted on her. I noticed that Nick was still filming, but that he seemed stunned by what he was

192

hearing.

"I *did* graduate," Veronica said. "I can prove it. My last name is Gillis."

"Didn't you go to the police?" Bernice asked, putting the pitcher on the table. Thank goodness. It had been a wedding present from my grandmother and I didn't want to explain why it had been broken over somebody's head.

"I tried," Veronica said. "I got a restraining order. But he kept coming. He's a really bad person." She held her hands out pleadingly. "I didn't know what else to do." Riley gestured toward the female officer, who approached Veronica gingerly.

"You need to come with us," she said, helping Veronica to stand and placing cuffs on her wrists.

By now Nick's eyes were as big as saucers.

"What's going to happen to me?" Veronica asked. She turned to me. "Please, I really need this job. I have nowhere else to go." The tears were pouring down her cheeks again.

The police escorted her out of the house. Riley crossed the room in two steps. Impulsively he held out his arms and I stepped into them. "Jackie, Jackie," he murmured over and over, holding me and stroking my hair. Somehow Nick wedged his way into the embrace, followed by a trembling Maggie, who had been hiding under the table. One by one my friends increased the circle until we were all holding onto each other for dear life, sure of the unbreakable bonds between us.

# *Chapter Nineteen*

"I need a drink," Linda stalked to the liquor cabinet and pulled out the bottle of 20-year-old scotch Lars and I had kept for special occasions. Frankly, I'm not a scotch lover and hadn't touched it since he passed away, except drinking a tributary glass the day of his funeral. I had frequently thought of giving the bottle to one of my friends who appreciated hard liquor more than I do. However, right now I was glad I had kept the darned thing. A big swig didn't sound like such a bad idea.

"Here, here!" Bernice took my best Waterford glasses out of the cabinet. What in the world were we celebrating? Possibly still being alive? Oh, come on! Veronica hadn't been that bad. Or had she? Nick still looked as pale as I had ever seen him. Riley's face was grim, his eyes focused elsewhere, but his arm remained firmly hooked around my shoulders. I leaned against him, as much for his comfort as mine. He turned his head and studied me closely.

"Riley?" Linda held up a glass with a knuckle of gold liquid in his direction.

He hesitated. "Thanks," he said, reaching for the tumbler.

"Are you on duty?" Linda asked.

Riley shook his head. "No. I heard a call on the radio and realized it was coming from here."

"What about me?" Nick piped up.

"What about you?" I asked.

"I've been traumatized too," he announced.

I pondered a moment. I allowed Nick a small glass of wine at holiday dinners and the occasional sip of beer at a cookout. After all, he was going to be

194

eighteen soon and I'd rather he experience the taste of liquor (and possibly its effects) surrounded by family and friends I trusted. I nodded and Linda poured him a small (a very small) portion of amber liquid. Nick took a sip and made a face. "That's disgusting!" he said, pushing the glass away.

"Glad you think so," I said, taking a cautious taste. Nope, I still didn't like it. The ritual of a drink with friends might help soothe my nerves, but I probably should give the bottle to someone who appreciated the stuff. It was simply wasted on me.

"So," said Marcia, sitting next to Nick and patting his shoulder.

"That was exciting," Bernice said. "And look at that, it's barely noon."

"What in the world made Veronica bust in here like that?" Linda asked.

"I'm not sure," I said. "When Riley and I saw Judith on Saturday, though, she said she was going to confront Veronica about her resume. I suspect, from what I've seen of Judith lately, that she wasn't particularly diplomatic."

"And Veronica decided to take it out on you?" Marcia said. She thought a moment. "I suppose from some twisted point of view that makes sense."

"What's going to happen to Veronica now?" Linda asked, looking at Riley.

"I don't know for sure," he replied. "She could be charged with assault, or at least attempted assault." He gave me a twisted smile. "I'll bet you won't press charges, though."

"No, I won't," I said firmly. "If she's charged and I need to testify, I'll do that, but I'm not going to make things any harder for her than they already seem to be by bringing charges myself."

"Do you believe what she said?" Marcia asked.

"There's no reason not to," I said. I watched Nick taste his scotch again and make

195

another face. He stood up, pushing his glass to one side. "I'm going to take Maggie for a run," he said. "That will help me calm down better than alcohol any day." I hid a smile.

"Hey, Nick," Riley called as Nick headed toward his room with Maggie on his heels, "Would you send me that film you took?"

Nick gave him a thumbs up. He walked a few steps toward his room. He turned. "Mom," he said, "I'm glad you're all right." He jogged over and gave me a quick hug. "You were awesome. You handled her just right." This time he really did leave the room.

I couldn't help grinning. That had been high praise from a teenaged boy.

"What do we do now?" Marcia asked.

Riley thumped his glass on the table. Thankfully, he didn't thump it very hard. Like my water pitcher, which Bernice had put back in its place, the Waterford (or at least the first four glasses) had been a wedding gift from my grandmother. Also like the pitcher, it would have been hard to explain how the glass had been broken. How does one explain to a ninety-year-old grandmother that an irate police detective had put it down too hard on one's kitchen table? How does one explain to said grandmother that there is a police detective in your life anyway? And besides, I really liked the Waterford and I'd have to replace it and Waterford is really expensive and…oh, never mind.

"Nothing. You….do…nothing," Riley said, spacing out his words. My friends just sat at the table smiling pleasantly at him.

Riley stood up and he actually began to pace. "There is nothing for you to do. If there is a case concerning Judith, my department will work on it. Bobby and Lisa's murder is my team's responsibility. Not yours!" My friends weren't smiling any longer but were watching him with concern. It wasn't the liquor talking. He had taken no more than one or two sips. Riley ran his hands through his hair. "I'm getting gray hair!" he announced. "I never had gray hair before I met you. I'm having nightmares. And you're in them."

I could tell that my friends were getting more worried, as was I.

Riley stopped pacing and held his hands out. "Please," he said, "I care about you. I care about all of you. My biggest fear is that you will go too far and that one of you will get hurt." He pointed at me. "I care about you all, but this woman," I could have sworn his voice cracked, "This woman is important to me. I couldn't stand it if something happened to her."

The room was silent for a moment. Then Bernice, my gorgeous, regal friend, glided out of her chair and put her arms around Riley. He stiffened. "Is that too much affection?" Bernice asked, chuckling. Marcia and Linda joined in the group hug. I thought if a hole opened up Riley would happily drop into it.

"We're not going to get hurt," Marcia promised him. "I can't promise you that we'll stop trying to solve puzzles. But I can promise that we won't do anything stupid."

"Assuming we know it's stupid at the time," Linda said under her breath. I swatted her. Riley left shortly thereafter. I was certain from his unwillingness to meet our eyes that he was feeling utterly mortified. It was very out of character for him to express his feelings, particularly to a bunch of women. I'm sure he was praying that none of us would mention what he had said to Ray or Bob. It would feel too personal to him. It probably had been difficult for him to say what he did in the first place.

"Well," said Marcia, "That wasn't exactly a declaration of undying love, but it was a start." She gave a thumbs up.

I frowned. It was clear that Riley was developing feelings for me. That was flattering but at the same time, a bit unnerving. I wasn't at all certain that I was ready to move into a more committed relationship. After all, we had only known each other a couple of months and our relationship had gotten off to a very rocky start. There were certain to be plenty of bumps along the way, more than normal if I continued my nosy behavior. I wanted to proceed very cautiously. And slowly. Sort of like a snail.

"Don't tease her," Bernice said, sensing my mood. She placed her hand on my arm. "Jackie, you know we only want what's best for you. If you think we're being too pushy," she cast a meaningful glance at Marcia, "tell us to back off."

"We want you to be happy," Linda agreed. "Sometimes we forget that our idea of happy might not be the same as yours."

"I'm sorry," Marcia said. "I just think…" she stopped. "Oh, phooey, who cares what I think?" I thought she was going to cry.

I smiled. "I care," I assured her. "I don't always agree, but I care. I simply need to take my time and think things through. OK?"

Bernice surprised me with her answer. "I'll give you one more thing to think about," she said. "Not everything in life should be thought over and analyzed every which way. Some things should just be allowed to happen."

Hmmm. Now that was something I definitely hadn't considered.

"As I was saying earlier," Marcia said, straightening our pile of papers, "What do we do now?"

"It should be easy to find out whether Veronica Gillis really graduated from Cornell," Linda said. "I think we should do that."

"Assuming that Veronica Lake *is* Veronica Gillis," Marcia said. Now that truly was an interesting observation.

"How are we going to do that?" Linda asked.

"Let's start with looking at Cornell year books," Bernice said. "I'll take care of that. You'd be amazed at what university librarians can get their hands on. I'll get one of ours to help me."

I nodded. "I think that's a great idea. In spite of all the drama, I have a feeling we still don't have the whole story where Veronica is concerned."

The door slammed and Maggie came charging past us. She skidded to a stop in front of her water bowl and lapped up water like she hadn't drunk anything in a month. Nick followed her. His hair was pressed against his forehead and his tee shirt clung to his lean form like a second skin. I took the sight in. My, but my son was growing up. I'd be willing to bet that more than a few female hearts skipped a beat when girls saw him pass by. "Did you run Maggie too hard?" I asked, concerned at the rate at which she was drinking.

"No, Mom," Nick assured me. "I took her fold-up water bowl and some water. She's fine. We sprinted back the last couple of blocks and that made her thirsty again." He sprinted back two blocks. I'd die if I tried that.

"I have news," Nick said, grabbing a bottle of water for himself.

"What?" I asked.

"I was talking to Kelly," he began.

That totally confused me. How had he been talking to Kelly if he was running? Was she running with him? Did he go by her house? Then I noticed an ear bud. My son was totally wired for sound. Modern technology amazed me. Possibly some day I'd catch up to it, but I wasn't holding my breath.

"What did she have to say?" I asked, expecting to hear about some innocuous conversation.

"The girls who were on the homecoming court with Lisa have decided to hold a memorial for her," Nick said, looking proud of himself when he saw that he had captured our attention.

"That's nice of them," I said cautiously.

"When will it be?" Linda asked.

"Day after tomorrow," Nick replied.

"That's awfully quick," I said. "How are they going to get it organized that quickly?"

"It's all over social media," Nick said. He did something on his phone and turned the screen to face me. Sure enough, there was an announcement, quite nicely done in fact, with Lisa's high school graduation picture prominently featured. Technology again. I was impressed. Maybe I'd look into taking a class at the community college so that I could join my son in the twenty-first century. Then again, I was perfectly happy bumbling along as I was. On the other hand, I would be able to monitor Nick's social media life, something I couldn't do now. On the other hand, did I really want or need to do that? After all, my trust in Nick and his decision making was an important lynchpin of our relationship. On the other hand, one hears horror stories about bullying and other things that happen in the internet universe. On the other hand – how many hands were there, anyway? Apparently, there were a lot. And now, when my darned book still wasn't finished, wasn't the time to think of putting anything more on my plate. So that idea was tabled. For now. In the meantime, I suspected one of my friends could show me a trick or two.

"Kelly's sister is coming down from Richmond for it," Nick said. Kelly's sister was a sophomore at the University of Richmond. "She's going to give the what do you call it?"

"Eulogy," Bernice said helpfully.

"Yeah, that's the word."

"It sounds as though they're trying to make this something special," Marcia said.

"I guess so," Nick said. "I thought you'd want to know so you could go snoop."

"Nick!" I exclaimed.

"Well, that's what you do, isn't it? I figured you could see who was there, maybe talk to some of the kids who knew her. Kelly and I could nose around too."

"I'm not sure I want you involved," I said.

"Why not? I'll bet some people who would talk to us won't talk to you." He thought a moment. "I should tell Riley," he decided. "The only problem is, he'd stick out like a sore thumb. I wonder if they have any detectives that look like teenagers, sort of like Jump Street." I gave myself a mental head shake. My son was starting to think like a detective himself. I had no idea where this new interest of his was going to lead.

"Wouldn't we look like sore thumbs too?" Bernice asked.

"Well…" Nick looked a bit sheepish. "I sort of promised Kelly you'd help with refreshments." He surveyed our group. "I told her you'd all bake cookies or something."

"I don't bake," Linda reminded him.

"Bringing something will give you a cover," he told her. "Pick up some bottles of water or something."

We all laughed. He certainly had Linda's number.

"Thanks for the help," Nick said. "This is going to be really fun."

A memorial service fun? What was my son thinking? My friends looked equally unsure.

"I'm not sure 'fun' is the right word," Bernice murmured after Nick had departed to take a shower. "Why do I think we're going to have a squad of teenaged detectives on our hands?" That was a terrifying thought.

"I'll make brownies," Marcia said. I eyed her thoughtfully. Actually, with her wild hair color and petite form she probably could be mistaken for a teenager.

"Stop squinting at me," Marcia commanded me. "I'm not going undercover." Now Linda and Bernice were also watching her thoughtfully.

"I'm going as myself," Marcia said firmly. "It would only take one question for someone to realize I didn't know a thing about Lisa." We were silent. "On top of that, if just one person recognized me as my boys' mother, my cover would be blown and no one would talk to any of us." She was probably right. And it had seemed like such a good idea.

# *Chapter Twenty*

"Thank you for the cookies, Mrs. Olsen." Nick's girlfriend lifted a full tray from the back of my car. She was dressed demurely today, with a black and white skirt that stopped just above her knee, a black sweater set and silver necklace and earrings. She had let her jet-black hair swing free to her shoulders as opposed to wearing it in her usual bun or French braid, but she maintained her ramrod-straight gymnast's posture. From the middle of the picnic pavilion her mother, who was setting up trays of food for consumption after the memorial service, gave me a wave. She was a tiny Asian woman with the same straight posture and trim figure as her daughters. Kelly's older sister, dressed in a simple black dress, was helping her mother set the tables. Car doors slammed as my friends and some other parents delivered food and beverages. As promised, Marcia had made several platters of brownies. Today she looked the quintessential high school student's mother, wearing tailored slacks, a blazer and a turtle neck sweater. Her hair was back to its normal color. She spotted me and gave me a quick smile. Close to her Bernice was carrying platters of vegetables and dips. Behind her came Linda, true to form, with bottles of water and seltzer.

We finished setting up the tables and grouped together, each of us holding a flyer to be used during the ceremony itself.

"Well," Linda said, looking around. "It seems there's going to be a good crowd for the service."

Indeed, young people were moving toward the park's central pavilion from the surrounding parking areas. For the most part they were dressed in dark colors and tailored clothing, although you could see the rebels and individualists dressed in grunge (I think that's what you call it), high fashion, or faded jeans and tee shirts. The atmosphere was subdued, as though even the more unorthodox sensed and understood the solemnity of the occasion.

I spotted Bernice's husband, Ray, working the crowd, stopping to chat with current or former students. To one side stood a young man and woman with two small children, looking very solemn. The woman held a handkerchief wadded up in her hand. I wondered if they were Bobby's brother and his family. I also saw Lisa's parents and her siblings, huddled in a small group but accepting the greetings of various people waiting for the service to begin.

"This kind of thing just shouldn't happen," Marcia muttered, dabbing at her eyes. "When is Riley going to catch the person who did this?"

"He's trying," I said soothingly. He and I had spoken briefly earlier in the day and his frustration had telegraphed itself over the air waves.

There was the squeal of a P.A. system. Kelly's sister, who was the principal speaker for the day, cleared her voice and asked for quiet. "I'd like to begin with a quick prayer," she said, "and if you're offended, so be it." Wow! That was quite the start. She went on to sketch a vivid picture of Lisa, talking of her beauty queen and cheerleader days, but also about her volunteer work at a local food pantry and an animal shelter, and her love for her family and friends. I doubt that there was a dry eye anywhere when she finished. The eulogy had changed my perception of Lisa. I had assumed she had been one of the popular, pretty girls who tormented me during high school. Apparently, there was more to her than that. I was ashamed to have jumped to a conclusion about someone I had never met. And you know the old saying about 'assume' – it makes an ass out of you and me. Too true. Would I never learn?

204

To Bernice's obvious surprise, Ray spoke next, acknowledging Lisa's family and mentioning that Bobby had died alongside Lisa, giving a nod to his brother and his family. Apparently, loner Bobby hadn't been known by enough people to merit his own memorial. I choked back a sob just thinking of how isolated he must have been. Several of Lisa's former classmates belonged to a band, and they set up their instruments and played in the background as attendees began to mingle. Thank goodness they had the common sense not to play rap or hard rock, I thought, as I stepped to the refreshment table to help serving.

Nick sidled up to my side with a tiny, red haired girl in tow. She looked like a beautiful elf. Her curly hair hung to her shoulders in natural waves. She had milky skin spattered with freckles that I would be willing to guess she hated. Her emerald green eyes would have been mesmerizing, except that they were overflowing with tears and the poor thing was crying so hard that she was hiccupping. Nick was awkwardly patting her on her back. His eyes telegraphed panic in my direction. "Mom, this is Peggy," Nick said. "She was one of Lisa's best friends." Help! his entire body language cried. Just like Riley, this male didn't know what to do with a crying female.

"Hi, Peggy," I said, wrapping an arm around the girl's tiny waist. "Why don't we walk over to the lake? It's quiet over there."

Peggy nodded, fighting for breath. I gently led her to a bench on the lake shore. We sat down and I rubbed her back as Nick had been doing. "This is so hard for you," I said encouragingly.

Peggy nodded, her sobs and hiccups gradually subsiding.

I had stuffed a handful of paper napkins into my pocket and now I handed her one. She blew her nose and wiped her eyes.

205

"I'm sorry," she whispered.

"I hope not," I said stoutly, continuing to rub her back.

"Most people didn't really know Lisa," Peggy said softly. She blew her nose again and I handed her another napkin. She gave a small smile of thanks. "She really cared about people. She was always trying to help others." She gave a very unladylike honk.

"Like Bobby?" I asked.

"Bobby?" Peggy raised her head and looked toward the lake. "Yeah, like Bobby. She kept saying he was good to her and she knew he would straighten out if she just stayed with him."

"Straighten out how?" I asked.

Peggy gave the typical teenaged shrug. "She thought he was hanging around with some bad people and he was getting sucked into something that would really get him into trouble. But she was so sure she could fix him." Peggy balled a napkin up in her hand. "She always talked about how his brother's wife had saved Tommy. She was certain she could do the same thing."

"It's hard when you see someone you care about going in the wrong direction," I volunteered.

Peggy nodded vigorously. "I kept telling her that Bobby needed to figure things out for himself, that he was dragging her down. She didn't want to listen to me." Another honk. "Looks like I was right. My friend is dead and so is Bobby." She gave an unladylike snort. "Some of the other girls think it's so romantic." She started to cry again. "It's not. It's not Romeo and Juliet. It's…" She was at a loss for words.

"It's such a waste," I said softly.

Peggy nodded. "I get what you mean. Lisa wasted her life on someone who didn't deserve it." She straightened her spine. "I'll never do that. And I'll do anything I can to keep my other friends from doing it too."

Peggy rose from the bench and straightened her skirt. She gave me a brave smile. "Thanks for listening to me," she said. "Nick's a great guy. I hope Kelly knows how lucky she is."

I hoped so too. The same thing applied to Nick. I hoped he realized how wonderful Kelly was.

We walked back toward the pavilion. As we approached, I noticed a tall blonde man leaning against a tree. Henry Byrn. Well, he *had* been a friend of Lisa's. I shouldn't be surprised that he was attending her memorial. A slim young man with curly black hair approached Henry. He said something that made Henry turn away. The dark-haired youth placed a hand on Henry's arm and talked rapidly. Henry shook his arm off. Beside me, Peggy had tensed, her eyes becoming narrow slits and her mouth turning downward.

"Who is that?" I asked.

"Alan Wallace," she replied.

"Nice looking guy," I said casually.

"If you judge a book by its cover," Peggy said sourly. I lifted an eyebrow. Well, I tried to. Mr. Spock I was not. "Good old Alan, he can get you anything you want." She scowled at the duo. Henry was moving away from Alan. "Henry sure knows that." Interesting comment.

"I heard Henry and Lisa were friends," I said.

Peggy nodded. "They were. They dated for a while. Henry was a lot more interested in Lisa than she was in him. But they always stayed in touch, even

207

when Henry went away to school." Peggy sighed. "He was another one Lisa tried to help. Poor Henry, born with a silver spoon in his mouth, like he needed help. His parents gave him everything." She threw another glance in Henry's direction. "He wasn't satisfied, though. Lisa said he complained a lot about his grandmother. He claimed she was always interfering and he kept trying to think of ways to get her to stop snooping on him."

"Snooping?"

Peggy nodded. "He complained that his grandmother figured out how to get into his Facebook account and his Instagram account. It really made him angry, but she told him it was for his own good."

"What did he do?" I asked, recalling my earlier internal debate about monitoring Nick.

"He set up another account with a different name," Peggy replied. "It's not hard to do. He kept the ones she knew about innocent and posted other stuff on that second account."

"What kind of stuff?" I asked.

Peggy slid her eyes in my direction. "I'm not sure I should be talking to you about this."

"Why not?" I asked.

"I don't want to get anyone in trouble."

"I could hazard a guess," I offered. "Would you tell me if I'm right?"

Peggy looked skeptical but nodded her head.

"I bet he talked about parties he went to, who he took, what they did, maybe even about getting high?"

Peggy looked at me in astonishment. "How did you know?" she gasped.

I tried to look all knowing. "I have my sources."

"Henry didn't do anything hard core; you know what I mean?"

I nodded, thinking to myself 'not really'.

"It's not like he's hooked on anything. In fact, I don't think he even goes to that kind of party anymore."

"And Bobby?" I asked.

"Bobby!" Peggy scoffed. "He was always ready to help Alan Wallace out, went to some parties with him, was sort of his sidekick. He kept seeing Alan even when Lisa begged him to stay away." She paused. "I don't think he ever used drugs though."

"Are Henry and Alan friends?" I asked.

"Not really," Peggy said, "but like I said, Alan can get you anything you want. Sometimes Henry wants something." She thanked me politely for my help and walked away.

I watched as Henry leaned back against a tree studying the crowd, ignoring the young man at his side. After a few minutes Alan Wallace gave up and walked toward the parking lot. He hopped onto a motorcycle and roared away.

I was picking up empty cookie trays when Henry Byrn approached me. "I guess I shouldn't be surprised you're here," he said, grabbing a leftover cookie.

"Where's your boyfriend?" He made a show of looking around the park.

"If you're referring to Detective Furman, he isn't here," I said coolly, continuing to clean up.

"Are you still sneaking around with my grandmother?" Henry asked.

"I don't know what you mean," I said.

"Of course, you do," he answered. "Going riding, hanging around, asking tons of questions, poking your nose into our family business."

I straightened and tried to send my friends a signal to come in my direction. Henry was definitely making me uncomfortable.

"Someone threatened your grandmother," I said. "She asked my friends and me to try to help her figure out who did that." I tried to seem nonchalant. Out of the corner of my eye I saw Linda and Marcia moving closer. Bernice was keeping an eye on us but staying at a distance. Good. They were picking up on my discomfort.

"Maybe it's all in her head," Henry scoffed.

I decided to take the bull by the horns. "You know that's not true," I said. "Don't you care about your grandmother at all? If you know something, why won't you help her?"

Henry had the grace to look embarrassed.

"I would think you would want to protect her," Marcia said from behind him. Henry jumped.

"You don't know anything!" he yelled. "Keep away from our family! The only way to keep Gran safe is to stay out of it." He took off at a run and soon disappeared into the parking lot.

Linda lifted an eyebrow. "I'm starting to be glad I wasn't born into that family," she said.

I kept an eye on Henry's departing form. "I don't know why, but I think Henry may be our missing link," I said.

"Or our weak link," Bernice said, frowning.

"Or both," Marcia contributed.

# Chapter Twenty-One

Riley called the next morning to see if I could meet him for coffee. The truth was, I was up to my eyebrows in galley proofs, the last step before my book went to press. I should have said no. I knew that. But I hadn't seen him in a couple days, and I wanted to see him. Of course, I said yes. To heck with proofs. I could work late tonight if I really needed to. I fluffed my hair around my face, redid my makeup, and surveyed myself in the mirror. Not bad. I stopped for a second before I slipped into my really, really cute form fitting jeans and a cowl-necked sweater. Was I actually missing the man? I needed to think about that. Or possibly Bernice was right, and I didn't need to think about it. For once I could try going with the flow.

When I got to Camille's, I spotted Riley sitting at a high-top table, nursing a cup of coffee. I gave him a quick wave and stepped to the counter to place my order. Was it my imagination or did he wave but not smile? Uh oh. Was I in trouble again?

I perched myself on the stool across from Riley and gave him my best smile.

"Hi," I said.

"Hi," he replied. He returned my smile but somehow it didn't seem to reach his eyes. The sparkle I had grown used to was missing.

"How are you?" I asked. "You look stressed."

"Do I?" He studied his coffee cup instead of looking at me.

A pain was developing between my eyes and radiating into my shoulder. Something was wrong. Very wrong.

Riley studied his coffee. What in the world was he looking at? It's not like he had ordered a cup of tea and was trying to read the leaves. Actually, most tea was filtered these days and you couldn't see the leaves. And if the leaves were in there they got stuck between your teeth and it was really disgusting. And…oh, never mind. Why was I thinking about tea? I snuck another glance at Riley; what I saw wasn't good. I must have really screwed up somehow. My headache intensified.

"I made a fool of myself the other day," Riley said. What day? I searched my memory. Oh, when he told everybody that he cared for me and accepted a group hug. It didn't seem bad to me. But he was a man, so I understood he'd be embarrassed.

Riley raised his head and looked me in the eye. "I meant what I said," he declared. "You have become very important to me." I attempted a smile, but the headache was now accompanied by a pounding in my chest. Riley took a deep breath. "My feelings for you have developed very quickly," he said.

Oh, my God, was he going to propose to me? What would I say? I heard something like the rush of waves pounding on the shore.

"I've never had this happen before," Riley said, staring at his cup again. Why wouldn't he look at me? He took another shaky breath, and I had the uncomfortable feeling that I spotted tears in his eyes. "I understand, Jackie," he said, looking up, "that you may not be ready for a relationship. Your marriage to Lars was strong and important, and moving on must be very difficult for you." I stared at him. Yes, I had adored my husband, but I thought I might (emphasis on the word might) be ready to try something new. I opened my mouth, but before anything could come out Riley held up his hand. "I don't want to pressure you," he said. "I don't want to rush things." He looked at me pleadingly. "But I also don't want to spend every day caring more and more about you without the hope that you might feel the same way." He took a sip of coffee, put his cup back on the table and rose. "I think you'll agree, under the circumstances, that we should stop seeing each other." What? *What? Stop seeing each other? Was he crazy?* He shrugged into his jacket and turned to leave.

"No," said a little voice. I sat up straighter. Was that *my* voice?

Riley turned and looked at me. "Excuse me?" he said.

"No," I said more strongly. "I don't agree."

Riley just stared at me.

I held out my hand toward him and he dropped back into his chair. Now my head was really pounding, but I had to make a choice. "Lars and I had a good marriage," I said softly. "It wasn't perfect, but nothing is. We made and raised a wonderful son and I see Lars in Nick every day." It was my turn to take a shaky breath. "But it was Lars who died, not me." Now I was crying. "I'd like to see what happens between us. You are an incredible man and I think that maybe, with a little more time..." Riley was staring at me. I noticed that suddenly the coffee shop had become quiet. Was I talking loudly? Was I making a scene? Oh, to Hell with it. I reach across the table, grabbed Riley's lapels, pulled him toward me, and kissed him. I mean I really kissed him, tongue and all. After a second, he reciprocated.

The couple next to us laughed and started applauding. Gradually, more people joined in. The barista banged his cups on the counter. The applause continued. I looked Riley in the eye and saw that his mouth was twisting into a genuine smile. I laughed and rested my forehead against his. "What do you say?" I

213

asked.

"I say let's keep going," he said. He took my hand and we drifted away on cloud nine. Or, at least, we managed to leave the coffee shop, although we seemed to have left our dignity behind.

As could be expected, I found it hard to concentrate on my proofs after I returned home and tried to work. I don't know how many times I read each sentence. Nothing seemed to sink in. I sat back in my chair and studied my favorite family picture, a candid shot of Lars, Nick and me on a beach somewhere. I blew air through my bangs. My goodness, I loved that man. But he was gone and Riley was on the scene and…and what? I stood up, grabbed a used tennis ball and headed to the back yard for a game of fetch with Maggie. Unfortunately, Maggie was a typical boxer. She was brilliant in some areas, but the concept of bringing a ball back so I could throw it again completely escaped her. I threw the ball, she ran excitedly after it, picked it up, and laid down to gnaw on it. Or she picked the ball up, started back toward me and got sidetracked, leaving the ball in a flowerbed. Or she watched the ball bounce along the ground and turned as though to inquire what she was to do about such an unpredictably moving object. This time, after a half-hearted attempt to catch the ball and bring it back, she fell over and ground her back into the lawn, grinning like a lunatic.

"She's pretty hopeless, isn't she?" Ray leaned on a tree behind me, hands in his pockets, smiling as he watched Maggie's antics.

I laughed. "She has other strong points," I said, picking the ball up and grimacing as I realized how much slime Maggie had left behind.

"You OK?" Ray asked.

"Why wouldn't I be?" I retorted.

He shrugged. "I don't know. Maybe because I called your name half a dozen times? Maybe because I've been standing here for five minutes? I know that even with Maggie a game can't be all that consuming. Besides, it looks as though only one of you is playing."

I managed a smile. "It's crunch time on my book," I said lightly. "I tend to be in another world right about now."

"But you're not working on the book," Ray said gently. "In fact, it seems to me that you're avoiding it."

"I have some things on my mind," I confessed.

"Hmm," Ray said. "Does his name happen to be Riley Furman?"

I looked sharply at him. "Why do you ask?" I squinted at him suspiciously. "Have you been talking to him?"

"I have," Ray said, "but not about you. At least not directly."

I raised my eyebrows.

"Believe it or not," Ray said, "some men have intuition too. You ladies don't have a monopoly on it."

I decided to remain silent. I adored Ray, but I wasn't sure I wanted to share my confused thoughts with him.

"Anyway," Ray said after a moment, "You will remember that we had talked about Riley interviewing Tommy, Bobby's brother."

I nodded, tossing the tennis ball from hand to hand. Now both my hands were slimy. Terrific. I started to wipe one on my pants but caught myself. I focused on Ray.

"Well," Ray told me, "After the memorial for Lisa, Tommy has decided that he

215

would like to talk sooner rather than later."

That was interesting. "Do you think he knows something about the murders?"

"I have no idea," Ray said. "But it sounds like he has something he wants to get off his chest. Is this afternoon all right with you?"

"You still want to meet here?" I asked, thinking about the rumpled clothing piled up in the laundry room and the dirty breakfast dishes in the sink and the fingerprints on the hall bathroom's medicine cabinet and Nick's unmade bed and the kibble Maggie had spewed all over the kitchen floor and the staggering pile of galley proofs on my desk and...

Ray seemed to read my mind. "Jackie," he reminded me, "This is not a social occasion. There will be no refreshments. He's not going to ask for a house tour. It's just Tommy, Riley and me and you sitting very unobtrusively in a corner, if Riley even lets you do that. I suspect he won't." I suspected Ray was right. He hesitated. "Oh, and Tommy's lawyer will come."

"His lawyer?" I asked.

Ray nodded. "Apparently that gentleman has been protesting this unorthodox arrangement but Tommy's not giving in to him."

"Is Tommy in trouble?" I inquired.

"I certainly hope not," Ray said. "He's come so far from his high school days. I pray that he hasn't done anything foolish where his brother is concerned." Ray frowned. "You don't know how hard I'm praying."

In spite of what Ray said, as soon as he left, I ran into the house. I stuffed a load of laundry into the washing machine and tossed the remaining clothing and hamper into my bedroom closet. I emptied the dishwasher, stacked the dishes inside, ran a cloth over the kitchen counters and dried the sink with a

216

paper towel. Nick walked into the house with Max, and I immediately thrust the vacuum cleaner into his hands and asked Max to make Nick's bed for him. They looked at me as though I had lost my mind, but did as they were asked. I cleaned the guest bathroom, putting out fresh hand towels (really cute paper ones I saved for company) and picked up Maggie's toys. I took out a bag of frozen cookie dough and turned on the oven. After all, one never knows. By that time, Maggie had picked up on my anxiety and was running around the house with a terrible case of the zoomies, as we liked to call it. Finally, Nick called a halt to the insanity.

"Is Grandma coming to visit?" he asked, picking up a wayward sock.

"No," I said, pushing my hair off my forehead. "Why would you think that?" I paused for a moment from dusting the coffee table.

"Because I can't think of anyone else who would make you act like this," he said, taking cookies out of the oven.

"The house looks very nice, Mrs. O," Max volunteered, putting the cookies onto a cooling rack.

"Riley's interviewing Bobby's brother here," I explained, vigorously polishing the dining room table.

"Oh, yeah, I forgot he wanted to do that," Nick said, straightening chairs around the table.

The beeper on the washing machine went off. "I'll get it," Nick said. He grabbed my elbow and led me to the couch. "This is really crazy, Mom," he said, as Max finished cleaning the sideboard. "Read a magazine or something."

"It will be really interesting to listen to a police interrogation," Max said, putting the furniture polish back in its place. That just went to show how much

217

time he spent at our house.

"What?" I exclaimed. "Oh…no, no, you guys can't be here. Why don't you go shoot some hoops? Or how about taking Maggie for a walk? Or if you want to go the movies, I could spot you some cash."

Nick neatly arranged the cookies on a platter.

"Or we could just hang out in my room," he said with a smile, filling a small plate of goodies for himself and Max.

"And listen?" I exclaimed. "That is a really bad idea. In fact," I said, "It is completely out of the question."

"We'll be very quiet," Nick said as he and Max, with Maggie trailing behind, headed toward his room.

Oh, this was promising to be a fiasco. I thought quickly. Everyone could sit on the porch. That way the boys couldn't possibly eavesdrop. Right on cue a jagged bolt of lightning lit the sky and it began to pour. Sideways. Rain pounded the front door and windows. Of course. I put my head in my hands. This was feeling like a really, really bad idea.

# Chapter Twenty-two

Ray was the first to arrive, dashing through the rain and taking his shoes off before entering the house. "What in the world?" he asked. "I thought it was supposed to be partly cloudy this afternoon."

"Meteorology is an imprecise science," I said, taking the wet windbreaker he held out to me and hanging it in the laundry room.

"The only field in which you can consistently be wrong and keep your job," he said. His nose crinkled. "Do I smell cookies?"

"Yes," I said in a small voice.

"And coffee?" Ray asked.

I nodded.

"Oh, Jackie," he chuckled. "I should have known we couldn't stop you from being the consummate hostess."

Riley arrived on Ray's heels. He stopped, looked at Ray's stocking clad feet, backed onto the porch and removed his highly polished broughams. I kept my laugh to myself. He looked a bit awkward in his charcoal grey suit, paisley tie and white shirt with no shoes on. "What?" he asked.

"Nothing," I said.

Riley sniffed the air. "Cookies?" he said. "Jackie…" he sniffed again. "And coffee?"

"Icebreakers," I told him.

He shook his head.

Ray and Riley settled in the living room and immediately started up a conversation about a sports team I had never heard of.

219

The doorbell rang. I opened the door. On the stoop, getting wetter by the second as the rain continued its horizontal deluge, stood Tommy and his lawyer. "Come in," I said, opening the door wide. The men looked at the shoes sitting outside the door, looked at each other, and promptly began to peel their own shoes off. "You don't have to do that," I protested. Nonetheless, Tommy pulled off his work boots and the attorney removed his own fancy shoes.

"Please come in before you drown," I said.

They moved into the living room. Tommy was a well-built man with broad shoulders and slim waist and hips. He was tall also, easily topping six feet. It appeared that he had come straight from work, as he was wearing a pair of well-worn jeans and a flannel shirt. His lawyer was lean and smaller, with white hair and an aggressive nose that some might have called a beak. He wore thin-rimmed glasses and sported a navy designer suit with a blue shirt and yellow and blue power tie. Sharp blue eyes sparked behind the lenses of his glasses and he didn't look at all happy.

Riley and Ray stood.

"Tommy," Ray said, reaching out to shake the younger man's hand. "It's good to see you."

"Thanks for being here, Mr. Bradley," Tommy said, returning the shake.

"I'm Detective Furman," Riley said, offering his hand to both Tommy and his attorney.

"Jim Wilson," the lawyer said.

Riley gestured to me. "This is our hostess, Mrs. Olsen."

I didn't bother to shake hands. I could sense that Riley and the lawyer were taking stock of each other, sort of like two lions trying to scent weakness.

"Please sit down," I said, gesturing to the living room sofa and chairs.

They moved toward the sitting area, but before they could settle in Attorney Wilson spoke. "I object to this unorthodox means of interviewing my client," he said, staring at Riley. "I have encouraged him not to participate in," here he paused to look around the room, "whatever this is."

"I'd be perfectly happy to conduct this interview at the station," Riley said calmly. "Shall we go?"

At this point I have to interject that two grown men in designer suits and stockinged feet with their pant legs dragging on the floor, facing off in a professional dispute looked pretty ridiculous. I caught Ray's eyes and saw that he also understood the surrealism the scene presented.

"Tommy asked me to be present when he spoke with Detective Furman," Ray said in his mellifluous voice. "We agreed to meet in neutral territory. This is convenient for me. I live across the street and would have offered my own home, except that I have two younger children who would in all likelihood have been very distracting." Ray gestured toward Jim Wilson. "When we set up this meeting Tommy didn't say anything about having an attorney present. I would be happy to bow out and allow you to make other arrangements."

"No, please," Tommy said. "I really would appreciate your being here, Principal Bradley."

Riley and the lawyer were still eyeing each other suspiciously. "This is not an interrogation," Riley assured him. "I'm simply hoping to gain more insight into the killing of Tommy's brother."

"Will you assure me that if at any time during this conversation my client becomes a suspect of any crime, at least in your mind, you will so inform us and allow us to terminate this discussion?" the lawyer asked.

"Absolutely," Riley said.

Jim Wilson sighed. "I continue to object," he said turning to his client, "and advise you not to proceed."

Tommy squared his shoulders. "I understand," he said, "but I've done nothing wrong. If I can help the police solve my brother's murder, I will."

The men settled themselves in my living room.

"Would anyone like a cookie?" I chirped.

Riley rolled his eyes.

Ray bit his cheek to keep from laughing. "I'll have one, thank you," he said, helping himself to an oatmeal cookie and a napkin. He beamed at the gathering. "Jackie's the best cook on the street," he said, "other than my own dear wife. How can I say no?"

Riley was giving me the evil eye.

"What about coffee?" I pressed on. Jim Wilson accepted a cup and Tommy took a cookie.

I put the cookie platter on the table. "The coffee's in the kitchen," I said, feeling Riley's eyes burning into my skull. "I'll just be...ummm...over there." I pointed vaguely in the direction of my office, "if you need anything." The good thing about my office was that I would be able to easily hear what the men were talking about. As I passed the closed door to Nick's bedroom, I heard a snuffling sound. Either Maggie had her nose stuck under the door or the boys had their ears pressed against it, or both. I said a quick prayer that I wouldn't go to Hell for not revealing their presence. As I moved into my office, I felt Riley's eyes continue to burn holes into my brain. Oh, boy. I certainly hoped this hadn't derailed our plans for the future. Whatever they were.

I was settling down close to my office door when I thought I heard the back door to my house creak. I really needed to do something about those hinges. It was another thing on my list. But why would the hinges be creaking? Surely it couldn't be the wind.

Dressed in black from head to toe, Marcia crept into my office. "What in the world are you doing?" I hissed.

"I wanted to hear what they were saying," she explained, as though her sudden appearance were the most rational thing in the world. "But I didn't want them to see me." She beamed at me triumphantly and pulled a stocking cap off her head.

"But it's the middle of the day," I protested. "You don't blend in. They could see you just fine."

Marcia pouted. "Well, it will be darker when I leave."

The door creaked again. Oil. I needed to buy oil.

"How's Ray doing?" Bernice whispered. "Have you heard any good tidbits yet?"

What in the world? I was speechless.

Linda was the final entrant, shaking rain water off her curly hair and tossing her raincoat onto the floor. "What did I miss?" she asked.

"Nothing," I said. "Nothing at all. What are you doing here?"

"We want to hear what Tommy has to say," Marcia explained, looking at me like I was an idiot.

"But…"

Marcia curled up next to the office door and put her finger on her lips. Linda, ever limber, eased into a lotus position next to her. Bernice pulled up a chair and motioned to me to do the same. I hesitated for a moment. Actually, it was more like a millisecond. I tugged up another chair to sit next to her.

Riley spoke. "You wanted to talk to me, Tommy," he said. "I'm here. What do you want to say?"

"I think my brother got himself into some trouble just before he was killed," Tommy said in a low voice.

"What kind of trouble?" Ray asked.

"I warn you once again," Attorney Wilson began.

"I know," Tommy said. He took a ragged breath. "But you need to understand that he was my brother. I have no idea whether I know something important, but I want to help. I only brought you with me in case Detective Furman decides he wants to arrest me."

"Would you like another cookie, Tommy?" Ray asked. Did he seriously say that?

"No, thank you, Sir," Tommy replied. "But I could use a glass of water." We heard someone move to the sink.

"Bobby and Lisa got together in high school," Tommy said. "I couldn't see the attraction myself, at least on her part. They were so different. It didn't make sense to me. I mean, she was a nice girl, but she was really social and popular and my brother..." he paused.

"Wasn't?" Ray supplied.

"I guess that's it in a nutshell," Tommy admitted. "He was crazy about Lisa, though. He'd have done anything for her." Tommy sighed. "I'm not sure she felt the same way, but Lisa seemed to have this complex."

224

"What kind of complex?" Riley asked. We could hear the scratching of pen upon paper.

"She seemed to think she could change Bobby," Tommy said. "She thought she could set him on the straight and narrow, make him into something he wasn't."

"Isn't that what your wife did with you?" Ray asked gently.

"Yes, Sir, it was," Tommy agreed. "But there was a difference. In my heart of hearts, I wanted a normal life. I wanted a woman who loved me, and children, and a nice home. I wanted to go on family vacations, and coach Little League and do all those things normal people do. My wife made me believe it was possible. And I was willing to change. You'd be the first one, Principal Morton, to tell these gentlemen I really needed to do that. And you'd be right. Fortunately, I was determined to make that life I wanted happen. I was willing to work for those things I was just talking about."

"And you've done a wonderful job," Ray said encouragingly.

"Thank you, Sir," Tommy said. "I've tried real hard. My family is everything to me. My wife and I have made a good life together, and I'd do anything for her and our kids."

"Was Bobby different from you?" Riley asked. I thought I heard understanding in his voice.

"Yes, Sir, I think he was." Tommy replied. "Bobby thought he wanted what I had, but I don't think he wanted to work for it like I did. Even before high school, he was into short cuts. He wanted to be a big man, but he wanted things to just fall in his lap. I tried to tell him that isn't how things work, but he wasn't interested in listening to me."

"What makes you say that?" Riley asked.

Tommy sighed loudly. "A couple months ago, he came by the house to visit. I saw a couple joints in his shirt pocket. I took them and threw them out. I told him that he wasn't welcome at my home if he was using drugs."

"What happened?" Riley asked.

"Let me caution you, Tommy," his lawyer said.

"I hear you, Mr. Wilson," Tommy said. "But I don't think the detective is going to take me to jail because I saw some reefer in my brother's pocket."

"Nonetheless," the lawyer started.

Riley broke in. "You're right, Tommy. I don't care about that."

"Did something else happen?" Ray asked.

"A few weeks later he came by again. Everything seemed fine. I can't remember what we were talking about, but Bobby opened the glove compartment in his car." We heard his voice break. "I saw a bag of pills."

"Tommy," his lawyer said again.

"It was a lot of pills," Tommy said, ignoring Mr. Wilson. "I asked him about them. He told me he was keeping them for a friend."

"Then what?" Riley asked. The pen was scratching again.

"I told him I didn't believe him. I told him to give them to me and I'd flush them down the toilet. He got really upset, said they weren't his, that he'd be in trouble if he didn't give them to this so-called friend."

"What did you do?" Ray asked.

"I told him to leave," Tommy said. "I told him not to come back if he was involved with drugs. I meant it. That looked like serious stuff in that bag." He seemed to be crying. My friends and I exchanged stricken looks. "He begged me. He swore he wasn't dealing drugs, that he was just doing a favor for a friend." Tommy was crying harder, from what we could hear. "I told him to leave. He drove off. I never saw him again."

Riley's voice was sympathetic. "Is there anything else?"

"He called me a week later, really upset. He said Lisa had found the pills. She told him he had to stop seeing this friend of his, to get rid of the pills, or they were finished."

"Did he say what he was going to do?" Riley asked.

"He claimed he was going to do what she said. He was going to give the pills back and change his life around. He wanted to be with her and he knew she was right." Tommy paused. "Next thing I knew, he was dead."

"And so was she," Linda whispered.

"Who was this friend, Tommy?" Riley asked.

"That's the problem," Tommy replied, just as his lawyer tried to interject. "I'm not one hundred percent sure."

"But you have an idea," Ray said encouragingly.

"There's one guy he went to school with," Tommy said. "Bobby used to help him sell stuff out of his car sometimes. I tried to warn him the guy was trouble, but he didn't listen."

"Alan Wallace," Bernice mouthed. The rest of us nodded.

"What's his name?" Riley asked.

"Alan Wallace," Tommy replied. We looked at each other knowingly.

"But he's not the only one," Tommy said. "Bobby said he met a bunch of other people at some of the parties he went to. From what he said, they may not have been selling, but they were involved somehow with Alan."

227

"Do you know any of their names?" Riley asked.

"There were a bunch of them," Tommy said, listing some people we had never heard of. "Then there was Henry Byrn." Tommy laughed. "Good old Henry, he'd never get his hands dirty, but he wasn't far from the action."

Once again, my friends and I exchanged glances.

"And Henry had a girlfriend for a while, a real looker. I don't know her name, but she and Alan were pretty tight too, from what Bobby told me."

"What did she look like?" Ray asked.

"Tall, blonde, shaped like…" here he must have made a gesture with his hands.

"Anyone else?" Riley asked.

Tommy appeared to think for a moment. "I think there was some older woman involved at some point, but I don't know who it was. Or maybe the girlfriend was older. I'm not sure."

Tommy had apparently run out of steam. My friends and I leaned against the door, but heard nothing but muted breathing.

"Thank you, Tommy," Riley said finally. "This is helpful." He paused. "Attorney Wilson, your client is free to go. I appreciate his cooperation."

We could hear people move toward the front door.

"Be careful on the steps, gentlemen," Ray advised them. "It looks pretty slippery out there." Tommy and his attorney took their leave.

"Jackie?" Riley called. "You can come out now."

We heard footsteps moving toward my office. "Hey, Riley, you want some coffee?" Ray asked. He knew. Somehow, he knew we were all in my office.

"Quick! Hide!" Marcia ducked into the closet, pulling Linda behind her. They squeezed the door shut.

228

"Suck it in!" Linda hissed.

"Me!" Marcia whispered. "You suck it in! You're bigger than me!"

Bernice slipped out the door and into the back yard. I tucked one of my editing pens behind an ear and stirred around the papers on my desk to make it look as though I had been working. "Coming!" I called.

Riley pulled the door open. "They're in here, aren't they?" he demanded.

"Who?" I asked innocently.

Riley's eyes scanned the room.

Nick popped out of his bedroom with Max and Maggie was on his heels. "That was so cool!" he said. "This detective stuff is amazing. I never thought I'd hear a real interrogation."

Riley's face was turning an unattractive shade of red. I was afraid he was going to have a heart attack.

Suddenly a sneeze exploded from the closet. Riley yanked on the door and Marcia and Linda tumbled out.

"What do you thing you're doing?" Riley asked. He turned to me. "I trusted you."

"This wasn't my idea," I protested. "I had no idea they were coming."

Ray held up his hands. "Me neither. I swear." He scowled at the rest of us.

Bernice poked her head inside. "Can I come in now?"

Riley grabbed the doorframe and started to rhythmically pound his head on it. "The lunatics are in charge of the asylum," he moaned. "I can't take it. I can't do my job." He stopped pounding and stared at us. "What if you heard something confidential? I mean, what you heard is bad enough, but do you know the trouble I could be in?"

"That lawyer made sure we didn't hear anything good," Max said. Ray glared at his son, who studied the floor.

"Thank goodness for that," Riley muttered.

Marcia opened her mouth. Riley pointed at her. "And don't you dare ask what we do next or I may shoot you."

Marcia's jaw snapped shut.

# Chapter Twenty-three

After everyone else had left, Riley paced my living room like a caged animal. I sat on the couch, my legs tucked under me, watching in consternation. Riley ran his hands through his hair again and again until it stood on end, making him look like a deranged porcupine. After he had circled the room at least a dozen times, he snorted. I watched him in alarm, having no idea what that snort meant. To my amazement, he started to laugh, softly at first, then breaking into guffaws. Now I was really worried. I'd never seen a grown man go into hysterics before, if that's what was happening.

"I'll never forget the sight of Marcia and Linda in that closet," Riley finally gasped. "I've never seen anything so funny in my life!" He sat next to me on the couch and struggled for breath. "I wish I'd had a camera."

I smiled tentatively. The scene *had* been pretty funny, assuming, that is, that my friends hadn't jeopardized Riley's investigation and that my budding romance wasn't finished before it had begun.

"Oh, Jackie, I don't know what to do with you and your buddies," Riley said, using a tissue to blot the tears of laughter dotting his cheeks.

"Did we damage your investigation?" I asked tentatively.

Riley shook his head. "No, I didn't learn much new from Tommy. In fact, he just confirmed the direction in which we're heading."

I sat up straight. "Henry Byrn is a murderer?" I asked.

Riley stopped me from commenting further. "I didn't say that," he said sternly, "and I didn't mean to imply it."

"But," I began.

"There is no 'but'," Riley said. "The only 'but' I can think of right now is the one with two t's... as in 'butt' out."

He rose to his feet. "I have to go," he announced. "I'll call you later." He narrowed his eyes at me. "Don't let me hear that any of you have been within 100 miles of Henry Byrn, or Alan Wallace, for that matter."

"Do you think the girlfriend is Veronica Lake?" I asked.

Riley put on his cop face and frowned at me. The problem was I now knew that, at least as far as I was concerned, there was a marshmallow behind that face.

"And an older woman," I mused, "I wonder who that might be."

Riley strode across the room and grabbed my shoulders. He put his face close to mine. "Work on your book," he instructed. "Do anything but meddle in my case any further." He kissed me quickly. "Now, before I go, could you pack up some of those cookies? My team would love them."

I laughed and complied with his request.

Riley had barely pulled out of the driveway before Marcia, Bernice and Linda appeared on my doorstep.

"He isn't coming back, is he?" Marcia asked, peering at Riley's departing vehicle.

"Not right now," I said, ushering them into the house.

"That's good," she said. "I really don't want to get shot."

"You just have to say it, don't you?" Linda asked, shaking her head.

"Of course." Marcia grinned. "What do we do next?"

"Nothing," I said firmly. "I think Riley has a good idea about who committed the murders. We need to let him do his job."

"But what about Judith?" Bernice asked. "We told her we'd try to find out who threatened her."

"I have a feeling that Riley will have the answer to that also, very soon." I replied. "So, we do nothing."

Marcia shook her head. "I disagree."

"Why?" Linda asked, settling onto the couch.

"We made Judith a promise," Marcia said staunchly, "and we need to deliver on it ourselves." She hesitated a moment. "For some reason, I think there's more to the picture than we're seeing."

"Like what?" Bernice asked.

"Like maybe there's some third party involved in all of this," Marcia replied. "It's clear there are a lot of family issues swirling around her, what with the business control and all. But I can't help but think there's more to it."

"Do you have a suggestion?" I asked, knowing that, unfortunately, she'd come up with something.

"I say we follow Henry," Marcia announced.

"What?" I said, incredulous. "Are you nuts? He knows us. How are you going to explain it to him when we're there every time he turns around?" And how could I possibly justify this to Riley?

"I've thought about that," Marcia said. "Henry knows you and Bernice, especially Bernice, since she chewed him out. I think Linda and I should do the tailing."

"Me?" Linda exclaimed. "How did I get dragged into this?"

"He didn't see much of you at the party," Marcia said, "and I doubt he saw you at the park at all. You're perfect. Besides, you can blend into a crowd pretty easily."

Linda raised an eyebrow.

"I mean," Marcia said hastily, "it's not that you're not gorgeous. You're just gorgeous in a more subtle way than Bernice." She saw Linda's displeased expression and stumbled on. "You're certainly less conspicuous than I am." Well, there was some truth to that.

"So how do you propose we do this?" Linda asked.

"We wait for him outside his house tomorrow morning. I already know his address. He lives in Windsor Farms," she said, naming one of Richmond's swankiest neighborhoods.

"He's a young man," Bernice protested. "He probably stays out until all hours and sleeps in late. He might not come out at all. This sounds like a terrible waste of time."

"Well, I'm going," Marcia said stubbornly.

"I'll go too," Linda said, "if only to protect you from yourself."

Marcia beamed. "We can meet in town for lunch and we'll tell you what we learned."

"If anything," Linda said repressively.

"Riley said to stay away from Henry," I protested. "I can't be part of this."

"You won't be," Marcia promised. "You'll only hear our report."

"Did you promise we'd stay away from Henry?" Linda asked.

"Well, no," I admitted.

"Did you pinky swear?" Marcia asked.

"No."

"Then it's settled."

"I thought you wanted me to have a relationship," I wailed.

"We do," Bernice assured me. "But one thing at a time."

I grabbed a cookie.

The next day dawned cool and clear, yesterday's rain having blown away. I spent the morning on my proofs and then drove into town to meet my friends at a local café. When they arrived, Marcia looked crestfallen and Linda looked irritated.

"Well, that was a bust," Marcia admitted. "Stakeouts are incredibly boring. I don't know how cops stand it."

"What happened?" Bernice asked, holding back a smile.

"Nothing, that's what happened," Linda said. "We sat in the car and I played about a million games of solitaire. Henry finally came out about 10:30. He drove to the gym and worked out for about an hour. Then he picked up some dry cleaning, ran into the grocery store and went home."

"That's it?" I asked.

Marcia nodded.

"Ok," I said. "We're off the case unless something falls into our laps. Agreed?" My friends nodded glumly.

"We can't win every time," Bernice said consolingly. "At least we tried. Now, let's have a nice lunch and then we can decide what we want to do this afternoon."

We followed her suggestion and passed a pleasant hour or so eating and chatting, the way friends do.

"I think I'm going to go home and work," I said as we walked toward our cars.

"Look, Jackie, there's something on your windshield," Linda said. She reached out and removed a piece of paper from under my wiper.

"It's probably an ad for something," I said, reaching out my hand, "or someone complaining about my parking job. After all, we know I'm the world's worst parallel parker."

Linda's face had paled. "I don't think so," she said, handing me the note.

I read it out loud. "Mind your own business or your precious pup is history." I gasped. The paper rattled in my hands as I read it again.

"What?" Bernice exclaimed, reading over my shoulder.

"Oh, my God!" Marcia said, leaning on my car.

Maggie! My darling little boxer puppy. The light of my life. Someone was threatening my dog. I felt myself starting to hyperventilate. "Deep breaths," Linda commanded. "Take slow, deep breaths."

Marcia dug into her pocketbook. She pulled out a pair of rubber gloves and a baggie. What did she have in there anyway? "Fingerprints," she said, snapping on the gloves, removing the note from my shaking hand and putting it in the baggie.

"What are we going to do?" Bernice asked frantically.

"Nick! I have to call Nick!" I said, fumbling with my phone. For once he picked up.

"What's up, Mom?" he asked.

"Where are you?" I asked without preamble. Nick sounded startled "I'm home. Why?"

"Where's Maggie?"

"She's right here," he replied. "What's going on?"

"Don't let her out of your sight," I commanded. "Stay with her at all times, even if she's playing in the back yard. Don't let her eat anything you don't give her and don't let her near anyone you don't know well."

"Mom, you're scaring me," Nick said.

"I'll explain when I get home," I told him. "Please just do as I say." I hung up.

"What now?" Linda asked.

I thought for a moment. "I'm going to call Judith," I said. "I'll show her this note, see if the handwriting's the same as on the one she received." I pounded my fist on the hood of my car. "I wish she still had that note." Judith answered her phone and agreed to see me. I slid in behind my steering wheel. The passenger doors opened and my friends piled in.

"We're going with you," Marcia said. "No one's going to threaten you and get away with it. Not on our watch."

"Roger that," said Bernice, clicking her seatbelt.

"Shouldn't we tell Riley?" Linda asked sensibly.

"We will," I said grimly. "Let's see if we can get some more information first."

We made the drive to Judith's house in record time. I noticed Bernice's tight grip on the door handle as we took the turn into Woodford Hall. I eased up on the accelerator. Bernice gave a shaky sigh. "Sorry." I muttered.

She just shook her head.

Judith was waiting for us when we pulled up.

"Jackie," she said, coming to greet us. "Is everything all right? You sounded so distraught on the phone."

"Something's come up that we need to talk to you about," I replied.

"Of course," she said, leading us inside.

"Is Veronica here?" Bernice asked, looking around.

"No," Judith said. "She has the day off." She sighed. "I've decided to let her go. I simply can't trust her, after she lied on her resume and how she behaved

237

at Jackie's house." She sighed again. "I suspect she knows it. I'd be willing to bet she's out interviewing for a new job."

"I guess you'll have to change your will too," Linda commented, "since you said you left her some money."

"I hadn't thought that far, but you're right," Judith said. "Thanks for reminding me. I'll let my attorney know." She smiled sadly. "Life doesn't often go smoothly, does it?"

"That's an understatement," I said.

"You seem upset," Judith said. "What did you want to talk to me about?"

"Did you happen to find that threatening note you received?" I asked.

"No," Judith said. "I looked for it some more after you left, but there's no sign of it. Why?"

Marcia pulled the bagged note out of her pocketbook and handed it to Judith. "What's this?" Judith asked, starting to read it. We heard a sharp intake of breath. "My heavens!" she exclaimed. "This is awful!" She looked up from reading the note. "Is your dog all right?" Judith's own dog, a King Charles Cavalier spaniel, seized the moment to wander into the room and jump onto her owner's lap. Judith hugged the dog close to her chest. The dog licked her chin and nestled into her lap.

"She's fine," I assured her. "My son is with her. But I'm terrified for her. And I'm scared for him too."

"Of course, you are," Judith said, absentmindedly smoothing her dog's fur.

"We're wondering if this is tied in with the note you received," Bernice said. "Does the paper look the same? Is the handwriting similar?"

Judith scrutinized the note more carefully. "My note was on garden variety

238

white paper, probably copy paper," she said. "There's nothing special about this paper that I can see either."

"No watermarks, huh?" Marcia asked hopefully.

"That only happens in Sherlock Holmes stories," Linda informed her.

"The writing's completely different, too," Judith said, squinting at the paper. "The writing on my note was very messy, sort of scribbly. That could have been done to disguise the writing, of course."

"Or the person could have terrible handwriting," Bernice said.

"That's a possibility, too," Judith agreed. She continued to study the note. "But I'm guessing that if he or she tried to disguise the writing they'd do the same thing this time. I'd say we're dealing with two different people."

"Now *you're* turning into a detective," I said with a shaky smile.

"There's something about this writing," Judith mused, holding the note closer to her face. She paled. "Hold on a second." Grabbing her dog and balancing her on her hip, she headed to her office. We could hear her rummaging around on her desk. When she returned, her face had lost all color. "Look at this," she said, handing me a handwritten list of items.

I frowned. "It looks awfully similar."

Judith took the note and laid it on the coffee table next to the one we had found on my car.

Linda gasped. "I think the handwriting's the same."

Marcia nodded. "Practically identical."

"That's my daughter-in-law's writing," Judith said. "Elizabeth wrote that note."

239

# Chapter Twenty-four

Marcia opened her mouth to speak.

Bernice held up her hand. "Don't say it."

Marcia closed her mouth and pouted.

"I can't believe Elizabeth would do something like this," Judith said.

"She must be trying to hide something," Linda contributed. "Why else would she do something so nasty?"

"We're going to find out," I said, rising to my feet.

"Where are we going?" Bernice asked. I heard her mutter "I have a bad feeling I know the answer."

"I'm dropping you off at Marcia's car," I replied. "Then I'm going to have a conversation with Elizabeth Waters Byrn."

"Oh no, you're not," Linda said. "Either we all go or no one goes." She grabbed my car keys off the coffee table where I had deposited them.

"You may need witnesses," Marcia said. "What if she attacks you? Or you attack her?" I glared at her. "Not that you would, of course," she said quickly. "I know you'd never do that, but she might. She's clearly not stable."

"Oh, all right," I said, snatching the keys from Linda's hand. "Nobody's going to attack anyone. I'm just going to ask her why she would do this. Then I'm going to call Riley and report her."

"I think you've got it backwards," Bernice said.

Maybe I wasn't thinking straight, but I started the drive toward Windsor Farms without further comment. All right, I *know* I wasn't thinking straight. After all, I was normally the voice of reason in our group. But with the threat to my puppy, all my reasonableness seemed to have vanished.

We were sailing along back roads when my phone rang.

"Mom?" Nick's voice came through the speaker. "Are you there?"

"Yes," I answered tersely, swerving to avoid a branch in the road.

"What is going on?" I heard a small yelp. "Oops! Sorry! I think I was holding Maggie too tightly."

Bernice looked at me, silently asking permission to speak. "Your mother received a note threatening Maggie," she said. "She's very upset."

We heard Nick's sharp intake of breath.

"We're pretty sure we know who sent the note," Bernice continued, holding onto the door handle as I maneuvered around a curve. "I don't think you need to worry about Maggie any longer." She gulped as my car tires squealed. "Your mother is driving," she began.

"And not very well!" Marcia yelled from the back seat.

"That's why she can't have the phone," Linda chimed in.

I slowed down.

"This is probably not the best time to talk," Bernice continued. "But we should be home soon."

"Well, OK," Nick said, sounding very uncertain.

"It's fine, Nick," I said, "or at least it will be once I…"

Linda leaned forward and punched me in the shoulder.

"Why don't you go to our house and hang out with Max and Ray?" Bernice suggested. She shot me a glance that told me she still didn't approve of my driving.

"All right," Nick said. "Just don't do anything stupid. I need my mother in one

241

piece."

"Roger that," Bernice said, as I slowed down even more and entered the Windsor Farms development.

Windsor Farms is one of the most desirable neighborhoods in Richmond, Virginia. It houses two remarkable houses disassembled in Britain and brought to the United States; Virginia House and Agecroft Hall. Agecroft Hall is a Tudor beauty with extensive gardens offering many musical and theatrical productions each year. Virginia House was actually built in the 1600's, long before the United States came into being. It was carefully taken apart in England and put back together in Richmond. The lots in the subdivision tend to be wooded and deep, and streets bearing British-sounding names meander attractively through the neighborhood. At the center sits a church and a square, which is the meeting place for residents. Windsor Farms sits just south of Cary Street, home to some of the most sought after addresses in Richmond, as well as the site of a charming multi-block development of stores and restaurants. It is almost impossible to find a home in Windsor Farms valued under a million dollars, and the majority are priced at closer to two million. The place is incredibly attractive, and when we were young Lars and I would drive around the neighborhood, imagining what it might be like to live there one day. In later years we decided that, as beautiful as it is, we would not enjoy the environment and settled happily in our little college town, we didn't have to worry about whether we wore the right type of clothes or drove an acceptable brand of car. Chances are that our worries about being faced with snobbishness were overblown, but we opted not to find out.

The Byrns made the opposite choice. Naturally, they lived in one of the grander homes in Windsor Farms, a meandering Tudor that occupied over an acre of landscaped grounds.

"That's it!" Marcia pointed to the brick and stucco confection.

I pulled up to the curb. "Nice," I admitted.

"Wow!" Bernice breathed.

"Not my taste," Linda said, "but they've done a nice job with the landscaping."

Really? I couldn't remember Linda spending a lot of time in her yard, although she always had some attractive plantings out front.

"What now?" Marcia asked.

I spotted Elizabeth's jaunty convertible parked in the driveway. "We pay a visit on Elizabeth Waters Byrn," I said, jerking on the steering wheel and entering the driveway. I grabbed the vile note in its plastic baggie and stepped out of the car, ready to do battle. My friends followed me, the sound of car doors closing reverberating through the unnaturally quiet street. I strode up to the front door and pushed the door bell. Elizabeth opened the door. She stood completely still, the color draining from her face as she took in our group.

"What can I do for you ladies?" she finally asked, her chin tilting toward the sky.

"We'd like a moment of your time," I said politely. "May we come in? Elizabeth hesitated.

"Thank you," Marcia elbowed her way past me. "Nice house," she said neutrally, eying the vestibule with its twenty-foot ceiling.

"I'm sure you remember me," Bernice said, stepping regally past Elizabeth and joining Marcia in the foyer. Linda slipped in behind, surreptitiously taking pictures with her phone.

"What do you want?" Elizabeth asked, crossing her arms.

"We want to talk to you about this," I said, brandishing the note. I shoved it into her face.

What's that?" she stuttered, taking a step back.

"Something your mother-in-law says you wrote," I said, stepping forward.

"I don't know what you're talking about!" Elizabeth said. "What is that thing? You need to leave!" She moved as though to open the front door.

"I don't think so," I said softly. "Let me read this to you. 'Mind your own business or your precious pup is history.' Sound familiar?"

"No," Elizabeth said, trying again to open the door. "You need to leave now."

"Not quite yet," Linda said. "Judith recognized your handwriting. You left this note for Jackie."

"Why would I do that?" Elizabeth asked. "That's just mean."

"Yes, isn't it?" I asked. "But I think I know what this is about."

"Mom?" queried a disembodied voice. "What's going on?"

We looked up to see Henry peering over the second-floor balcony.

"Nothing, Henry," his mother replied. "Go back upstairs."

"It's not 'nothing' Henry," Marcia called up. "Your mother is trying to protect you and she's threatening our friend in order to do it."

Henry started down the stairs. "This is crazy," he said. "Mom wouldn't threaten anybody."

Bernice squinted at him. "Is it? I'd say that if she isn't protecting you from something, she's covering for herself." She turned and pointed at Elizabeth. "You tried to scare Judith, didn't you?" she asked. I was taken aback. In truth, that had never occurred to me.

"No!" Elizabeth exclaimed. "I would never do that! I don't know who tried to frighten her, but it wasn't me."

"Well, if it wasn't you, maybe it was Henry," Linda declared, shooting daggers in his direction.

"You ladies are nuts!" Henry said. "I would never hurt my grandmother. You all need to leave now or I'm calling the cops."

"Be my guest," I said, waving the baggie with the note in his direction. "That's my next step anyway. Take a look at this." Henry stepped closer and read the note. He blanched. "No one is going to get away with threatening my dog. Not even Ms. High and Mighty Elizabeth Byrn."

"I have another theory," Marcia said. "You're afraid it's going to get out that Henry is using drugs. That would be quite a scandal, wouldn't it?"

"What?" Henry and his mother asked, eyeing each other.

I nodded. "We've heard about those parties you go to, Henry," I said. "We know there are drugs there." I turned to face him squarely. "I don't know if you use drugs rarely, or occasionally, or opportunistically, or regularly. You have chosen some unsavory people to spend time with, but I don't care and I'm not interested in your drug habit, whatever it may be."

I turned back to Elizabeth. "If that's your concern, and you're trying to keep other people from knowing Henry's little secret, it has nothing to do with us. Anyway, Henry's secret isn't a secret. A lot of people from the high school know. I suspect half your lovely neighborhood knows. I also suspect half of the kids here are just like Henry. Here's the bottom line – *who cares?*" I took a deep breath.

"You should," Marcia muttered under her breath, staring at Elizabeth.

Linda continued to glare at Henry. "I think you know something about the threat to your grandmother and I also think you know who messed with her saddle. And if you don't know, I suspect you have a good idea who it was."

"I think you know more than that," Bernice said, stepping closer to him, causing him to back into the stairs, "I think you know who killed your friend Lisa and her boyfriend." She narrowed her eyes at him. "Or at the very least you have a strong suspicion."

"You really need to talk to the cops," Marcia said. "Preferably before they come looking for you."

I thought Henry and Elizabeth were both going to faint.

I waved the note in Elizabeth's face again. "I felt sorry for you when I heard about your miscarriages," I said. "But I don't anymore."

"What miscarriages?" Henry asked. "Mom?"

Elizabeth was crying but refused to look at her son.

"Here's the deal," I said. "I'm sending a copy of this note to my attorney, along with a letter telling him who wrote it. I am giving all of my friends," here I made a sweeping gesture, "a copy. And I am giving the original to Detective Furman." I walked toward Elizabeth until she was backed up against the wall. "If anything happens to my dog, or my friends, or their children or husbands, or my son, or my friends' dogs," here Linda cleared her throat "or Miss Kitty," (did I really say that?) you will regret the day you were born." I turned on my heel and strode out of the house. It would have been a grand exit, except that I caught my heel on the top step and started to tumble, having to grab the railing to prevent being unceremoniously dumped to the ground.

"Let's go home," Bernice said. She held out her hand. "I'll drive."

246

# Chapter Twenty-Five

I was emotionally exhausted by the time we reached my house. I turned to my friends, "Thank you so much," I blurted. "I don't know what I would have done without you."

"You would have handled it just fine," Linda said, patting my shoulder.

"Well," I said, smiling tremulously, "It certainly helps to have my posse with me."

"Always," Bernice said, giving me her normal gentle smile. She hugged me tightly. "We love you, Jackie."

"All for one, and one for all," agreed Marcia, also giving me a hug. "Actually, that was kind of fun."

"Only you would think that," Linda told her, kissing my cheek. "But we do make a good team."

Nick was perched on the edge of the couch when I entered the house. He was holding a wiggling Maggie next to him. The treat jar was open, and apparently Maggie had been feasting as Nick tried to keep her in place. I just hoped she wouldn't throw everything up on the rug. Nick stood up and put his arms around me. "Mom," he said, "You need to tell me everything that happened. Right now." His entire body was tense and the skin around his eyes was tight as he concentrated on me.

I took the note from my purse, explaining how I had found it and what had happened since then.

"Henry's mother sent it?" Nick gasped, falling onto a chair. "That's insane. Is she nuts?"

"She's far too protective of her son," I said. "I'm sure she's going to regret this. I know Judith will confront her, and I'll bet Judith will tell all the other family members what she did."

"Man, if I were her husband, I'd leave her," Nick said. "She's unhinged."

I thought a moment. That had never occurred to me. After this stunt, it probably should have. I tried to feel badly for Elizabeth and on some level I did. On the other hand, what she had done had scared me to death. On the other hand… no, my sympathy was definitely limited at this point.

The door bell started to jangle incessantly. Someone wouldn't stop pressing the button and the noise reverberated through the house.

"All right, I'm coming!" Nick called. He looked through the peep hole and glanced over his shoulder. "Riley," he mouthed.

Riley charged into the house and directly toward me. "Jackie!" he cried. "Are you all right? What's happened? I got this crazy message from Marcia babbling about a threatening message and then I got a call from Henry Byrn saying he needed to talk to me and that he might know something about Lisa and Bobby's deaths, but he wasn't sure if he knew anything…None of it made any sense." He stared at me, his grey eyes searching my face for clues and, to my embarrassment, I started to cry. No, let me be clear. I started to sob. Uncontrollably. Nick moved to my side, looking uncertain as to what he should be doing. Riley cleared the distance between us in a bound and took me into his arms. He held me tight against his chest, stroking my hair and kissing my head, murmuring reassurances. "Jackie," he whispered over and over. "It's all right. I'm here. Whatever it is, I'm here." Apparently, I was one wo m an whose crying he was prepared to tolerate. Maggie bounded from her

248

place on the couch, standing on her back legs and inserting herself between us, insistently licking my leg. At long last I stopped wailing and stepped back. "I'm sorry," I whispered.

"You'd better not be," Riley said, pulling a handkerchief from his pocket and wiping my cheeks. "Now, tell me what's wrong."

"You need to take a look at this," Nick said, handing him Elizabeth's note. Riley read the note quickly, then more slowly. His face paled, then turned an unhealthy shade of red. "Do you know who wrote this?" he asked. I nodded. "How do you know?" he asked, in full cop mode. I explained that Judith had recognized Elizabeth's writing and what had transpired after we found the note.

"This is a crime," Riley said. He reached for his phone. "I'm going to have a chat with Ms. Byrn." He hesitated for a moment and took a deep breath. "On second thought, I'm going to have my sergeant do that. I don't want Ms. Byrn claiming I have a conflict of interest. There have to be consequences for what she did. No one should get away with this behavior." He reached down and scratched Maggie's head. "You look ok, little girl," he said. "Thank goodness," he added under his breath.

The door bell rang again. Before I could reach it, the door swung open and Bernice charged in with Ray on her heels. Her complexion was mottled with a strange, slightly pale tone I had never seen before. "There's been another one," she said, handing a baggie to Riley.

Another what?

"You have a beautiful little daughter," Riley read out loud. He blanched, I gasped, and Nick collapsed onto a chair. Ray's eyes were shooting fire.

"Someone is threatening our family," he proclaimed.

Riley reached for his phone again. "Ms. Byrn is going to have a visit from the police sooner rather than later," he said.

"No, wait," Bernice said, putting her hand on his arm.

He looked at her questioningly.

"I don't think Elizabeth wrote this," she continued. She turned to me. "Do you remember Judith telling us that the handwriting on the note she received was messy and almost illegible?"

I nodded and peered at the paper in Riley's hand. "This is a mess." I raised my head. "Do you think this is from the person who threatened Judith?"

Bernice nodded. "I think we have two note writers."

Riley frowned.

"We've sent the kids to my parents," Ray said. "Max took them."

Bernice gave a shaky laugh. "They think this is a great lark. I told them they could take a day off from school tomorrow." She gulped. "Max didn't want to go until I convinced him that he was their bodyguard. I doubt he'll take his eyes off them."

Ray paced the room agitatedly. "I have a gun," he stated.

"Now, Ray," Riley said, holding out a hand.

"I know how to use it," Ray stated. "I *will* use it if anyone tries to hurt my family."

"I know how to use it too," Bernice said.

"Please, guys," Riley pleaded. "Let's not do anything foolish. I'll arrange protection for the kids and Ray's parents." This time he dialed his phone and spoke urgently with the person on the other end, pausing only to get the details about Ray's parents and their address.

I put my arm around Bernice, who was shaking like a leaf. Ray was clenching and unclenching his fists, breathing heavily and staring at Riley.

"Ok," Riley said. "A uniformed patrol is heading to Bernice's parents. One officer will be in the house and one outside." He reached out and grabbed Ray's shoulder. "We're going to protect your family, Ray," he said. "We won't let anything happen to them."

Ray continued to breathe heavily. Suddenly he collapsed, sobbing, against Riley's chest. Riley looked panicked for a second, but then he wrapped his arms around the big man. "It's going to be all right, my friend," he said. "It will be all right." He included Bernice and me in his glance. "I'm pretty sure I know who did this, and he's being watched. He's being watched very carefully. I don't have enough yet to bring him in, but we're very, very close."

The door bell rang again, but before I could answer it someone pushed the door open. Marcia, Bob and Linda charged into the house.

"What's going on?" Bob demanded, panting slightly. He must have literally run across the street. He saw Ray's red eyes and Bernice's shaking body. In two strides he was beside Ray, wrapping an arm around his shoulders. "I'm here for you, bro," he said. "Just tell me what you need." The sight of the slender accountant caring for the huge football player brought tears to my eyes.

Riley slid his eyes toward me. "Don't you ever lock your door?" he asked.

"Usually," I said apologetically. "Things are a little crazy right now."

He shook his head.

Marcia and Linda had circled Bernice, who had begun to cry, with their arms. Bob challenged Riley. "Are you going to tell us what's happening or not?"

251

Riley explained about the threatening note and the Mortons' children being taken to a safe place.

Linda gasped. "This is getting out of control," she said. She held Bernice tighter.

"No kidding," Riley muttered.

Linda glared at him and tightened her grip even more.

"I can't breathe," Bernice protested, half laughing and half crying. "You two don't know how strong you are." Linda and Marcia moved away slightly, but each held one of Bernice's hands.

"I have a gun," Bob said. "If you need me to stand watch, I'll be happy to."

"NO!" Riley shouted. I looked around the room. How many of my friends owned guns, anyway?

"I have one too," Linda said. "I'm a really good shot."

"STOP!" Riley roared. "No one is using a gun. At least not one of you."

Everyone else in the room was absolutely still.

"Promise me," Riley said, pointing at my friends, "that you will lock your guns away and not take them out again until this is over."

Clearly, each person with a gun was pondering their decision.

"All right," Linda sighed finally. "Mine's pretty low caliber anyway. It probably wouldn't be much use."

Riley slapped his hand against his forehead.

"I agree," Bob said finally. "I have to trust Riley."

Reluctantly, Bernice and Ray agreed.

"OK," Nick piped up. I had forgotten he was in the room. Oh my God, was he going to need counseling after all this? Was he damaged for life? Should I make him leave in case things got even wilder? Maybe he and Maggie should be staying with Ray's parents also. That way they'd be safe. I made a mental note to run the idea by Ray and Bernice.

"Now that's settled and all the guns are staying locked up," Nick announced, "it's booze all around except for Riley. And I don't mean wine. I mean the real thing." In a matter of minutes, he had set a glass in front of each of us other than Riley. I gave him a weak smile.

Riley's phone rang and he snatched it out of his pocket. "Talk to me," he said tersely. There was a pause. "What did she say?" Another pause. "So, she admitted writing the note?" Pause, pause, pause. "WHAT? She says Jackie did what?" Riley listened intently. "Hold on." He turned to me. "Jackie, Elizabeth claims you pushed her and hit her. Is that true?"

My eyes were as big as saucers. "Never!" I gasped. "I never touched her! I never even thought about it!"

"We were all there," Marcia interjected. "Jackie has witnesses."

"Yes, but those witnesses are Jackie's best friends," Riley replied. He listened to the voice on the other end of the phone. Riley turned to me. "She wants to press charges against you for battery."

I felt my entire body go cold. "It never happened," I said pleadingly. "I would never hit anyone, even over something like this."

"Jackie," Riley said gently, "she has the right to press charges."

I felt myself start to collapse.

"Wait a minute," Linda commanded. "Look at this." She took out her phone, pressed the video button, and thrust the phone in Riley's face. He began to smile.

"You smart girl, you!" Marcia exclaimed. "You videoed the whole thing."

Linda nodded.

"Well, so did I!" she handled Riley her phone.

"You wonderful, smart women!" I exclaimed. Next to me I felt Nick exhale.

Riley addressed the person on the other end of the phone. "We have two videos showing that Elizabeth Waters Byrn is lying," he said. The phone squawked. "Henry's there? Will he talk to you?" He listened. "Not about his earlier call, but about what his mother said? He wants to go into the hall? Fine." Riley tapped his foot nervously as he waited for the officer on the other end of the phone to return. "He said what?" he exclaimed. He turned to us. "Henry told my sergeant that his mother is lying, that Jackie never touched her."

We exchanged amazed glances.

Riley returned to his phone call. "Ok, Annabella, good work," he said. "Thank you. I'll see you back at the station." Annabella? Somehow my mind conjured up a long-buried image of a gorgeous Hispanic woman accompanying Riley at the crime scene when our neighbor was murdered. Should I be a teensy, weensy bit jealous? No, I decided, definitely not. She was a career woman in a difficult job. Being pretty was irrelevant, and maybe a handicap sometimes. You go, girl! You can do whatever you set your heart on.

Riley puffed out a breath. "Annabella has charged Elizabeth with threatening Jackie, along with lying to a police officer."

"What a screwed-up family," Linda muttered.

"Jackie, do you want to press charges against her?" Riley asked. "If so, you'll need to talk to the Commonwealth's attorney about that."

Normally my motto is forgive and forget. I thought a while. "Yes," I said finally. "She obviously needs psychiatric help. Any deal that makes sure she gets it will be fine with me."

"You're a good woman, Jackie Olsen," Riley said, rising. "I'm heading to the station." He turned to Bernice and Ray. "Your kids are safe," he said. "I promise you." Ray shook his hand and Bernice gave him a hug.

Marcia opened her mouth. Riley pointed at her. "Don't say it," he commanded. He headed toward the front porch. "And lock your door," he said to me. Nick followed him to the door and turned the lock once he had left.

Marcia looked at those of us who remained. "What do we do now?" she asked.

# Chapter Twenty-six

I couldn't recall many times in all the years we'd been friends that Bob hadn't been happy with Marcia, but this was definitely one of them. He drew his eyebrows together and drummed his fingers on the table. "Marcia," he said in an exaggeratedly patient voice, "our friends are going through a really bad time right now. You don't need to be thinking about detecting or doing anything but supporting them."

"I know that," Marcia said sharply. "But what do *we* do, Bob? Do we take our kids somewhere else to be safe? Do we get Ray and Bernice to stay with us? Do we all leave until this is settled?" The tears came. "I really, really mean it. What do we do?"

"Oh, Honey," Bob said, pulling her close to him. He puffed out a breath. "I don't know. I wish I did."

Ray intervened. "I trust Riley. Our family is going to be fine. I think that to the extent possible we keep our routines. We go to work. We check in with each other. We stay far away from Riley's case."

"But what about Judith?" Bernice asked. "I'm afraid she may truly be in danger."

"Frankly," Linda said, "at this point I don't care. That family is so goofed up I'm not sure it can be fixed. Anyway, that's not what we signed on for."

"Let's have dinner," I said. I walked into the kitchen and pulled a frozen lasagna from the refrigerator. Thank goodness I always had several premade casseroles ready just in case the entire track team stopped by. It had happened, believe me. Bob opened a couple bottles of red wine and we settled in the living room.

Nick moved into the kitchen and began preparing salad and garlic bread. "Do you want me to thaw one of your pies?" he called.

"Sure," I called back. "Thanks,"

"I don't know when I've ever felt so helpless," Bernice confessed, snuggling against Ray's chest, her feet tucked under her.

"I'm going to get my mother to take the boys tonight," Marcia announced, reaching for her phone.

"Good luck with that," Bob said. Their twins were classmates of Nick and Max as well as being good friends with them. "They're unlikely to go without a fight."

Marcia punched buttons on her phone. "Oh, they'll go, believe me," she said.

The doorbell rang. "What is this, Grand Central Station?" I complained, heading toward the door.

"Check to see who it is," Ray advised, moving behind me, "before you open the door."

"Why didn't I bring my darned gun?" Linda muttered. Oh dear.

I peered through the peephole. Judith, her daughter Ann, and goddaughter Emily stood on the stoop. "Now what?" I groaned. I turned to my friends. "Can we just pretend we're not here?"

"Somehow I don't think they'll believe you," Bob said. "I'll see if I can get rid of them." He pushed Ray to one side and opened the door. "Can I help you?" The ladies were visibly startled to see a tall, serious-looking man staring down at them, his body blocking the doorway.

"We're looking for Jackie," Judith said. She thrust a giant bouquet of flowers toward Bob, who reflexively reached for them. "This *is* her house, isn't it?"

Bob retained enough presence of mind not to step back, even with his arms laden with flowers. "Yes," he said shortly. "But she's busy."

Ann stood on her tiptoes and tried to see beyond Bob. Ray stepped up to his side. "What do you ladies want?" he asked without any pretense of being polite.

Emily, shorter than the others, attempted to duck under his arm. "We heard about what Elizabeth did," she said, finally finding me with her bright blue gaze. "We just had to come over and say how sorry we are."

"Fine." Ray said. "You've said it. Thank you. Goodbye." He started to close the door.

"Please!" Judith called to me. "Can't we just talk?"

I waivered and sought guidance from my friends. One by one they shrugged, although Marcia had crossed her arms over her chest, evidencing her unhappiness.

To my surprise, Nick walked to the door with Maggie at his heels. "This has been a really bad day," he said, standing between Ray and Bob. "Elizabeth threatened our dog. That means she threatened my mom and me." I almost expected him to say 'we are not amused' as he tossed his hair and stared down his nose at our unwanted guests. I was so proud of my son I could burst. But when had he gotten so tall? He was towering over our visitors. "Now someone else has threatened our friend's daughter," Nick continued. "I think you should leave us alone."

At his last words I heard a collective gasp from the three ladies.

"Please let's talk," Judith pleaded again. "Rosalinda has started to remember things, and I thought you'd want to know what she said."

Oh, crap. Just when I thought Nick had convinced these people to go away. "Come in," I said reluctantly. Immediately they were standing in the living room. Well, here they were, in my house, facing a distinctly unfriendly crowd. I had to give them credit. But this wasn't a social occasion. I wasn't going to invite them to sit down. I wasn't going to offer them a glass of wine. No sir. And I certainly wasn't going to feed them. "Would you like something to drink?" I offered. Behind me Linda sighed heavily and moved toward the cabinet where I kept the wine glasses. I slid my eyes toward Bernice, who shrugged her elegant shoulders, but made no attempt to welcome the trio. The men adjusted the seating arrangement so that there would be enough room for all of us. Bob opened yet another bottle. Man, was I going to have to make a run to the wine store in the near future. Nick cocked one eyebrow at me, shook his head to indicate his disapproval, and returned to his work in the kitchen, taking Maggie with him. She would have stayed to entertain our unexpected company but the pup knew that when Nick cooked there would be treats in the offing and she wasn't about to miss that opportunity, no matter how interesting these newcomers might prove to be.

"We can't begin to tell you how sorry we are about what Elizabeth did," Ann offered, taking a small sip of the wine Bob had poured.

I remained silent, examining my feelings. I try, I swear I try, to be sympathetic to others, but I found that I didn't care about their apology. I said nothing. Marcia had taken the huge bunch of flowers to the kitchen island and was vigorously snipping stems in preparation of putting the flowers in a vase. Snip. Snip. If she kept up her current pace, there would soon be no blooms left. I felt a brief twinge of regret, as they truly were lovely, but I didn't stop her cutting them apart.

"We appreciate the apology," Bernice said, always gracious, "and understand you're upset. But apologizing for someone else's behavior is rather meaningless, isn't it?" Ouch!

Snip.

Judith stared into her glass for a moment, then into our eyes. "My son has decided to stay with Elizabeth," she said. "but he's insisting she get psychiatric help."

Emily issued a harsh laugh. "I thought he'd take the opportunity to run," she said, "but I obviously was wrong."

I still couldn't think of a thing to say.

Snip.

"This seems to have totally shaken Henry," Ann offered. "He said he's moving out of the house. He also said he had called Detective Furman and was waiting to talk with him."

Snip. Snip. Snip, snip, snip!

Bernice moved to Marcia's side and gently removed the scissors from her hand. Linda handed them a vase she had retrieved from a cupboard.

"You said Rosalinda seemed to be regaining her memory?" Bob asked.

Judith nodded and leaned forward. "She doesn't remember anything about being attacked," she said. "However, she has a clear recollection of seeing a young man with a motorcycle near my house the day that note was left on my car. She didn't think anything of it because she frequently saw my neighbor's grandson with his motorcycle."

"Does she recall what this young man looked like?" Ray asked.

"She has very vague memories, unfortunately," Judith replied.

"But there's more, Mom," Ann said. She turned to us. "Rosalinda also saw that same motorcycle parked in the woods near the stables when she took one of her lunchtime walks."

"Does she remember any details of that?" Bob asked, leaning forward. He had guided Marcia to the sofa and was sitting close to her with his hand on her knee. For her part, she was glaring at our visitors as though they were enemy aliens invading my home.

"There's a little more," Emily said. "She thinks she saw a woman with the man at one point. She said they were talking for a few minutes but that they both disappeared pretty quickly."

"Have you told Riley about this?' I asked.

Judith nodded emphatically. "Indeed, we have. He seemed very interested and was going to talk to Rosalinda himself."

Nick thumped a beautiful tray of cheese, crackers and accompaniments on the table, along with a stack of napkins. He was doing an amazing job of hosting, although he wasn't being particularly gracious. I decided that was just fine with me.

Judith reached out to me. "I truly am sorry," she said. "I know you didn't bargain for any of this." She looked around the room. "Whose daughter was threatened?"

"Mine," Bernice replied tersely. Ray put an arm around her shoulders.

"Is there any chance you kept the note?" Judith asked.

To my surprise, Ray nodded and reached into his pocket. "I made several copies." He handed one to Judith, who frowned over it.

261

"I would swear on a stack of Bibles that this is the handwriting from the note I found."

I couldn't say I was surprised. I sipped my wine, thinking intently. I wasn't going to say it to Judith, but her revelation supported my belief that her accidents had nothing to do with her family business. I thought a moment longer. Was I convinced all the incidents had the same root cause? I thought harder, back to what I had learned about the family, what Linda had seen happen between Henry and Veronica during Judith's party, about the motorcycle.

Emily seemed to read my mind. "I know Judith was afraid one of us was trying to take over the business, but in light of this note I think we can agree that isn't the case."

Judith was staring at her hands. Ann watched her intently. "This note you received is terrifying," Judith said to Bernice and Ray. "Is there anything I can do? Can I send your children away somewhere? Can I send your entire family away? I can't help but think that if I'd never contacted you, this wouldn't have happened." Judith had tears in her eyes.

Bernice seemed to thaw toward her and put a hand on her arm. "We're confident our family is safe," she said. "Riley Furman has several people protecting them." She looked intently into Judith's eyes. "You must have seen something threatening to someone. I'm sure that whoever is feeling threatened by you and Rosalinda killed those two young people. Think. Think hard."

Ann gestured to her relatives and stood to leave. "Mom will keep thinking," she said. She opened the front door. "Now I'm starting to worry about Henry." I thought Marcia might throw something at her. Obviously, she didn't care for the young man. "Henry wants to talk to Detective Furman," Ann continued.

262

"He thinks he knows something about the threats to Judith or the murders or both. He won't share whatever it is with us." She surveyed us for a moment before she moved onto the porch. "I have to wonder," she said. "Is Henry safe?"

The three women took their leave and left us pondering the answer to Ann's question.

# Chapter Twenty-seven

Ann's parting words haunted me long after my friends and I had finished dinner and they had left for their homes. So much seemed to be swirling around Henry. It seemed he had made some poor choices concerning friends and drug use. Apparently, he had now decided to disclose everything he might know about Lisa and Bobby's deaths. Now that he was cooperating with the police, would he be the next person targeted by whoever was sending threatening letters? When would this ever end?

I slept poorly, tossing and turning frequently. At one point I woke up sweating, shaking from a dream that had Nick, Maggie and me chasing Henry along a dark and winding path. I spent longer than usual in the shower, still shaken by the dream that seemed unusually real. I did the laundry, vacuumed the floors, and dusted, thinking of Henry. The only other thought that intruded was the idea that I really needed to hire a cleaning service.

I remembered that we hadn't received one important piece of information. On impulse, I called Bernice. Knowing her fear about her children's safety, I was reluctant to do so, but I realized she might have a key to our puzzle. Bernice picked up on the first ring. "I'm so sorry to bother you," I started.

Bernice stopped me in mid-sentence. "You're not bothering me. In fact, you're welcome to distract me from worrying about my kids."

"How is everything going with Ray's parents?" I asked.

Bernice actually laughed. "The younger kids are having a great time with their grandparents. Max is bored but on duty. And everyone seems to have fallen in love with the officer who was in the house last night. Apparently, he plays a mean game of Monopoly. It seems that he and his family have been invited to Sunday dinner."

"Oh, my," I said appreciatively. An invitation to Sunday dinner with Ray's parents was much prized. In the summer Ray's father usually manned the grill. He wasn't as adventurous a cook as his son, but he turned out a tasty variety of meats, chicken and seafood while Ray's mother supplied a multitude of side dishes along with a variety of pies whose crust I simply couldn't duplicate. In other seasons, you were likely to be treated to her delectable pot roast or succulent roasted chicken. "Lucky man," I said enviously.

Bernice chuckled. "Why did you call other than to check in?"

"Did you ever find out if Veronica Lake went to Cornell and if her real name is Veronica Gillis?"

I heard Bernice slap her forehead. "I completely forgot!" she exclaimed. "I have a stack of Cornell yearbooks. Let me bring them over. And call the others so we can go through them together."

Linda, Marcia, Bernice and I sat at my kitchen table, nursing cups of coffee, each with a yearbook in front of us. We flipped through the pages, looking for a picture or mention of Veronica.

"Got it!" Linda yelled triumphantly. "Here she is!" She turned the book so we could see Veronica's head shot. She looked quite a bit different, with tousled brown hair and chic eyeglasses.

"I knew she wasn't a blonde," Marcia said.

Bernice nodded. "I knew that the moment I saw her. That blonde hair color is completely wrong for her."

Linda agreed. "I think she really did style herself after the actress, but I'm not

265

sure why. There are many other looks that would have been more attractive."

I sat back and thought. "I don't think she cared about that," I finally said. "I think she might have been telling the truth about running from an abusive boyfriend. In that case, she would have wanted to look as different as possible, but she could still keep the name Veronica."

"I wonder if there are any other pictures in here?" Linda mused. "There seem to be a lot of vacation or social activity pictures."

She paged through the yearbook pictures slowly, the rest of us peering over her shoulder.

"Wait!" Marcia exclaimed. "Look at this picture in with the spring break photos."

I studied a picture of three people wearing bathing suits and smiling broadly at the camera. I shook my head and looked at my friends. They were staring back with expressions of shock on their faces. "Do you see what I see?"

Bernice pointed at the picture. "That's Veronica. I guess that's the boyfriend. And that…" she zeroed in the third person.

"That's Alan Wallace!" Marcia exclaimed.

We sat back in shock.

"Wait a minute," Linda said slowly. "Let's think about this."

Marcia, always the scribbler, grabbed a piece of paper from my kitchen junk drawer. "What do we know?" she asked, pen at the ready.

"Obviously, that Veronica knew Alan Wallacebefore she moved here."

"That Veronica and Henry had some type of relationship," Linda contributed. "And may still have it."

"Do we really know that, or do we suspect it?" Bernice asked.

"We heard Tommy talk about Henry having a good-looking blonde girlfriend, who might have been older than him," Marcia contributed.

"And that hand brushing I saw at Judith's party wasn't accidental," Linda chipped in.

"OK," I said. "Assume we know something was going on there."

"Alan Wallace, Henry, Bobby and Lisa, all knew each other." Marcia said.

"Ray suspected Alan of dealing drugs," Bernice contributed.

"Let's agree that we don't know for sure that he was doing that, but it was a possibility," Linda said.

We all nodded.

"Alan Wallace and Henry Byrn both ride motorcycles and those motorcycles are similar to the one

Judith saw at the overlook where Bobby and Lisa were killed."

We were gathering speed.

"Rosalinda saw a motorcycle near the stables at Woodford Hall and near Judith's house," Marcia said, writing furiously.

"Someone tried to scare Judith with various tricks," I said.

"The most serious one, the one with the saddle girth, happened around the time Rosalinda saw a motorcycle near the stables," Bernice said.

"Tommy saw drugs in his brother's possession twice," Linda noted. "And Bobby said he was going to give them back to someone."

"Henry and Alan Wallace were at parties where Henry obtained drugs," I said.

"It looks like Veronica may have been at those parties also." Marcia looked around the table, seeking signs of agreement.

I expelled a breath. "What does this all mean?"

267

"I think," Linda replied carefully, "that Alan Wallace and Veronica whatever her name is were tied together and that Henry somehow ended up in the middle of it."

"What if…" Bernice offered hesitantly, "what if Bobby was helping Alan sell drugs? Lisa talked him into going straight. He tried to give the drugs back to Alan Wallace, his old friend, but Alan killed them to keep them quiet."

"Riley said they were watching someone closely. I'll bet it's Alan Wallace!"

"I'll also bet he's the one who threatened your daughter!" Marcia exclaimed.

"That bastard," Bernice said softly. I suspected that at this moment in time it was good that Ray's gun was locked up. At least, I hoped it was.

# Chapter Twenty-eight

I called Riley. Of course, the one time I had something I thought was important to tell him, the call went to his voice mail. I informed him of the connection between Veronica and Alan Wallace and where we had found it. Then I sat back and thought.

What did we really know? We had a lot of individual facts, but what conclusions could we draw? I had a feeling that Alan Wallace had killed both Bobby and Lisa to keep them from talking about his drug peddling business. From what Riley had said earlier, I believed that he and his team had already reached the same conclusion and were carefully gathering their facts before moving in.

As far as Veronica was concerned, we knew that she had been seen with Alan. The new information was that she had known him while she was still in college, long before she began working for Judith or dating Henry. What did that mean? Was it a coincidence? Like Riley, I don't like coincidences. Had Veronica been working with Alan in the drug business? If so, what did that have to do with the threats against Judith?

My head felt like it was going to explode. Clearly, I needed to move onto something else and let Riley tie together any loose ends. I took two aspirin and settled down with my galley proofs. I was hard at work when the phone rang. A breathless Judith was on the other end of the line.

"Jackie," she said, her shaky voice barely above a whisper, "I think I found something. I think I know who was threatening me and who attacked Rosalinda. Can you come to the house?"

I glanced at my watch. It was just early afternoon. I had time to take a ride to

Woodford Hall and still be home in time to make dinner. Of course, the more sensible thing would have been for me to advise her to call Riley. Naturally, that's not what I did. "Sure," I said. "I could use a break anyway."

"Great!" Judith said. "Come quickly, before…"

The line went dead.

"Judith?" No reply. I grabbed my bag and car keys and headed toward the door. On my way I wondered if I should call Riley before I left. If I did, what would I tell him? That my phone call with Judith had been disconnected? That didn't seem to be a reason to call out the calvary. Phone reception could be spotty where Judith lived. That was probably all the dropped call meant. I would check on Judith and call if I found anything wrong when I got there.

All was quiet when I arrived at Judith's house. Veronica's car was parked in the driveway. I guess that meant Judith hadn't fired her. I wondered if she was going to. I almost turned around. After our encounter at my home, I was none to eager to have another interaction with Veronica. Certainly Judith knew that. 'Oh, be a big girl!' I told myself. I would turn around and leave if Veronica got confrontational.

I rang the doorbell and waited. No one came to the door. I rang again. Still nothing. I tried the doorknob, remembering that Judith often left her door unlocked. "Hello?" I called, stepping over the threshold.

"We're in the office," Judith replied.

I turned into that doorway and stopped dead in my tracks. Judith was seated in a chair facing the office desk. On the other side stood Veronica. She was holding a gun. In front of her on the desk lay a large stack of money and a pile of expensive-looking jewelry. The door to the wall safe behind her hung open. When I turned my head toward Judith, I saw that she was tied – fastened, actually – to the chair. Duct tape was wrapped around her ankles and wrists, securing her tightly to her seat. Duct tape for everything, wasn't that what they said? I reined my thoughts back in. I couldn't lose it now. Remembering old product slogans certainly fell in that category. I tried slowly backing away.

"Stop!" Veronica commanded, shifting the barrel of the gun in my direction. "Come back and sit in that chair." She motioned toward the chair next to Judith. "I'll shoot her if you don't do what I say," Veronica threatened, aiming directly at Judith.

When Judith looked at me her eyes were huge, her pupils enlarged and the whites visible all around the irises. "I'm sorry, Jackie," she whispered, tears running down her face. "I had no idea it would come to this."

I slumped into the chair. Holding the duct tape in one hand and the gun in the other Veronica approached me. "Wrap this around your wrists," she said, handing me the tape.

"You must be kidding," I blustered. "You want me to tie myself up?"

The gun twitched and Veronica's finger moved slightly on the trigger. Yep, she definitely wanted me to do that. I took the tape and wrapped it around my wrists and the arms of the chair. Still holding the gun, Veronica managed to cut the strips. She moved behind the desk and began to shove money and jewels into a tote bag.

"Why are you doing this?" I pleaded, trying to buy time as my mind frantically sought an escape.

"I have to get away from here!" she exclaimed, panting slightly. "If I don't, he'll kill me!"

"Who will kill you?" I asked, although I was certain I knew the answer. I wriggled my wrists. My feet were free, but I hadn't figured out how that could help me. I supposed I could try running with the chair strapped to me, but that didn't seem to hold much potential.

"Alan Wallace," she replied with a rough laugh. "He killed those kids and he'll kill me too."

"How do you know he killed them?" Judith managed to ask. I saw that she had slightly loosened the tape on one of her hands.

"He told me!" Veronica said, looking at us like we were morons.

"How do you know him, anyway?" I asked.

"I met him when I was on spring break at Virginia Beach with my old boyfriend." She took a minute to collect her thoughts. "What I told you about him was true," she said. "He was horrible after we had been together for a while. What I didn't know until later is that he's a major drug dealer and he and Alan were working together." She shoved more money into her satchel.

"You might consider not keeping so much cash around in the future," she said to Judith. At least that was encouraging. It sounded like she didn't intend to kill us. On the other hand, Veronica wasn't what one would call mentally stable.

"I came here to disappear. I changed my name and my appearance and started a new life. Then I went with Henry to a party and there was Alan. At first, I didn't think he recognized me. I was wrong. After those kids were killed, Alan got in touch with me. He said he had killed them because he was afraid they were going to rat him out to the police. And he said that unless I did what he wanted me to he'd tell my ex-boyfriend where to find me. I knew I'd be dead for sure if that happened." She paused and

272

slipped a diamond ring onto her finger.

"What Alan doesn't know is that the police were already onto him," I said. "In fact, they may have arrested him by now. If you tell them what you know, I bet they'll go easy on you."

Veronica laughed again, a chilling sound. "Not after what I've done."

"What you've done?" Judith wondered. "Other than make a very foolish mistake, what have you done?" Her face clouded. "You played those pranks on me, didn't you?'

Veronica shrugged. "I did the first couple. Henry had told me how you were preventing his father from getting control of the company and how you were holding him back. I figured if you thought someone was after you, or if you were losing it, you might turn the company over to Bert."

"And then what?" I asked. I surreptitiously rubbed the duct tape against a metal stud I had found on the chair. Why in the world did this stuff have to be so tough, anyway? "You'd marry Henry and live a life of leisure?"

"Something like that," Veronica admitted. "Only Alan told me he was certain Judith could identify him because she saw him at the overlook where he killed Bobby and Lisa. He cut the girth and left the note on your car." She nodded in Judith's direction.

"What about Rosalinda?" Judith asked.

"I don't know anything about that," Veronica claimed. "That must have been Alan." She fastened her tote and pointed the gun at Judith. "Now that I've spilled the beans, I realize that I have to do something about the two of you after all. Sorry."

"Are you crazy?" I blurted. Veronica's face turned a nasty shade of scarlet.

273

Oops. Poor choice of words. "I mean, you've left evidence all over the place. The police will pick you up in a heartbeat. "

Veronica chewed on her lip, seeming to ponder my words.

"You haven't done anything terrible yet," I persisted. Nothing terrible other than be an accessory after the fact to two murders, I thought. "But if you hurt us or kill us, that's another story."

Veronica seemed to hesitate although the gun was still pointing loosely in our direction.

"Put the gun down, Veronica," ordered a male voice. My head whipped to the right. Henry Byrn was standing just to one side of the doorway. In his hands he held a rifle, and he had it pointed directly at Veronica. "I'm not going to let you hurt Gran, Veronica," he said. "I can tell you don't know a lot about guns, just from the way you're holding that one. On the other hand, I do. I'm a crack shot. My  grandfather taught me and he taught me well. I promise I will shoot you if you try to hurt my grandmother or Mrs. Olsen." I thought it was very gallant of him to include me, particularly since Veronica now had me in her sights. "Put the gun down."

Veronica hesitated.

"Listen to him, Veronica," chimed in another voice. Riley's voice. My heart did somersaults. "You're not a killer, Veronica," Riley said, his voice smooth and reassuring. "Put the gun down and let us help you." He was crouched to the opposite side of the office doorway from Henry, training his gun on Veronica. I thought I could see fellow officers positioned in the living room.

Slowly Veronica began to crumple. She laid the gun on the desk.

"Now put your hands on your head and leave them there," Riley continued in his soothing voice. She obeyed his command. At a gesture from him a uniformed officer trotted into the room and lowered Veronica's hands, cuffing them behind her back. He and a colleague led Veronica, who was now crying uncontrollably, toward a waiting squad car. One officer was talking quietly, apparently reading Veronica her rights.

"I'm sorry," she mouthed at Henry before she exited the house. He turned his head away.

'You may not be a killer,' I thought as I watched her go, 'but your elevator does not go to the top floor. In other words, you're crazy.' That would probably be her defense at her trial. She could spend some time in a cushy mental health facility and then be out. What a wonderful world.

As soon as Veronica had left, Henry handed his rifle to a police officer and ran to his grandmother, where he frantically sawed away at the duct tape holding her in her seat. As soon as she was freed, he swept her into his arms, holding on to her as though he would never let her go. In the meantime, Riley grimly worked on freeing my hands.

"How did you know what was happening?" I asked Riley.

"Henry called me," he replied, still working on the duct tape. "He came to visit his grandmother, came in through the garage and heard and saw everything."

Suddenly there was a loud clamoring outside the door, and my friends burst into the room. "So did we!" Marcia shouted. "We heard it all!"

"And we called Riley!" Linda added.

"Oh, Honey," Bernice said, rushing to my side, "Are you all right?"

Riley finished cutting me loose. I stood shakily and immediately three pairs of arms were wrapped around me. Riley backed away, looking bemused. "But

275

how can you possibly have heard?" I asked.

"You must have sat on your phone," Bernice said. "You accidentally called me. And as soon as I heard what was going on I grabbed Marcia and Linda. We headed over here and called Riley along the way. We kept my phone on so we could hear everything."

"What did you intend to do if you got here before me?" Riley asked curiously.

"Oh, we'd have thought of something," Marcia assured him. He rolled his eyes.

"Don't you ever go off like this without us again," Linda scolded me. "You scared us out of our wits. All for one and one for all, remember?"

Riley made a strange noise and tried to hide it with a cough. "Don't be rude," I said, slipping into his arms.

# Chapter Twenty-Nine

Two days later Riley and I were setting the table for a communal dinner. Marcia was bringing lasagna, Bernice had made a salad, I was contributing fresh-baked bread and a cheesecake and Linda (of course) was bringing wine.

"I see you got your man," I said, watching Riley carefully.

"Indeed, we did," he replied. "Two charges of first-degree murder, one of attempted murder, and multiple unrelated drug counts. Our Mr. Wallace will be going away for quite a while." He paused. "At least I hope so. Things in the courts have gotten so crazy lately that you really don't know what to expect."

"At least this should give some closure to Bobby and Lisa's families," I said.

Riley nodded. "To some degree. I'm hoping it will also encourage parents around here to pay more attention to what their teenagers are up to. A lot of kids were going to those parties Alan Wallace threw."

I thought of Nick, whistling in the kitchen as he put together an appetizer tray.

"It's hard to be a parent," I said. "I'm sure most of those parents are doing their best. But there are so many ways of connecting on the internet that I doubt even the most diligent parent can keep up with them all."

"You're probably right," Riley sighed. "And there's probably someone waiting in the wings to pick up where Alan Wallace left off." What a depressing thought.

"Changing the subject," I said "you looked very handsome on television." I batted my eyes at him. Riley smiled sheepishly. His face had been all over the local news when Alan Wallace's arrest was announced.

"I do my best," he replied.

"And you do it very well," I said, moving in for a kiss just as the front door opened and my friends streamed in.

"Left the door unlocked again, huh?" Riley murmured, turning to greet the group. Oops. I knew I should lock the door. On the other hand, if Judith had locked her house door the other day, what would have happened? Certainly no one else, like Henry for example, could have slipped in unnoticed. So maybe I shouldn't worry. On the other hand…The doorbell rang.

I opened the door to find Henry Byrn standing on my doorstep. "Oh, I seem to have come at a bad time," Henry said, thrusting a large box into my hands. "I'm sorry." He turned to leave.

"No, Henry, come in for a moment," I replied. I looked at the box. It bore the name of a local confectionery store. "Candy!" I said. "I hope it isn't poisoned." Henry paled. I patted him on the shoulder. "I'm sorry, I was kidding. That was in very poor taste."

"It sure was," Marcia said cheerfully. "Don't let her bother you, Henry, she has a weird sense of humor." Talk about the pot calling the kettle black.

Henry spotted Riley. "Hello, Detective Furman," he said tentatively. "Hello, Henry," Riley replied, holding out his hand. Henry took it in his own and gave it a firm shake. "You did a very brave thing the other day, Henry," Riley said. "I wish you'd waited until we got there, but who knows? Things could have turned out very differently without your action."

Henry actually blushed.

"Have some cheese and crackers and set a spell," Ray said. "Dinner won't be ready for a while. Of course, you could join us if you like." He looked around the room. All of us indicated our agreement.

"No, thank you, Principal Bradley," Henry said, "but I'll have a little cheese."

"Would you like something to drink, Henry?" I asked.

"Do you have any soda?" Henry asked. I indicated that we did and listed the choices. After he had his drink in hand, Henry sat on the edge of the sofa and took a deep breath. "I know I should have called before I came," he said, "but, frankly, if you had said I couldn't come I would have chickened out and never tried again."

"Why is that, Henry?" Ray asked.

"I have a lot to apologize for," Henry replied. "Especially to Detective Furman. You see so much wrong with our police system, and in college you hear about the bad things over and over again so that you forget about the good parts. I am truly sorry for the things I said, particularly at Gran's party. Particularly now that I know you a little and I've seen you and other cops in action, I know I was wrong." Henry saw the surprised look on Riley's face and held up a hand. "Don't get me wrong. I'm not signing up for the force any time soon."

We all laughed. "Let's just say I understand things better."

"Fair enough," Riley said, popping a piece of brie into his mouth.

Henry turned to Ray. "I owe you an apology too, Sir."

"You do?" Ray queried, raising an eyebrow. There was that one eyebrow thing again. Was I the only person on the planet who couldn't do it? "You didn't give me a tremendous amount of trouble when you were in school."

"No," Henry agreed, "but you're right about that attitude adjustment. I'm working on it."

"What are you doing?" Ray was clearly curious.

"For one thing I'm spending a bunch of time with Gran. We've talked a lot of things out. We'll never agree on everything, but that's OK. She's helped me

279

see some things more clearly. I apologized to Aunt Ann and Uncle Steven, and even to Emily." Henry gave a weak smile. "I was a real jerk to them."

"How did they take that?" Bernice asked.

Henry looked surprised. "Surprisingly well," he replied. "Dad even gave me my inside job back again." We all laughed. "I think Aunt Ann and Emily made that happen," he said. "They didn't have to do that."

"How is your mother?" I asked, sounding as gentle as I could.

Henry gave a deep sigh. "I'm not sure. She's in counseling, but after what she did, I don't know if things will be the same."

"Maybe they shouldn't be," Linda contributed.

"What do you mean?" Henry asked.

"You could have a better relationship in the long run if she can loosen her hold on you."

"She needs to vanquish some of her demons, whatever they are, too," Bernice said. "Hopefully she can find a way to be happy."

"I hope so," Henry said. "I don't know if my parents' marriage will make it. They're trying, but I'm not holding my breath. Dad was really clueless about what Mom was feeling, and my mother...well, let's just agree she has some serious problems. Uncle Steven is helping them a bit. He's really a terrific person, you know. He's hooked them up with a good therapist he knows, so only time will tell." He stood. "In the meantime, I've moved out. I'm going to stay with Gran until my apartment is available at the beginning of next month." Henry cast his glance over all of us. "Well, this was the last stop on my apology tour." He saw our faces and shook his head. "I didn't mean that the way it came out. Truly, thank you for everything. And once again, I'm sorry.

Have a good Thanksgiving." He stood and left.

We were all silent for a moment.

"Speaking of Thanksgiving," Marcia said, nudging me.

"What?" I asked.

"Have you asked him yet?"

"Asked who?" I said, thinking that somewhere along the line I had lost track of our conversation.

"Riley, of course," Linda said impatiently. "Have you asked him to Thanksgiving dinner yet?"

"Erm, that would be a no," I admitted.

"Oh, for Heaven's sake," Bernice muttered.

Riley was looking at me quizzically.

"Riley, would you join us for Thanksgiving dinner?" I asked. "I mean I know you have family, and that they probably want you there and that you might want to be with them…" I sputtered out.

Bob shook his head. "Now, there's a gracious invitation if I ever heard one."

Riley's lips twitched. "I would be delighted," he said.

"You would?" I asked.

"I would," he confirmed. He leaned over and kissed me.

Linda spoke up. "I'm thinking of families," she announced. "I'm thinking of Henry's family and then I'm thinking of all of us here tonight. We're a family." She gazed around the room and raised her glass. "To family."

We all clinked glasses.

Maggie barked and rested a paw on Riley's knee. He bent over and tickled her ears. "To family," he said and smiled at me.

Made in the USA
Columbia, SC
16 May 2022

# Pierre Teilhard de Chardin
# on
# People and Planet

---

edited by
Celia Deane-Drummond